MW00462787

Narkotika

A *Greenland Undercover* novel

~ Book 1 ~

by Christoffer Petersen

Narkotika

Published by Aarluuk Press

Copyright © Christoffer Petersen 2019

Original Cover Image: Annie Spratt

Christoffer Petersen has asserted his right under the Copyright, Designs and Patents Act 1988 to be identified as the author of this work.

This book is a work of fiction. The names, characters, places and incidents are products of the writer's imagination or have been used fictitiously and are not to be construed as real. Any resemblance to persons, living or dead, actual events or organisations is entirely coincidental.

All rights reserved. No part of this publication may be reproduced, stored in a retrieval system, or transmitted, in any form or by any means, without the prior permission in writing of the publisher, nor be otherwise circulated in any form of binding or cover other than that in which it is published and without a similar condition including this condition being imposed on the subsequent purchaser.

ISBN: 978-87-93680-63-0

www.christoffer-petersen.com

narkotikum
1.b
OVERFØRT person, fænomen, sanseindtryk m.m.
som har beroligende eller stimulerende virkning, og som
er vanskelig at undvære

narcotic
1.b
TRANSFERRED person, phenomenon, sensory
perceptions etc. that have calming or stimulating effects,
which are difficult to do without

Narkotika

I

1973

Chapter 1

I ignored the protestors as I had nothing to protest. Only the lack of change in my purse, and the lack of heat in my apartment. They were happy today, waving their anti-war banners. Just a small group of white Scandinavians, college age, my age, too young to think moderately, too removed to be affected. Just like me – *removed*. They, at least, were not strangers in their own land, nor were they protesting a war on their own borders. I lived far beyond my own borders and coped with my strangeness by hiding inside dark movie theatres, spending my last *kroner* and *øre* on a couple of hours of entertainment, escaping from the world, and the diamond-patterned wallpaper, blistering above the damp rising from the skirting boards in my rooms.

I had *rooms*, a place to stay, a place to hide. But the city was always there, bustling beneath the window, knocking on the door. I was hemmed in by brick and mortar, asphalt and glass, trapped inside a city, breathing its air, the smoke and the petrol fumes. I had a longing for something cleaner and quieter, but I didn't know what. The vague memories I had of that *other place* were like wrinkled photographs, scratched and blurred. If I concentrated, I would see shapes but not faces, strong walls of rock set at sharp angles, but no sense of distance, only that things were far away, and that when the wind blew it was sharper and drier than the city wind.

I put the photographs away, filing them in my mind like I filed the invoices at the offices of Bruun and Son, small time solicitors who paid small time wages. I checked my purse, slipped the coins under the glass of the theatre booth, and reached for the door, pausing for one last look at the poster – Brigitte Bardot, the female *Don Juan*. I caught myself, hands on my hips, smoothing my fingers over the hem of my tight-knit banded sweater, picturing myself in the Bardot bikini on a beach, or in a bedroom. The thoughts were delicious, primitive and exciting. I smiled for Bardot, and then for myself in the glass of the theatre door, wishing for the tenth or twelfth time that week that I had not bobbed my hair with the scissors I borrowed from my neighbour. But I would never be a Bardot blonde, nor would my skin ever be pale, white and creamy. I frowned for a second at my thick black hair, the deep nutty tones of my skin, but then I caught that tickle of dry air, the same one that blew on my cheek whenever I wondered who I was. It held a promise in the sharp breath of air that tickled my nose, that I was more than *this*, that there was a deeper layer to Evnike Rasmussen, the twenty-three-year-old secretary with two tiny rooms hidden in the heart of Copenhagen.

The brass door handle was cold but smooth to the touch. I gripped it, pushed, and paused for a second at the reflection of a man in the glass. He leaned against the bonnet of an open-top car parked across the street, staring at the theatre as he smoked. He looked away when I turned, the light wind teasing at the thin grey hair on his head. *A coincidence*, I thought, as I entered the theatre, found my seat and slid down the cushions, kicked off my shoes, and pressed my stockinged feet onto the back of the chair in front of me. The lights dimmed, the adverts crackled onto the screen and I waited for Brigitte, her curves and her curls.

The man was waiting in his car when I came out of the theatre.

"Frøken Rasmussen?"

I blinked in the afternoon sun as he crossed the street and joined me on the theatre steps.

"Yes," I said, straightening my sweater and staring at the man's round face, the stubborn patch of white whiskers around a mole on his chin, and his grey eyes beneath bushy grey brows. There were dark rings around his eyes that gave him the look of a tired panda. "But how do you know my name?"

"I knew your mother," he said.

"Better than me then," I said, wrinkling my nose at another breath of dry wind.

"Your *foster* mother. I knew Clara when she was a nurse. Before the cancer," he said, lowering his eyes for a second.

Even as a small girl, I understood that Clara was not my real mother, but that she loved me, sometimes too much. The boundaries she set, her rules, prickled at my curious nature and we fought, even more when I entered my teenage years. I didn't remember this man. He seemed old enough to be Clara's uncle, perhaps. Or even a family friend. But not a lover. She didn't have any of those.

The panda patted the lapel of his jacket and slipped two fingers inside the pocket. He took out a packet of cigarettes and offered me one, lighting it as I pinched it between my lips and leaned forwards.

"I thought we could go for a coffee," he said, as he lit his cigarette. He tucked the box of matches into his trouser pocket and crumpled the empty cigarette packet in his hand. I saw the moles and freckles of old age on his skin, stretched across the backs of his hands. He tossed the crumpled packet into the rubbish bin outside the theatre and pointed a wrinkled finger at a coffee shop on the street corner. "They have good coffee," he said.

I blew a lungful of smoke into the air above his head. Even though we stood on the same step, I felt like a giant beside him. Another look at his skin, especially his face, and I wondered how many of his wrinkles were from age or from the sun; his skin was peeling on the bald patch of his head between the sides of his thin wispy hair.

"I don't think I should go with you," I said.

"It's a public place, Evnike," he said. "Just one coffee. Consider it a courtesy for an old friend of Clara's." He tapped the ash from his cigarette, and then tossed it onto the step and ground it beneath his heel. "I'm trying to quit," he said, as he held out his hand. "My name is Frode Worsaae. I'm a policeman, of sorts, and I would very much like to talk to you."

"A policeman?"

"You've done nothing wrong, Evnike," he said. "I just want to talk."

I thought about the pot I had smoked the night before. It was Erik's. He bought it. Julie brought it. We all smoked it. That's what young people did on a Friday night in the city. Frode Worsaae didn't have the *look* of a narcotics cop, but the thought that he might be one, tipped the balance of my thoughts in his favour, and I nodded.

"One coffee, then," I said, and followed him down the steps.

The bell behind the door rang once as I followed Frode inside. He suggested the table in the window, tucked into the alcove and a discreet distance from the other tables closer to the counter. I sat down and stubbed out my cigarette in the ashtray, blinking as the late sun caught the gold lettering in the window. Frode ordered two coffees and pastry, and I pressed my palms against my stomach to stifle a low growl at the promise of food. Frode commented on the weather as I ate. I listened and nodded, brushing pastry crumbs from my lips as he sipped at his coffee. I caught the eye of the couple sitting closest to us. They were old enough to frown at the sight of a younger woman with an older man, or was it the colour of my skin and the wild cut of my bobbed black hair? Frode didn't seem to notice, or care. He sipped his coffee and pushed his pastry towards me as I finished mine.

"Inniki," he said, as I bit into the pastry. "That's your real name. Clara gave you the Danish version." Frode looked away as I stopped chewing, placing my pastry on my plate, losing my appetite, all of a sudden. "She meant well, of course. These are difficult times, as they were then, but," he said, turning to look at me, "You must have heard the latest from Godthåb?" He took another sip of coffee and gestured at the couple watching us from the table by the wall. "People in Copenhagen don't understand the anti-colonial sentiment," he said. "The popular opinion is that you should be grateful, and that you should shut up."

"Me?"

"The Greenlanders," he said. Frode leaned back when the waitress returned to top up his coffee. He waited until she was gone, took another sip, and then nodded for me to finish my pastry. "It's like the cigarettes," he said. "No good for a man of my age. I'm trying to quit."

"I'm finished," I said, pushing the plate with the half-eaten pastry to one side.

"Then I'll begin."

It was like a little ceremony, the smoothing of his fingers along the tablecloth at the table's edge, the rearranging of the plates, the position of his coffee cup, turning the saucer just so with the cup handle pointing towards the window. Frode leaned his elbows on the table and laced his fingers together as if in prayer. I felt the first crease of a frown on my forehead, only to feel it flatten as he started to talk.

"Inniki Rasmussen," he said. "You were born on the east coast of Greenland. Your real mother died when you were just five years old. Nobody knows who your father is. Clara Pedersen worked as a nurse in Angmagssalik. She took you in and brought you back to live with her in Denmark. You know this, of course."

"Yes," I said.

"Then we can skip over your schooling – the time when you bit Eva Schultz…"

"She asked for it," I said, remembering the sharp tug of Eva's fist wrapped around my long black hair.

"And Viggo Eriksen," Frode said. "Did he ask for it too?"

I couldn't remember.

"You were nine," Frode prompted.

"I thought we were skipping over my schooling?"

"Of course." Frode paused for a sip of coffee. The cup rattled on the saucer as he put it down. "Somehow, you graduated high school, and found a secretarial job, one that you have had for a few years now."

"Yes." Although I couldn't remember the number of times I had been fired, and how Clara had pleaded for them to take me back, and for me to behave, to at least try to fit in. Frode's smile suggested he knew how many times, exactly.

"Are you happy, Inniki?"

"Happy?"

I didn't know. But neither was *happiness* my most immediate concern. I was far more interested to learn how Frode Worsaae knew so much about me, and why?

"Why?" I asked.

Frode checked the position of his cup and saucer, smoothed the edge of the tablecloth, and laced his fingers in front of me. I looked at the wrinkles, the moles, and the hairs between his knuckles, thicker than those at the sides of his head. He reminded me of a priest, like the ones they had in the village, berating the drunk mothers and fathers and youths of Greenland, while the children ran free. The Sunday sermons were long and full of strange words that floated above our heads, as we crawled between the wooden pews, snaking in and out of guilty, penitent legs.

"Why what?"

"Why do you know so much about me?"

"I didn't," Frode said. "But I have made it my business to learn everything I can, so that we might meet one day, *today*, and that I might make you a job offer."

"I have a job," I said.

"Yes, you do." Frode smiled. "But tell me, Inniki, how often do you feel that breath of wind on your face?"

"I never…"

"It's all right," he said. "Clara told me. She described this look you would get in your eye. When you were quiet – between the bouts of stormy weather – she said you would get a faraway look, and that your nose would twitch, as if something was tickling it."

"Like wind."

"Exactly." Frode smiled again, and the wrinkles became creases, lines of laughter. Each smile sloughed years off his face, making him at once more familiar, and for want of a better word, *interesting*. The tired panda's eyes lit up, and he continued. "I feel that same wind, albeit not quite as strongly as before. But your wind, it's your identity, a breath of air from your past, and possibly your future, if you listen to it, and answer it." He dipped his head forwards and lowered his voice. "You're not destined to work in an office. And without Clara, the next time you are fired will be your last time. But you have a keen mind, Inniki," he said, pointing at my forehead. "An inquisitive nature, and a stubbornness that suits my purpose."

"Your purpose?"

"Yes," he said. "For the greater good."

Chapter 2

We outstayed our welcome at the café, and surprising myself, I suggested another. Perhaps it was that wild streak of mine, or maybe I was testing him, but the café I had in mind was in Christiania, the hippy commune in the centre of Copenhagen. Frode's gait stiffened as he realised where I was taking him, but he left his mature sensibilities at the gates to Christiania, shrugging them off like a cloak. He relaxed, and so did I, entering a more familiar environment suited to my youth, my aspirations, and far from prying eyes and prudish stares; most of the eyes on Frode and me were glazed. We found a seat at a small wooden table outside a café with bright wooden walls, painted with lazy murals and sharp slogans. Here was the uprising, the rebellion, and I looked around, half expecting to see the protestors I met earlier, wondering if it was here that they folded their banners and blazed passionate discussions until their minds were fogged with pot. I grinned at Frode as he refused a joint and settled for coffee.

"How often do you come here?" he asked.

"Now and again," I said, tucking my hand beneath my elbow and waving a cigarette lazily between my fingers. I blew a ring of smoke towards him, laughing as he waved it away from his face. The chatter around us flickered in all directions, from the war in Vietnam, through complicated chess moves, new potatoes freshly unearthed, new sex positions recently tried, and a warm hubbub rising between thick and thin clouds of smoke, all kinds of smoke, all kinds of people. I could hide here, become invisible.

"Shall I continue?" he asked, and I raised my eyebrows, *yes* – Greenland style. Frode fidgeted on his seat, beckoning me to lean closer across the thin slats of the wooden table, as he pressed his knees beneath it and turned towards me. "You have certain qualities and attributes that I need," he said.

"You make me sound like a machine."

"Not a machine," he said. "Although…"

Light flickered across his grey eyes. I only just caught it, before it dissolved into something else – the set of his chin, and a resolve, as if he had just made a decision.

"Can we go for a walk?"

"Does this place make you uncomfortable?"

"No," he said. "But I want to show you something. It's not far."

Frode paid for our coffee, refused another toke on a fat joint, the end blistering and curling behind pungent yellow smoke. We weaved between the tables and walked back to the bustle of the city. He slowed to talk.

"Back there," he said. "That was a test."

"*Imaqa.*"

"*Imaqa*? What's that?"

"It means *maybe*. Maybe it was a test."

"You were testing me," he said. "What did you achieve?"

"I don't know."

"Then it was a waste. Next time be sure to know the

purpose of a test. Otherwise you might as well not bother." He stopped at the kerb, waited for a break in the traffic, and then crossed the street. I followed, slowing to a stop when I saw where we were headed. "This," he said, "is also a test."

He stepped to one side, watching my face as I looked at the group of Greenlanders, swaying across the cobbles to greet one another, voices raised, words slurred, beer bottles clinking. These were my people, and like a mirror, I saw a little of myself in each of them. I looked away, avoiding their eyes as they heckled, calling out in Greenlandic – cackles of the western dialect, whispers from the east. Frode pressed wrinkled fingers around my elbow and guided me to a bench, far enough to dissuade contact with the Greenlanders, close enough to observe.

"Pathetic," Frode said. "Is that what you're thinking?"

"No."

"Tragic then. But what if I told you that it could be worse?"

"Worse?" I struggled to imagine a more pitiful scene.

"What if I told you that there is something worse than alcohol creeping into Greenland? It's there already, but it has the potential to grow if unchecked. Do you know what I'm talking about?"

"No," I said, and I didn't want to. There was a reason I didn't walk this route through the city.

"But you took me to Christiania – that was your test. This is mine. I want you to look at these people, *your* people, and imagine them addicted to another drug."

"Pot?"

"Cannabis, yes, and other drugs. Harder drugs that would rip through a community. It would destroy a small village. It would flatten a settlement."

"But I don't live in Greenland," I said, turning to look at Frode. "And I'm not a policeman."

"No," he said. "You're not. But I know someone who does live in Greenland, who used to be a policeman. Actually," Frode said, as he leaned back on the bench, "he was a *kommunefoged*, a bailiff. But I'm getting ahead of myself. Let me walk you back to your apartment."

We left the last of the Greenlanders' jeers at the corner of the street, but not before I felt another breath of wind on my cheek. It had a sharper bite to it than usual, something tangy, old fish perhaps. I looked at the shop fronts, searching for a fishmonger, but found nothing. I picked up the pace to walk beside Frode, putting thoughts of the strange wind to one side as I listened to what he was saying.

"The qualities I mentioned," he said. "You have a connection to your past, to your country, but you are lost. He'll pick up on that. He'll want to do something about it."

"Who will?"

"The bailiff."

"Does he have a name?"

"Yes."

"Are you going to tell me?"

"No," Frode said. "Not yet." He slowed between two groups of people, letting the couple behind us pass before he spoke again. "I won't tell you anything before you agree to the job."

"But I don't know what it is yet."

"Which is why we will part company now. My car is parked just over there, and I'm sure you can find your way home, or…" He pressed a handful of coins into my hand. "Treat yourself to a meal while you think it over."

"Frode…"

He held up a finger, pulled a business card out of his lapel pocket, and handed it to me. There was a number printed beneath his name, but no indication of title or vocation.

"I work for *Politiets Efterretningstjeneste*, the Danish Security and Intelligence Service. I have a job for you Inniki, but you must trust me before I take you into my confidence."

"Is it a secretarial position?"

Frode smiled. "More of an *assistant* than a secretary." He paused and I shivered as he appraised my body for a moment, long enough for me to feel uncomfortable, but not so long that I thought he took any pleasure from it. It was difficult to imagine what Frode Worsaae might find pleasurable.

"What?" I said. "More of my qualities?"

"More of your *potential*, really," he said. "What you might become, if circumstances allow."

"I said I wasn't a policeman, and I don't want to become one."

"And neither would I want you to. But how do you know what you want? You've hardly begun to live." Frode cut short my comment with another wave of his hand. "You've led a sheltered life, Inniki. Clara made certain of that. Apart from a boisterous schooling, and the challenge of keeping a job, you are no different from a thousand young women of your age, and yet…"

"I must be," I said. "Or you wouldn't have come."

"Exactly," he said, smiling as that same light flickered in his eyes. "Clara said you can feel the winds of Greenland, and I want you to hold on to that, to explore it, and to let those winds fill you up, Inniki. But of course, you don't yet know how. I do. I can help you; this job will help you fulfil your potential and become who you were meant to be."

"A policeman?"

"No," Frode said, with a shake of his head. "A *Greenlander*. That's who you need to become."

"To save people like them?" I gestured at the street with the drunken Greenlanders, a few city blocks behind us.

"And others," Frode said. "Do you know, there are 49,000 Greenlanders in Greenland, including a few thousand Danes, of course. If I told you they were all at risk, would you do something to stop it?"

"At risk of what? Drugs?"

"It doesn't matter. Would you do what you could to save them?"

"Yes," I said, without hesitation. This little grey man had stirred something inside me, as ambiguous as it was, elusive but enticing. He had my attention, if not my full understanding. It occurred to me, that it wasn't necessary, as long as I listened. The promise of self-discovery was narcotic, and yet sharper, like the wind of my past, blowing towards my future.

"Keep the card," he said. "Think about what we've talked about, then call me. I can be reached nearly all of the time at that number."

He took a step towards the kerb and I reached out to take his arm.

"You still haven't told me about what I would have to do. I don't know what the job is. How can I say yes?"

Frode looked at my hand on his arm and patted it. He moved away, and I caught the light in his eyes once more as he flashed a smile, before crossing the street. He had told me nothing, leaving me with a handful of change and a slightly battered calling card. I should have seen James Bond at the movie theatre, not Brigitte Bardot.

I emptied Frode's coins into my purse and walked home, stopping at the shop on the corner for more coffee, the cheap bread that had crusted behind the glass, and a thick slab of butter. My neighbour was on the payphone in the corridor between our apartments. She had moved a chair out there at about the same time she started dating her boyfriend. I waved as I fiddled the key from my pocket and let myself in. I could still hear her talking as I made coffee, buttered my crusty bread, tapping Frode's card on the pitted surface of my kitchen table as I thought about the details he hadn't told me, about the job I was supposed to accept on blind faith.

"And curiosity," I said.

It had been curiosity that led me to cuddling Viggo Eriksen before he tried to touch me between my legs, and I bit him on the arm. It amused me that Frode knew about that, but I wondered when Clara might have told him, and how long he had been watching me? I had qualities and attributes that Frode could make use of. That's what he had said.

I left his card on the table and carried my coffee into the bathroom. The mirror was cracked in the corners and chipped at the edges. I really wanted one in my room, but once the couch was made up into a bed, there wasn't the space. I sipped my coffee, then pouted for the mirror, wondering if my attributes included my brown eyes, my black hair, my hazelnut skin. Or were they my *qualities* and my attributes were a reference to my hips, my breasts, and the other parts of me that Viggo tried to explore.

There was a danger that Frode Worsaae was not who he said he was, and that all his talk of Greenland and protecting his people was just that, *talk*, like a worm dangling on a hook.

"There's only one way to find out," I said, tilting my head to one side as I heard my neighbour hang the phone on the hook.

I picked up Frode's card from the kitchen table, swapped my mug for my purse and took out a coin for the telephone. Frode answered on the second ring.

"What are my attributes?" I asked, as soon as he answered. "Is it my skin?"

"Yes," he said.

"My body?"

"Not necessarily. In fact, I'm not sure."

I frowned in the pause, as Frode coughed.

"But the way you looked at me on the street."

"I was looking at your muscles, your bone structure," he said, with a laugh. "I'm far too old for anything else. But I'm almost pleased you thought it *was* something else."

"I don't understand."

"And I don't expect you to. Not yet. I just need an answer." He paused again, and this time I could almost see him, see the light in his eyes. "I need a Greenlander," he said. "No-one else will do. No-one else could do this job. I promised your mother, Clara, that I would look out for you, and now I'm offering you a job."

"I accept," I said, ending the call before I could change my mind.

Chapter 3

Frode fussed over my choice of clothes when he picked me up at my apartment the next morning. He preferred the slim-fitting sweater I wore the day before, together with a mini-skirt instead of the long cord trousers I pulled on moments before he arrived.

"It's all about first impressions," he said, as he waited in the kitchen. "And lingering ones," I heard him say, as I swapped my cords for a short skirt, tugging on my sheer tights and slipping my feet inside flat-soled shoes. He nodded appreciatively as I emerged from the bathroom. "Perfect," he said.

I followed Frode down the stairs and straight to his car. He took the main road out of the centre of Copenhagen, glancing at his watch every time we stopped at a red light.

"Are we going to be late?" I asked.

"Not late, but visiting hours are restricted." Frode accelerated as soon as the lights changed. He was different behind the wheel.

"Visiting time? Are we going to a hospital?"

"Sort of," he said, cursing again at the next light. Frode glanced at the intersecting roads, gauged the traffic and sailed through the red light, waving his hand above his head at the sound of horns blaring.

He parked outside Blegdamsvej Prison fifteen

minutes later. I sat in the car, staring at the four sandstone columns of the prison's façade, as Frode checked his watch for the fourth time.

"We've got a little less than an hour."

"Here?"

"Yes," he said, opening his door. He waited for me to join him on the pavement.

"This is the job? Working in a prison?"

"Visiting a prison," Frode said. He hurried me to the door with a gentle grasp of my elbow. I waited as he signed us in, and then followed him through the dark corridors, past heavy iron doors, to a visiting area with six tables, and four chairs at each, all of which were bolted to the floor. "A precaution," he said, as I tried to pull a chair out from beneath the table.

Frode slid onto his seat and I did the same, conscious that we were the only visitors, or perhaps just the first ones to arrive.

"Simigaq?" the guard said, as he approached our table.

"Yes," Frode said. "Eko Simigaq. The Greenlander."

"I know who he is." The guard tugged a ring of keys from his belt and walked to the door in the wall opposite our table.

"Eko Simigaq?" I said.

"Yes." Frode looked at his watch.

"That's the name of the man we're meeting? The policeman?"

"Yes, yes. The bailiff." Frode bumped the table as he stood up. "Here he comes."

The guard blocked my view for a second, but when he moved, I saw a thin man step through the door. His hair was jet black, like my own, but longer; it reached to his shoulders. It was tied tight and pulled smooth beneath a thin cord around his forehead. He glanced at me as he stepped around the guard, and I shrank onto my seat, while Frode stepped away from the table to shake the man's hand.

"Eko," he said. "It's good to see you."

Eko nodded as he greeted Frode, then slid onto the seat opposite me. He reached across the table and offered me his hand.

"Eko Simigaq," he said.

"Evni..*Inniki*," I said. "Rasmussen." It felt good to use my Greenlandic name. It felt right.

"From Angmagssalik?" he asked, as he let go of my hand.

"Yes, but..." I looked at Frode, suddenly unsure of what I should say.

"Inniki left Greenland a long time ago," he said. "Years, in fact."

Eko raised his eyebrows, sending a little thrill of recognition through my body. It had been such a long time since I had had contact with other Greenlanders, not including the drunks I avoided in the city. Eko was older than me, but perhaps younger than he looked. His cheeks were thin, pulling his face into a gaunt expression, haunted, almost. I wondered if he was eating enough, thought about asking him, but Frode beat me to it.

"No seal meat in prison, eh?" he asked, drawing his hand down in front of his own rounded face in a pinching gesture. "You've lost weight since the last time I was here."

Eko turned away from me to look at Frode, pulling that small charge of connection with him.

"The answer is still no, Worsaae," he said.

"Yes, of course," Frode said. He held up his palms. "I understand. But I wanted to come, anyway. Just to see how you were getting on. Perhaps I can find some coffee?" Frode stood up, and I realised that this was it, the job, or at least part of it. "Three black coffees?"

"Milk and sugar," Eko said.

Frode walked away from the table, waving to the guard as he walked to the door. I turned my head, curious to catch the words Frode whispered to the prison guard as he let him out of the visiting room, but when Eko coughed, I forgot all about Frode.

"When did you leave?"

"Greenland?"

He raised his eyebrows – *yes*.

"I was six. A Danish nurse brought me home."

"She took you from your family?"

"I had no family. She brought me up."

"But never took you back." Eko leaned back in the chair, lifting one leg and pressing his foot on the chair next to him. He looked comfortable, as if he could relax on even the hardest of surfaces. "She should have," he said. "Family is important."

"She's dead now," I said.

"Then you have none?"

"What?"

"Family. You're alone."

"Yes," I said.

Eko dropped his foot from the chair and leaned on the table. He beckoned me closer with his finger. I felt that charge again, a short burst of electricity as I caught the scent of his skin. Beneath the prison soap pressed between the fibres of his clothes, I caught something wilder, a hint of heather, hot sand, crisp lichen, scents from my early years, playing in the dirt, playing with seaweed and fish bones. Eko smelled of wild places, ever so faintly, but strong enough that I could picture him there, the wind tugging at the hair at his shoulders, the cord pressed into his forehead. As I leaned closer to him, I could see that the cord was leather.

"Sealskin," he said, as he followed my gaze. "Too short to hang myself. The guards ignore it." He smiled. "I don't want to hang myself. Don't worry."

"I'm not worried," I said.

"Why not?" Eko frowned. "You don't care about me?"

"But we've only just met…"

He laughed, and the skin around his eyes wrinkled.

"Inniki," he said. "It is a good name."

"Thank you."

"*Qujanaq*," he said. "It should be me thanking you. You came to visit me. You don't even know me." He beckoned me closer once more, and whispered, "He asked you to come?"

"Yes."

"*Aap.*"

"*Aap*," I said, remembering my Greenlandic. I couldn't remember when I last used it.

"Frode wants me to do something, but I am in doubt."

"What does he want you to do?"

"I'm not sure. But he brought you here to change my mind." Eko smiled as I started to speak. He pressed his finger on my lips. "Shh," he said. "It's okay. I'm pleased you came."

The wild scent was stronger now. But there was more. The skin on Eko's finger, the back of his hand, smelled of seal oil, and something caustic – the word *brimstone* came to mind. It was gunpowder, and blood. I smelled the trace of old blood on his hands, beneath the scratch of rough fingertips. Eko took his finger from my lips and crossed his arms.

"How old are you?"

"Twenty-three," I said. "I'll be twenty-four at the end of August."

"I'm twenty-nine." He laughed. "But you thought I was older."

"I did not."

"I can see it on your face," he said, pointing at me, as his brown eyes widened.

"Maybe I did," I said.

"*Imaqa.*"

"Yes. For a moment. When you first came through the door."

Eko looked over his shoulder, nodding as if he could see it now, see himself walking through the door, looking older, thinner. When he turned around his cheeks seemed fuller, fatter somehow. He drummed his fingers on the surface of the table, bobbing his head as if he could hear a beat.

"You like music, Inniki?"

"Yes."

"Who?"

"Ah, Elton John..."

"*Crocodile Rock*," Eko said. "Yes, it's good. They play it all the time on the radio. What else?"

"You'll laugh," I said.

"I won't." Eko stopped tapping the table. "Not about music."

"Dr Hook..."

"*On the Cover of the Rolling Stone.*" Eko slapped the table. "Yes. It's good. Very funny." He sang the first few lines, drawing a look from the guard and a shake of the man's head. Eko waved at him, before tugging at the light, wispy beard on his chin. "But what about *our* music," he said.

"I don't know any."

"*Piffiit nutaat,*" he said. "*New Times* by Sume. You'll love it. It's good music, powerful. Strong medicine to heal the sick."

"The sick?"

"Greenland is sick. The people are sick. They need healing."

Eko leaned back in his seat, as the guard opened the door for Frode to come in. He took his coffee from Frode's hand and then a handful of sugar cubes that Frode pulled from his pocket. Eko dipped a sugar cube into the coffee. He gripped it between his finger and thumb as he pressed it to his lips, sucking the coffee from the cube before dropping it into his mouth.

"Has Frode told you why I'm in prison?"

"No," I said.

Eko took another sugar cube, dipping his head over the coffee, before nodding for Frode to speak. The smell of his wild skin grew stronger as he sat, dipping cubes of sugar in the coffee, nodding at one point in Frode's story, shrugging at another.

"Eko was a police assistant – a bailiff – in a small settlement in Upernavik," Frode said. "The police would use them if they needed help in a settlement, or if they needed them to do something, before they arrived. One night, there was a disturbance in a house."

"A fight," Eko said. "Between sick Greenlanders."

"They were drunk," Frode said. "Eko sent someone on a dog sledge to fetch the police. He told them to hurry."

"I could not wait," Eko said.

"No, if you did more people would have died."

"More people?" I asked.

Frode paused to sip his coffee. Eko took the last sugar cube.

"Eko went to the house," Frode said. "The husband had been in Upernavik. He had beer with him. He and his wife were drunk. They were fighting…"

"The kids were hiding outside, with the dogs," Eko said. "It was winter."

"And you couldn't wait for the police."

"No time," Eko said.

"So, Eko went inside, and he broke up the fight. The man had a knife, and he attacked Eko."

"And I killed him," Eko said. "It would have been him or me."

"But," Frode said. "When the police arrived, the wife said it was Eko who attacked the man, that it was Eko who started the fight."

"The people in that place didn't like me very much," Eko said. I caught the crease of skin around his eyes, but it didn't last long. "So, I was removed. Taken from my country. Forced to spend my time here. Away from the sea, from the land, from the ice. Trapped." Eko pinched the cord around his forehead. "If this was just an inch or two longer, I would have killed myself already." He looked at me, stared straight into my eyes, and said, "Do you believe me?"

"*Aap.*"

"Good." Eko took a long gulp of coffee, wiped his

lips with the back of his hand, and looked at Frode. "Then get me out of here. I will do what you want me to do."

Frode sighed. He placed his hand over his mouth, rubbed the stubble on his chin. "Thank you," he said. "Thank you, Eko."

"On one condition," Eko said.

"Name it."

"First, I take her home," he said, pointing at me. "She needs to see her country."

Chapter 4

It seemed like we flew forever. My memories of my childhood in Greenland were vivid and full of contrasts, like the top red stripe of the *Greenland Air* plane, separated from the silver fuselage by a broad white band stretching from the black nose to the tip of the red tail. Eko said it was a *Douglas DC-6B*, and that I should remember such things. And there was another contrast – Eko the music-loving prisoner, just a few inches away from suicide, compared to the aviation enthusiast, his nose pressed to the frosted window, staring at the engines, while I looked over his shoulder and gasped at the ice.

So much ice.

My country, my *green* land, was white, apart from the thin strips of rock around the coast. These rocky stretches were dotted with the tiny squares of wooden houses separated with smaller turf and stone dwellings on the east coast, and the concrete blocks of flats on the west. The Greenland of my childhood had evolved, and I had been left behind, robbed of my parents and robbed of a nation. Eko told me he was going to give it all back to me.

"My mother is dead," I said, when he turned away from the window in anticipation of landing.

"No-one is truly dead," he said, pointing at the

mountains as we descended to the runway on the island of Kulusuk. "You will find her spirit here, in the mountains, and the sea. You will find your people."

I gripped the arms of the chair as the pilot wrestled the plane through a brief bout of turbulence. I felt Eko's hand on mine, felt the rough cut of his skin, the strength in his fingers as he squeezed my hand.

"One more bump, and then we'll be home."

The flight from Copenhagen to Reykjavík had been smooth compared to the flight across the roiling seas of the North Atlantic. The waves had surged beneath us, as if hurrying us along. Eko had begun talking of spirits the moment he had spotted the white caps and the horses' tails on the black see below.

"My body was trapped in the prison," he had said, somewhere over the ocean, "but my soul was free, but unguided, restless. Do you understand?"

"Yes," I said, and I told him about the dry wind I often felt on my cheek.

"Exactly," he said. "But different. That is the land calling to you. You have been away for so long, you long for it…"

"Yes. I suppose I do."

"There is nothing to *suppose*, there just *is*. You'll see."

This was before we landed, before the little aviation enthusiast crawled out of Eko to sit on his shoulders, to guide his hands to the window and his eyes to the propellers. A moment later he was silent, sipping his coffee, slumped in his seat, eyes closed, searching for something.

"I don't feel the wind," he said. "I feel something else, deeper. I know what it is I must do, but I am scared,

Inniki." He opened his eyes and reached for my hand. I twitched at his touch, shocked by the cold, tight skin of his fingers. "This is why I'm pleased you are with me. I will help you find your family, and then you will help me find mine."

"And what will we do after that?"

The image of a life in Greenland took hold in my mind and I could smell the tough Arctic grass, taste the blood-rich seal meat, and gasp at the ice-cold water. I wanted it more than I ever believed I could, and I imagined having it, having that life, sharing it with this man. Not in a romantic way, not as his wife. Perhaps we would be lovers, but it was his connection with our land that I wanted. The thought teased into a knot that clogged my mind until the turbulence dislodged it, and I gripped Eko's hand until we had landed, and the pilot taxied the short runway to the airport building.

I could smell Greenland the moment they opened the aircraft doors.

I could feel the wind.

The mountains were still capped with deep snow and layers of ice, but the rock below the peaks was parched brown, all the way to the coastline and to the sand beneath my soles and the dust lining my boots. I stopped at the foot of the steps, spinning slowly as I tried to take it all in. Eko laughed and tugged me into the airport.

He greeted three men as soon as we entered the building, shaking each man's hand in turn, and speaking a rapid Greenlandic that I struggled to follow. There were cries and shrieks as we moved through the passengers and families in the waiting area. It seemed to me that everyone knew Eko. But with a whisper here, a nod, and a nudge, he managed to turn all their attention from him to me, and I shrank under the scrutiny. The first to greet me was an older woman with heavy cheeks and brilliant brown eyes. Her skin was warm as she took my hand, tugging me down to a seat. She pressed her palm to my face, turning my head first left and then right, clucking and nodding as more women joined her, pressing their hands into mine, twisting their fingers gently in my hair.

"Inniki?" the woman asked, turning to Eko.

"*Aap*," he said.

The woman stood up and pulled my head to her chest. She pressed thin lips to my forehead, and I felt hot tears splash onto my cheeks. She wiped them away with stiff thumbs, then stood back to let the other women, of all ages, hug me in turn, their hands lingering on my shoulders, smoothing my hair against my head. I don't know when I started crying, but it was a warm wind that dried the many tears on my cheeks.

"You're home, Inniki," Eko said, and he led me out of the airport building to a flatbed truck. He lifted me onto the back and climbed up next to me. We waved at the women in the airport as we bounced along the gravel road to the docks, until the road dipped and we left them behind.

"They were all crying," I said. "All of them."

"They remember you," Eko said.

"But I was so young."

"They remember everyone."

We took a boat to Angmagssalik and I let the chill air from the icebergs cool my head. It felt like too much too soon, but we had only just begun. This part of the journey was mine. Eko had promised as much. The fresh air, the cloudless sky, and the wind – always the wind – brought a sense of calm to my mind that I had never felt in the city. All those afternoons I had spent hiding in the movie theatre, all those hours spent hidden amongst the hippies and herb-growers of Christiania, all those days inside the office, hidden behind the desk and piles and piles of papers – suddenly I was exposed.

I could feel the wind on my cheeks. I could taste the salt of it on my tongue. And, from the look on Eko's face, I knew he could too.

My foster mother had taken pity on me, that day she plucked me from the dirt. But that same dirt was on my boots again, some seventeen years later. I started to cry, gripping the rail of the boat as I felt anger boiling from my stomach, churning through my body as the driver of the boat sped between the larger bergs and I caught the first real glimpses of home. My real home.

Eko helped me out of the boat. He carried both our bags, lugging them up the sandy road, past the shipping containers, beneath the sharp-peaked mountains stretching around the deep blue fjord waters ringing the town and the island of Angmagssalik.

"Here," Eko said, as he stopped beside a wind-bleached wooden house. The rocky yard was full of children. Each of them was different in height, but they were all skinny, cheeky and inquisitive. Their hair was thick and black, twisted long, cropped short. The sun had darkened their skin from smooth almond to deep Brazil nut. They were all of them different, and yet each one of them could have been me. They watched as we entered the house, and then clung to the sills of the brittle-framed windows, pressing their chins into the flaky blister of paint to stare through the salt-stained glass.

"Are you all right?" Eko asked, as he dropped the bags onto the wooden floor.

"I don't know."

"It's a bit much, maybe?"

"Yes," I said.

"*Aap*," he said, with a gentle nudge "You're home, Inniki."

It certainly felt familiar, and I brushed a tear from my cheek as I realised this *was* my home. We were standing exactly where I had stood so many years ago. The children outside could have been me. The house was no different. Perhaps there were a few more shoes by the door, more coats on the rack. And if there were coats and shoes, then someone had to be living here.

Eko nodded for me to kick off my boots, before taking my hand and leading me into the kitchen. There was raisin bread on the counter and three flat fish on a square of cardboard on the kitchen floor. Eko tugged me gently to the floor and we sat beside the fish. I crossed my legs and hugged my knees to my chest. Eko picked up the knife lying beside the fish, paring the skin to one side and cutting small handfuls of soft white flesh from the bone. He pressed the first to my lips and I took it, letting the meat melt into feathers in my mouth. He cut another and I took it in my hands, teasing the meat with my fingers, letting the oil seep into my pores, tasting it on my tongue.

"The family is away at their summer camp," Eko said. "We can stay here for as long as you like. For as long as you need."

"*Aap*," I said.

"You can sleep in your old room," he said. "If you want to."

I nodded, held my hand out for another piece of meat. I wasn't ready to go upstairs. Not yet. Besides, the late summer sun would not set, and I wanted to explore the town, to recapture my childhood, and to tread those same roads that I once skipped and ran along, sometimes bleeding and crying with scuffed knees, sometimes laughing with a fresh *ammassat*, a silver Capelin, wriggling between my fingers.

I remembered that fish, dropping it on the road, wiping the sand and grit from its scales onto my fingers, chasing after the boy when he swiped it from my hand, and again when I caught him, and he dropped it.

The boy.

I could see him now. A year younger than me, an inch taller.

Kunuk.

"There was a boy," I said.

Eko cut another piece of fish, slipping it into his mouth and chewing quietly as he watched me.

"I think he was my brother."

"He didn't come to Denmark?"

"No."

"*Naamik*," Eko said, softly, nudging.

"*Naamik*," I said. "He stayed here."

"Stayed here, or…"

I remembered then. It was the day after we chased each other with the fish. Kunuk crawled onto the ice clinging to the rocks at the beginning of the summer. He jumped from one floe to another. I watched him, in awe of my little brother. How strong he was. How brave. He jumped a fourth time. I had my head down, studying something – I don't remember what. But I do remember the splash.

"He stayed here," I said. "*Naamik*, he died here. I was with him when he died, when he drowned."

"You forgot about him?"

I shook my head. "I didn't forget," I said. "I just forgot how to remember."

Chapter 5

The black lichen on the rocks covering my mother's grave crackled beneath my palm, as I pressed my hand above her heart. The white paint of the slim wooden cross had been thinned by the wind and flaked by the frost. It leaned to one side and I righted it, holding it steady while Eko filled the gap between the rocks with a handful of stones. We found Kunuk's tiny grave enclosed within a wooden picket, bleached grey by the same irreverent Arctic winds that plagued all the crosses and pickets in the graveyard. We spent a few minutes longer with Kunuk than my mother, as I sifted through the patchwork of memories, trying to fix his face from the anonymous looks he threw at me from the thin threads of my Greenlandic childhood.

"We can go," I said, just a few minutes later.

Eko took my hand, squeezed it once, and then led me through the graves and back to the town. He said we could stay as long as I wanted to, but I had seen enough, for the moment at least. I spent the previous night walking the gravel roads of Angmagssalik. It was too bright to sleep, but the house was too dark for me to spend another hour inside it. I didn't have the words to describe why, but I knew I would feel better if we left. It was too much, too soon, and I felt the need to keep moving.

"I can always come back," I said, as we sailed across the fjord to the airport.

"*Aap*," Eko said. "Now you know the way."

We flew across the inland ice – a vast sheet of lonely white – to the old American air base at Kangerlussuaq, landing beneath clear skies with a strong wind pushing at the tail of the aircraft. I waited as Eko arranged for seats on a military flight going north. There were more Europeans in Kangerlussuaq than Greenlanders, but the handful who were there greeted Eko with a warmth that I found both odd and amusing. When the men had finished shaking his hand, and the women had stepped back from his embrace, Eko beckoned to me, drawing me into their circle of warmth, reuniting me with my people.

"They don't really know me," he told me, as we waited in the cantina, sipping strong black coffee and chewing sandwiches made from old bread. "But I don't dissuade them. It's important to make friends, Inniki. It's important to know one's own people, to be connected."

"You *look* connected."

"*Aap*," he said. "But actually, I am *reconnecting*, just like you. But it will take longer for you. You have been away for so long. You must give it time."

One of the crew from the American Air Force flight to Thule Air Base called to Eko, as he corralled a group of scientists and their equipment spilling over the tables and chairs at the far end of the cantina. Eko grabbed our bags and we followed the crewman out of the airport onto the apron. He led us to the loading ramp at the rear of a large American transport plane. Eko's eyes widened, his lips curving into a broad smile.

"That's all you've got?" the crewman asked, with a nod at our two small holdalls.

"Yes," Eko said.

"And you're going to Thule?"

"And then on to *Thule*." Eko smiled as the crewman frowned. "The village, north of the air base."

"How are you going to get there?"

"There is still ice, no?"

"Yeah, there's ice."

"Then it won't be a problem."

Eko winked at me, and then carried our bags up the ramp, dumping them beside the bucket seats. The crewman secured them beneath a heavy cargo net, before nodding for us to sit and gesturing at the lap belts.

"Be sure to put them on," he said. "Keep them fastened."

I sat down, felt the stiff canvas beneath the seat of my jeans, and buckled my belt. The crewman sighed as the string of scientists cursed their way up the ramp. Eko pointed at the crewman and whispered something about *ilalaarneq* – patience, smiling as the scientists sweated under repeated trips up and down the ramp.

A thin man with a long white beard stuffed his jacket beneath a cargo net and slumped onto the bucket seat beside me.

"Do you speak English?" he asked.

"Yes," I said.

"First time to Thule?"

"Yes."

"Well, there's nothing there but ice, rock and snow." The man shrugged as he tightened his belt. "I'm sure you'll love it."

The man's companions filled the remaining seats, clicking the metal clasps of their belts, and swapping comments, wondering if the flags and stakes were with the core boxes, or if they would have to buy more fuel for the generators.

"Never mind all that," the thin man said. "So long as we packed the bourbon..."

The crewman pressed his palm on a large button to close the rear ramp, as the scientists laughed. I caught one of the younger men staring at me. He stopped when Eko took my hand, locking his fingers within mine.

"Sweethearts?" the young man said.

"Married," Eko said, with a smile. Eko curbed the wild thought in my head with a reassuring look and a quick squeeze of my hand. He leaned in close to whisper in my ear. "It's a long flight and you need to rest." He nodded at the young man. "He won't bother you now."

The man stared for a moment more, before turning to his companion, laughing at something as he nodded in my direction. His next words were drowned out by the roar of the aircraft's engines and Eko's hot breath in my ear.

"Lockheed C-141A *Starlifter*," he said.

The light in Eko's eyes stripped years from the gaunt cheeks and the wispy beard of his face. Eko grinned as the plane taxied to the runway and the crewman did a final check of the passengers, reaching down to fasten one of the scientists' belts. I closed my eyes, and as the plane sped down the runway, the image of Kunuk's grave rushed towards me, pressing me deeper into my seat than the force of take-off. I squeezed Eko's hand, digging my knuckles into his thigh as the plane roared into the air.

Eko leaned into the wind as he carried our bags off the aircraft, shortly after landing at Thule Air Force Base. I shivered beside him as we showed our papers to an officer waiting to process the passengers. He pointed to a vehicle to the right of the aircraft when Eko asked about a ride to Dundas.

"The driver will give you a lift down to the Eskimo village," he said.

I followed Eko to a dark blue Jeep, waited as he talked with the driver, and then climbed into the back. The driver sped between the uniform buildings of the base, slowing to wave at civilian contractors. He pointed at the flat top of Dundas mountain, and said something about hiking up it as soon as the ice had melted. I dipped my head and leaned between the driver and Eko to look at the mountain. The burnt granite rock contrasted sharply with the white sea ice at its base. Eko pointed at a ship, far out to sea, breaking the ice beneath its bow, as it forged a channel to the dock.

"It's real thick this year," the driver said, gesturing at the ice. "Maybe three metres."

Eko nodded, and then pointed to a small hut close to the edge of the ice. The driver swung the Jeep towards it, and then slowed to a stop. He shook Eko's hand and stared at me for a moment, as I climbed out of the Jeep. Eko grabbed our bags and the driver turned the Jeep in a tight arc, before accelerating back to the base.

I wiped the dust from my face and looked down at the gravel at my feet. The wind whipped at my hair, chilling the back of my neck. I shivered again. Eko dropped our bags at his feet, took my hand and led me to the door of the tiny hut. A bitch, heavy with pups, waddled towards us and I bent down to greet it. Eko smiled as a small man with dark brown skin and keen eyes opened the door. He looked at Eko and flashed his gums, curling his tongue around a single tooth as he smiled.

I had gotten used to Eko's reception each time we arrived in a town or landed at an airport in Greenland, the heartfelt handshakes, the light lingering touches. But this was different. The two men smiled for the better part of a minute before Eko took the smaller man's hand.

"This is Nassaannguaq," he said, after another minute. "My uncle."

I stepped around the bitch and took Nassaannguaq's hand, felt the familiar strength and warmth in his touch that reminded me of Eko. Height separated the men, but a closer look revealed the same thin cheeks, the same wispy beard and alert eyes. Only Nassaannguaq's tongue seemed larger, exposed as it was through the lack of teeth.

"This is Inniki," Eko said. "From Tunu."

I glanced at Eko as Nassaannguaq held my hand. *Tunu*, East Greenland, my home. Eko had insisted on taking me to Greenland, as part of the deal with Frode. He had taken me home to see my family, and now we were going to see his.

Nassaannguaq started to speak, and I frowned at the vague familiarity of the words. Where I expected a double 's' he used an 'h', challenging the reconstruction of my rusty Greenlandic. Eko smiled as he caught the frown on my forehead, adding the missing consonants as he translated for his uncle.

"It's the northern dialect," he said. "You'll get used to it." He added something for his uncle and Nassaannguaq raised his eyebrows in a universal Greenlandic *yes*.

"You need warm clothes," Nassaannguaq said. "Come."

He gestured for me to follow him inside the hut. The floorboards were thin and black with age, smooth beneath the soles of my boots. Nassaannguaq waved me into a small wooden chair with a thin cushion, while he pulled clothes out of a large sea chest. Between the chest and the bed, and a tiny table pressed against the wall beneath the window, there was little space to move. It was just as well that Nassaannguaq was a small man. He tossed a pair of sealskin *kamikker* onto the floor in front of me. I took the hint and unlaced my boots, glancing at the curled edges and faded print of the newspaper sheets pasted to the walls. The soft beige light from the window highlighted the tiny tears in the sheets of greased paper, several layers thick, tacked beneath wooden spars. Nassaannguaq added a sealskin smock and a pair of polar bear skin trousers to the pile at my feet. He waited for me to start dressing, before finding more clothes for Eko. Thinner and with signs of a lot more wear and tear, Eko's travelling clothes smelled used, and I wrinkled my nose at the wild tang that filled the hut as he dressed.

"I will take you to Thule," Nassaannguaq said.

"*Aap.*"

"The dogs are fresh."

"That's good."

Nassaannguaq took Eko's hand, holding it firmly, as he reached up to grip his nephew's chin, turning Eko's head from side to side.

"Why have you come back?" Nassaannguaq asked. "Were you called?"

"*Aap.*"

Nassaannguaq nodded. "Are you ready?"

"I am, uncle."

Nassaannguaq let go of Eko's chin. He squeezed his

hand and smiled. "You *are* ready."

"I would have come sooner," Eko said. "But…"

"I understand," Nassaannguaq said. "You were delayed."

"*Aap.*"

"But you are ready now. I will take you to Thule and then on, to the other place."

It wasn't just the missing consonants that confused me. I wondered if Frode knew what he was agreeing to, when he accepted Eko's terms, as I realised that bringing me back to Greenland was only a part of it. Eko was going home too, further north than I had ever been. And, from the little I understood, Thule was not the final destination.

Chapter 6

The wind curled around my neck as the dogs fanned out in front of Nassaannguaq's sledge. I dug my fingers into the smooth reindeer skins covering the thwarts, lashed in a zigzag pattern of sealskin cord. I teased the reindeer hairs beneath my nails, scratching back and forth as we left the flat top of Dundas Mountain far behind us. Eko and Nassaannguaq chatted behind me, and I caught the occasional cloud of smoke from the cigarette Nassaannguaq and Eko shared. I struggled to remember when I had last smoked a cigarette, and how awkward it would be to smoke like Brigitte Bardot, bundled in seal and polar bear furs, sitting cross-legged on a broad wooden sledge, creaking, twisting and bumping over the sea ice. I could feel the toes of Eko's *kamikker* just behind me, pressing into my bottom and the thick polar bear skin trousers trapping the chill Greenland air between the oily fibres. Surrounded by ice I had never been warmer.

The sledge creaked as Eko fidgeted behind me. He tapped me on the shoulder, and I turned around so that we could talk.

"You can sleep if you want," he said. "We will arrive late tonight."

"Tonight?" I lifted my chin and looked at the sun filling the sky above us. It would not set before late

September.

"You have to sleep sometime."

"I will." I curled my fingers inside the deep cuffs of the sealskin smock. "What about you? What are you and Nassaannguaq talking about?"

The corner of Eko's mouth curled into a smile, but the look in his eyes was far more serious, without the familiar crease of the skin around them. He slipped his fingers inside the cuff of my smock and pressed his fingertips against mine.

"I told Frode I would accept his job on one condition…"

"That you take me home to Greenland." I locked my fingers within his and smiled. "I'm pleased you did."

"Good," he said. "But I needed to come home too."

Eko looked over his shoulder and said something to his uncle. I caught only a little of the conversation, their soft consonants were lost in the wind, the padding of the dogs' paws on the ice, and the creak of the sledge within its bindings. Nassaannguaq caught my eye and smiled. He nodded at Eko, curled the dog whip into the air and adjusted our course with soft commands, and the snap of the whip on the ice. Eko turned around, squeezed my fingers once and then rested his hands on his knees.

"I have a purpose," he said. "A promise to my uncle and a duty to my people."

"A duty?"

"Something I must do." Eko plucked at the grazed knees of his sealskin trousers. The fur was bare in places, revealing parched patches of soft leather. "It will seem strange to you," he said. "Frightening, perhaps."

"In Thule?"

"*Aap.*"

Nassaannguaq cracked the whip, slapping the ice with the tip, turning the sledge to the left to begin crossing the fjord. Thule lay somewhere in the far distance, hidden within a tiny layer of brown rock squeezed between the inland ice sheet and the frozen white sea. Eko gazed at the long-tongued glaciers on our right, licking at the sea ice like children tasting lollipops, their tongues sticking to the frosted sides. He took my hand.

"This is your country," he said. "All of it. Just like it is mine, my uncle's, it belongs to the people, the Inuit, us Greenlanders. What I will do in Thule is a part of something bigger than me, but it will allow me to *see* all of this, and to protect the people."

"I don't understand. You're going to work for Frode."

"And I will. What I do in Thule will help me to help him."

"He wants you to work undercover," I said. "Doesn't he?"

"*Aap.*"

"In Greenland?"

"Some of the time." Eko tilted his head to one side; his eyes narrowed. "How much has he told you?"

"Very little. Only that he needed me to convince you." The chill wind blistered my lips as I smiled. "I think it worked."

"It did," Eko said. "And I'm glad. But what more will he ask of you?"

"He said he would tell me when we get back to Denmark."

"You must be careful, Inniki. Frode Worsaae is a nice man. Gentle. But he is like *terianniaq*, the fox, he will change his colour when he needs to. I think he has other plans for you. This," he said, waving his hand at the ice and the glaciers in the distance, "is just the beginning. He wanted you to see this, to reconnect with your country. He has plans for you, Inniki." Eko shifted on the sledge, uncurled his legs, sliding them along the reindeer skins as he stretched flat on the sledge. "I will sleep now."

Nassaannguaq grinned at me through a cloud of smoke from the cigarette jammed into the corner of his mouth. "Sleep," he said, and I nodded. But the sky was too bright and the sea too white for sleeping. I felt more alive than I had ever felt in the city. I was infused by the clean air, intoxicated by the thrill of travelling in the north, across the sea, beneath the bright polar sun. Eko's warning nibbled at the edge of my Arctic intoxication, coupled with the image of Kunuk's grave and the shadows lurking in my family home. My mind raced as the blood coursed through my body. I hadn't smoked, I realised, because I didn't need it. Greenland provided all the stimulation I needed, together with a sense of the unknown, lying just out of reach. Unfathomable, *dangerous* even.

Eko stirred as I lay down beside him. I turned onto my side, resting my head on my arm and curling my fingers into my hair. The bob of black hair I wore was growing, and I thought of the long locks of my childhood, when my hair reached down to my bottom, and I could sit on it. Or Kunuk could, when I was lying down, trapping me on the ground as I twisted to one side and rolled to the other, laughing and giggling until he moved, and I could pull myself free. I imagined myself with long hair, fashioned in the style of the Greenlander; Inniki the Inuit woman. The thought lingered as Eko pressed his fingers into my hair as he turned onto his side. We lay there, curled within each other's furs, as the sledge creaked and warped across the ice. I searched for the panting of the dogs, caught the steady rhythm of their gait, and the occasional soft snap of Nassaannguaq's whip, as he drove the dogs into the night, across the fjord, beneath the sun, all the way to Thule.

I woke with the sound of a hundred dogs. The sledge creaked as Eko stood up, and I sat at his feet. We were surrounded by a flotilla of wooden sledges. Some were full of children, the driver obscured beneath a tumult of furs and cheeky faces. The children of Thule waved at Eko as the drivers of the sledges pulled alongside, pulled ahead, and circled us. There were other sledges too, faster with twice the number of Nassaannguaq's dogs. Women smiled, waved and shrieked softly as Eko leaped onto the ice to catch a passing sledge, greeting the passengers, shaking hands with the driver, before leaping onto the ice once more, and racing for the next sledge. The children's sledge was his last, as they buried him beneath tiny bodies, crawling onto his back and pressing his body onto the skins stretched across the thwarts. I laughed and waved at the children seated in a row like birds on a wire, tapping the heels of their *kamikker* on Eko's body.

Nassaannguaq slowed his dogs as we approached the beach. The tide was out and the ice foot almost level with the sand, gravel and grit marking the division between the land and the sea. Hunters took hold of his dogs, separating the lines and anchoring the dogs to the ice, as Nassaannguaq coiled the whip around the sledge uprights. He shrugged the journey from his body with a sigh, stretched, and then smoked as the hunters fed his dogs with dried fish from the racks, seal bones with black, sun-leached meat, and polar bear scraps. The air was filled with the sound of runners scraping across the ice as more sledges arrived behind us. The children giggled across the ice. Two of the larger children, a girl and a boy, dragged their prize by the fingertips, while their smaller brothers and sisters curled their arms around Eko's ankles, forcing him to drag them from the ice to the beach. I laughed again, and then felt the warmth of slim fingers slide into the palm of my hand, tugging me from the sledge after Eko.

I looked down at a shock of black hair, pressed flat on either side of a little girl's face. The girl spoke with the same soft consonants that Nassaannguaq and Eko shared, and I wrinkled my nose in confusion. She tilted her head to one side, studied my face, and then resolved to take me to shore, and I walked with her across the ice.

There was blood on the ice. Loose dogs and puppies chewed and clawed at it, as the larger dogs ate, and the hunters shoved and nudged the teams to their anchors. The ice just in front of the beach was puddled with clear blue water as the summer sun did its best to release the sea from the grip of winter. The girl picked a path between the dogs, the blood and the surface melt water to where Eko stood, ringed with women and children.

"This is my family," he said, as I joined him. "All of them."

The girl let go of my hand and ran across the beach. She slipped into the huddle of sealskin pressed around Eko, and was lost, camouflaged in the spots and stripes of the skins, the jet-black hair, and the sun-dark skin of the Inuit.

The hunters gathered around Nassaannguaq, sharing news, cigarettes and lingering looks directed towards Eko. They smoked and chatted until Nassaannguaq clapped his hands and strode across the ice, parting the wave of children pressed around Eko as he stepped onto the beach. He spoke softly and pointed past the wooden huts and low sod-bricked dwellings, past the more robust colonial buildings, to a lonely graveyard to the right of the settlement. The Greenlanders hushed as Nassaannguaq walked across the beach to the dirt road. Eko followed.

"*Naamik,*" a woman said, as she shook her head. "You come with me."

She fussed at a tear in my smock, firing a stream of questions at me as we walked behind Eko and Nassaannguaq. She stopped at a small wooden house and led me inside, forcing me to bend in the tiny, spartanly-furnished room next to the kitchen as she gripped the cuffs of my smock and peeled it off my head. I looked up as she teased at my short hair, brushing her wiry fingers against my cheek. She fiddled with the braces holding the polar bear skin trousers in place, then slipped them over my shoulders, clicking and clucking with her tongue, gesturing for me to shrug my way out of the heavy furs. She brought me clothes to change into, a white smock, broad black shorts made of the thickest seal fur, and long white *kamikker*, soft thigh-length boots sewn from the smoothest skin I had ever felt.

"My name is Serseq," she said, as she fiddled with the fit of my *kamikker*. "I am Eko's mother's sister."

"Inniki," I said, jerking as Serseq adjusted the shorts to cover the top of the *kamikker*.

Serseq tucked the hem of the cotton smock inside the

waist band of the shorts and took a step back to appraise the fit. For the second time in as many days, I had been transformed. Gone was the wild, musky smell of travelling furs. Serseq had dressed me for the land, in the style of the women and people of Thule. She tapped my bottom and gestured for me to turn, and I jerked again with the tug and twist of Serseq's adjustments. She tutted and clucked as she fine-tuned my clothes, until, with a brief nod and a stream of soft sentences, Serseq was satisfied.

"It is a big day," she said. "You have to look right."

She guided me to a wooden chair and waited for me to sit, teasing my hair as soon as she could reach it.

"What is going to happen to Eko?" I asked.

Serseq clucked softly and shook her head. "Can't talk about it. You must wait."

Chapter 7

I slipped out of Serseq's house when she went upstairs. The gravel on the road between the houses was lumpy beneath my feet, but not sharp; the soles of the *kamikker* were thicker than most high street shoes I had worn in Copenhagen. I made my way up the road between the houses, smiling at the gaggle of children following me, as I walked towards the graveyard. The sun turned a low circle in the sky, leaving a sandpaper light in its wake, with layers of blue thinning to white above me. I stopped as one of the children scurried alongside me, tugging at the hem of my *kamikker*. She pointed at the entrance to the graveyard and shook her head.

"I'm looking for Eko," I said, but the girl just shook her head, and then ran to join the other children waiting in the shadow of the last house before the graveyard fence.

The fence was a boundary of stones, with the smooth sides turned upright and bleached by the long summer sun. I ignored the children and took another step, pausing at the sound of a skin drum beating on the light wind blowing up from the sea ice. I scanned the graveyard and saw Nassaannguaq tapping a length of bone against the wooden rim of the drum, tapping a steady beat as he swayed, his arms moving like a metronome, tapping one way and then the other. Eko would be close, and I took another step, felt the wind on my cheek, and stopped still when I saw Eko lying on the ground beside a grave. The mound of stones was barely higher than he was, the cross long since weathered to a thin stick, pushed to one side by the wind. He lay with his hands crossed over his naked chest. The wind lifted his long black hair and curled it across his face in soft waves. He wore a simple loin cloth at his waist. The rest of his clothes were piled to one side, discarded, not folded. It was as if he had shed the skin of the seal and was reborn – bloody. There were streaks of blood on his skin and his palms were wet and red. He gripped a flint knife in one fist.

I held my breath as I sank to my knees. Curiosity held my anxiety at bay as Nassaannguaq beat the drum and Eko lay flat on the rocky ground of the graveyard. The first scratch of claws on the gravel below the graveyard were masked by the drum, and it took a moment more before I realised that Nassaannguaq had stopped drumming. He held the drum at his side, and the stick flat against his thigh. He stood still, carved into the landscape, as the great body of a white bear emerged from the rocks below the graveyard. The bear huffed its way towards Nassaannguaq, and I pressed my hand to my lips, covering my mouth as it sniffed the air, neck forwards, snout low, then high, searching and scenting. It entered the graveyard, picking its way between the burial mounds until it was less than a few feet from where Eko lay.

I raised my head, opened my mouth to shout, only to feel warm earthy fingers clap the breath from my lips, as a boy pressed his hands on my face. He shook his head, plucked at my fingers and tugged me to my feet. I stumbled behind the boy, walking backwards, my eyes fixed on Eko, waiting for him to notice the bear, to rise, to flee.

The warning shout caught in my throat as the boy pulled me harder, and I followed him out of the graveyard, stepping over the boundary stones. The stones were electric, tingling through my body with a hidden power, as the boy crouched on his heels and gestured for me to do the same. He held my hand, and I could feel the grit between his fingers, charged with the power of the earth, just like the boundary was charged with the spent energy of the dead.

"Eko," I whispered.

The boy pointed and I looked, saw the bear twist its long powerful neck, as it turned towards Eko. The bear huffed, and I imagined its hot rancid breath on my cheeks, pushing into my lungs.

"*Angakkoq*," the boy said, grinning as he flicked the tip of his finger towards Eko.

The bear swayed to one side as Eko scrabbled to his feet. The loin cloth slipped and Eko stood naked before the great white bear, his bare feet pressed into the gravel beside the grave. The bear lurched to one side, raising its paw. I saw Eko twist at the waist to look at Nassaannguaq as the old man started to beat the drum. The bear swiped its paw to one side and Eko caught the blow within his hands and arms, tumbling onto the grave as the tempo of Nassaannguaq's drum increased.

"He'll be killed," I said.

"*Naamik*," the boy said. "Watch."

There was blood on Eko's chest, four thin lines of red stretching around his side, dripping blood beneath his arm. The stones beneath the bear's paws clacked and rolled to all sides as it scrambled up and over the grave, lunging at Eko, huffing with every missed strike. Eko darted to all sides, spinning the bear in tight circles. I looked for the elastic that bound them together, convinced that it was real, as I could not understand why Eko did not run, or at the very least, leap just a little farther from the bear's claws.

The bear struck Eko again, and I heard it roar as Eko clutched at his chest, smearing the blood across his skin as he turned his back to the bear. I gripped the boy's hand, convinced now that Eko would run, lifting his pale buttocks like the Arctic hare, and leaping out of the bear's reach. But the drum stopped beating, and Eko stood still. He let his hands fall to his sides, tucking his chin to his chest as the bear raised its paw and raked Eko's back with its claws. I scrambled to my feet as Eko fell out of sight, slipping behind the scattered rocks of the burial mound, as the bear took another step towards him.

Nassaannguaq cried out as the bear approached Eko, squealing and shrieking, beating the drum until the bear retreated. When the bear turned, Nassaannguaq threw grave rocks, chasing the bear towards the sea ice. The boy let go of my hand and joined the children and teens running and shrieking around the corner of the graveyard boundary, hands raised, lungs expelled. When the men and women of Thule emerged from their houses, the bear ran, loping at first, then lengthening its stride as it bounded towards the refuge of the ice.

I stepped across the boundary of stones, only to stop at a word from Serseq. She skittered towards me, hands raised, waving me out of the graveyard.

"*Naamik*," she said. "Wait."

"But Eko…"

"You must wait."

She took my hand and pulled me further from the graveyard, just as the children returned, red-cheeked, glowing. She ushered them towards the houses with one outstretched arm, the other curled around my waist.

Nassaannguaq's drum started to beat with slow, regular bone-taps on the wooden rim. Each tap seemed to anchor my feet to the ground, and Serseq gave up trying to pull me away. She stood beside me; her wiry fingers hooked into the sealskin shorts wrapped around my waist.

"Wait," she said. "Wait and see."

"Wait for what?"

"*Angakkoq.*"

"I don't understand," I said. "You're saying *shaman.* Why?"

Serseq pointed at the graves, and I turned to see Eko stand. He trembled on his feet, blood streaming from the ripped flesh on his back and side. Serseq gasped as he turned to face us, pressing his hands to his body. It looked like he was counting his bones. Eko's lips moved as he pressed his fingers into his skin, starting with his head, working down to his toes. His words were lost in the wind, his eyes, staring alternately at the mountain and ice behind us, then the Arctic grasses and the tiny-leaved crowberry bushes. I held my breath as his gaze drifted past Serseq and me. But his face showed no sign of recognition, only his lips moved with what I imagined were the names of every bone in his body.

"He lay with his father," Serseq said. "The bear carried him to the otherworld, and now he is returned, whole. *Angakkoq.*"

Serseq tugged at my arm. She turned me away from the graveyard and we walked down the gravel road to her house. She paused at the sound of a helicopter approaching, its rotors beating the thin summer air like an oversized hyperactive drum. I saw the sun reflected on its windshield, watched as the children gathered and pointed, squirreling left and right, running in small circles as the helicopter approached. The pilot flew low over the settlement, circling the graveyard and throwing up a cloud of dust as it settled on the road to land between Eko and me. The children peeked through the slits of their fingers, giggling as the pilot cut the engines and the rotors whined to a slow stop. They ran forwards as the side door slid open, and a small man climbed out of the helicopter, tugging the headset from his ears and pressing it into the hands of a crewman.

Frode Worsaae smoothed his thin grey hair to the sides of his head and dug his hands into his pockets. He pressed lollipops and paper-wrapped toffees into the children's fingers, reaching over the smaller ones to treat the teens pressing at the edges of the circle of Thule folk that buoyed Frode along the road towards me.

"You look very Greenlandic, Ínniki," he said, as he approached.

"Yes," I said.

"And Eko?" Frode gestured at the graveyard behind the helicopter. "Is that him I saw when we flew in?"

I nodded. "Yes."

"The pilot spotted a bear running from Thule. He pointed it out, but I didn't see it. Did you?"

"It was here," I said. "It attacked Eko."

"Really?"

Frode held out his hand to greet Serseq, frowning for a second as she turned away. The children followed her down the road, peeling paper from Frode's toffees. Frode waited until we were alone.

"He did it then," he said.

"Did what?"

"Became a shaman. He told me about it once, and then I did some reading. It's a passion of mine," Frode said. "Religious customs and practices. *Le Chamanisme et les techniques archaïques de l'extase.* It was translated into English just last year." Frode smiled. "A monumental work. Scholarly," he said, with an indulgent twist of his lips. "Fascinating."

"He nearly died, Frode," I said.

"Ah, but he must, you see. He must *nearly* die. He must return from the dead. Did he count his bones? Did you see him?"

"*Aap,*" I said.

"Ah, and now you are speaking Greenlandic. This is good."

"Is it what you wanted?"

"Oh, my dear Inniki, everything is turning out just as I wanted. But now, I'm afraid, time is running out, and I have come to take you back. Both of you."

"What happens now?"

"For Eko?" Frode gestured at the settlement between us and the sea ice. "He will stay in Greenland. His work is here, for the moment at least."

"And me?

"You will come with me to Denmark. I have a job for you, and I hope you will accept it."

Suddenly, it seemed as though Denmark was very far away. Far from Greenland, and far from Eko. Frode smiled, pointing at my wrinkled nose and the frown furrowing my forehead.

"You're wondering about Eko?"

"Will I see him again?"

"Yes, of course. Inniki," he said. "Eko is your job. But you need training to be able to do that job. Coming to Greenland," he said, "was only the beginning."

Frode turned at the sound of someone walking along the gravel road. We both stared as Eko walked towards us. The wind had dried his blood in streaks across his body, stripes across his face, and clumps clogging his wispy black beard. But the light of Greenland danced in his eyes, shining across his teeth as he smiled.

"*Angakkoq*," I said, as he stopped to shake hands with Frode.

"*Aap*," Eko said. He pressed his bloody fingers to my cheek, and I smelled the earth, the grit and the blood of Greenland on his skin.

Narkotika

II

Chapter 8

The first three miles from the camp were always the worst. After that, once we left the heath and started running through the dunes and onto the beach, I could feel the wind on my face, smell the salt of the sea, and for at least one more mile I could imagine I was in Greenland. But the sun in Greenland was stronger, the wind drier, and the people far more hospitable. The woman running behind me cursed my heels, shouting between breaths.

"Faster, bitch. Keep moving. You're slowing us down."

She was right, and I knew I could go faster. But the faster I ran, the sooner we were finished with the beach, and then it was back to the barracks, to the canvas deck of the boxing ring, the woman's fists, the instructor's constant shouting, in English, his mother tongue, although I often wondered if he had a mother. He seemed to enjoy cursing mine, questioning why she had ever pushed me out. I came close – three times – to telling him she was dead, and that if he really wanted to know, then all he had to do was throw himself off the top of the barracks. But I knew the fall would never kill him, that the barrack buildings were too low, hooped as they were into the ground, like long metal igloos with no light, no air, and nowhere to hide. The canvas was my only respite, and I would hug it each time I landed on it, blood dribbling from my lip as *she* stalked around my body, desperate for the instructor to drag me to my feet so she could knock me down again, just one more time, to put the little *Eskimo bitch* in her rightful place, at her feet, where she belonged.

I never knew her name, although I had many names for her. I whispered them over the surgical tape I peeled from my knuckles each night, just to let them breathe, to let the skin heal a little before the abrasive activity of the following day. I read a little each night, once I was done with my knuckles, the blisters on my heels and between my toes – once all my sores were airing, I would lean back on my pillow, measure the length of my hair, and read. I skimmed the words, letting my eyes follow the shapes of the letters, rolling the sounds of the words on my tongue while my mind wandered. I thought of Kunuk, teasing the memory of him with the promise of just a few more weeks and *then* he could sit on my hair. I thought of Frode – dark thoughts mostly, cursing him for conning me into coming to his little training camp, preparing me for some dirty little assignment that might or might not have anything to do with Eko.

Eko.

I thought of him a lot.

The last image I had of him, the one I chose to remember, was of his blood-streaked body, naked, cut and scarred, but with a powerful light shining in his eyes. He looked strong, he *smelt* strong, like the land, and I thought about him, our people and our land. Thinking of Eko and Greenland got me through each night, and out of bed each morning.

She had a bunk at the far end of the barracks, closest

to the door. The men slept in the adjacent barracks. On warm nights, when the windows were open and the wind barely licked at the sand between the dunes, I could hear them snoring. There were three men and two women in the camp, not including the male instructors. I don't think any of us knew exactly why we were there, or what our purpose might be. All I knew was that *my* purpose was Eko, and that thought helped me into my cotton shirt, my cotton pants, and the heavy army fatigues they called trousers. I used some of the surgical tape on the hems, taping them tight to my ankles, before pulling on the stiff leather boots for the morning run.

And there we were again, on the beach, the wind in my face, and the angry Danish woman just behind me, pushing, cursing, goading.

When I look back on it, I think that was the moment Frode had been waiting for, because as soon as it happened, the woman left the camp a matter of hours later.

"Slow bitch," she said.

I heard her hawk a gob of spit into her mouth as we ran. I glanced to my left, saw her chin rise just a little, and then I put on the brakes, digging my toes into the sand, and thrusting my elbows behind me. She ran straight into my back and we collapsed onto the beach.

I didn't wait for her to get up. As soon as I could roll clear, I grabbed a handful of sand and cast it into her face. The sand clung to the spit on her lips and the sweat on her forehead. The men were too far ahead to notice, and I was too quick for her to cry out. After the handful of sand I threw in her face, I scrambled to my feet and kicked another cloud of sand into her mouth.

She coughed and spat on the beach, coating her hair

and cheeks with fine sand as she brushed at her face. I looked down at her, wondering if this was how *she* felt when looking down at me during the daily boxing match. I wondered if the instructor would shout at her, if he would drag her to her feet, holding her steady for me to knock the wind out of her lungs her with a solid strike to the gut. I didn't wait for her to get up, nor did I think about waiting for the instructor. I simply pulled back my foot and slammed my boot into her chin.

The crack of her jaw breaking was the most satisfying sound I had heard in a month.

I didn't know why she was at the camp, what purpose she served, but I knew that the second my toe connected with her chin that it was over, that I had climbed some metaphorical wall, and that I was now on the other side.

Closer to Eko.

I didn't have the answer to that. No-one did. I hadn't seen Frode since he dropped me off at the camp shortly after we returned from Greenland. He said something about not wasting any more time, and the need to move things along quickly. Perhaps I had been dragging my heels. Perhaps he had been close by all along, waiting for this moment. But it was strange how quickly he arrived at the camp, only an hour after the ambulance scooped the woman out of her bed in the barracks, and out of my life for good.

I took the longest shower I had had in a month, peeled the tape from my fingers, heels, toes, knees and elbows, measured my hair, and then dressed for dinner in the third tubular building that doubled as a classroom, gym and mess hall. The three men sat with the gym instructor at the table closest to the kitchen, Frode sat alone at the other.

"Hello Inniki."

Frode nodded at the instructor and waited for him to lead the three men into the classroom at the far end of the building. A breeze rattled the hooped sheets of metal, and the men's voices were spirited away in much the same way the ambulance had removed the woman.

"Just us," Frode said, as I sat down.

"This is a horrible place," I said.

"Yes."

"I hate it."

Frode prodded at the meat on his plate. "Did you get the books I sent you?"

"Too scholarly," I said.

"But you read them?"

"*Aap*. There was nothing else to do."

"Tell me about them," he said.

There were so many, I didn't know where to start.

"The English ones were hard," I said. "They took longer."

Frode poured water into two glasses, pushing one across the table towards me as I thought about the different books he had sent me. They always arrived on a Monday morning – homework for the week. After the first week, I began to think of Frode's books as a challenge, and that if I finished all of them before the following Monday, he would let me leave. But, as fast as I read, the swollen eye *she* gave me one Tuesday, and the bout of diarrhoea we all had during my rotation in the kitchen, had slowed me down. Frode's books kept coming, and the pile to be read grew every week.

"You sent me the book about that man in the desert."

"Lawrence of Arabia," Frode said, and a smile tugged at the corner of his mouth. "It's a favourite, I confess."

"It's boring, Frode. Unless you want to learn about Arab divisions, and crossing deserts no-one should cross, to attack a city no-one thought could be attacked. Unless you want to read about *that*..."

"Which you obviously did," he said. "Clara always said you were a bright one, Inniki. And, you are growing your hair."

"*Aap*."

"Good."

Frode said *good* a lot, but in such a way that I never fully understood what he meant. After a month in the training camp, under the tutelage of caustic instructors and the fists of the *she-devil*, I had become bolder than I might ever have become if I had never left the city.

"What do you mean by that? That it *looks* good, or that it *is* good? And why?"

"Well," Frode said. "I think it looks good, and it is good that you look like a Greenlander. That's all I want, Inniki. For you to be Greenlandic."

"To help Eko?"

"Yes," Frode said. "And now we come to it."

If I could have grown another inch of hair in that moment I would have. The very thought of seeing Eko again, being near him, smelling the wild earth on his skin, I would have given anything for that. But Frode wore that *complicated* look that I had seen before, and I knew it wasn't going to be straightforward.

"About Eko...," he said.

"What about him?"

"He's very good, you know."

"At what?"

"At blending in. Now, I don't know if it has anything

to do with that shaman business in Thule, but he has a canny way of fitting in, so much so it's not always easy to know whose side he is on."

"You sent him undercover."

"Yes," Frode said. "And now, I simply don't know if he has been successful or if he has been successfully turned, against us. You understand?"

"Not really," I said. The scabs on my knuckles popped as I laid my hands flat on the table. "I've been here for so long – running, studying, and fighting. They even showed me how to use a gun. But no-one told me what I was going to do with it. No-one told me anything, Frode. So, perhaps now that you're here. Maybe you can tell me something. About Eko."

Frode took a sip of water, looking at me over the rim of the glass as he lifted it to his lips. He set it down heavily on the table, sloshing water up one side of the glass. He wiped at the drops on the table with the cuff of his sleeve, nodding as dried the surface.

"It *is* time," he said. "After today, well, it was a coincidence that you chose today to graduate."

"Graduate?"

"To make your mark," Frode said. He clasped his hands together and looked at me. "You have scored excellently in all your studies. Top of the class in map reading. Highly skilled with curious fingers in weapons handling and marksmanship. Of course," Frode said, laughing. "I told them that would be the Greenlander in you – good with your hands, especially with weapons that could be used for hunting. But they all agreed on one thing, you showed no signs of aggression. No matter how hard she tried, poor Heidi couldn't get you to fight, until today."

"Heidi?"

"Yes. I put her here, you know, just to test you. I didn't realise it would take so long. Neither did the instructors. They were ready to fail you. *Can't send someone into the field if they won't stand up for themselves.* That's what they said. Verbatim. So," he said. "Why didn't you fight back?"

The answer had been there all along, but I had never had to face it, or put it into words. But Frode asked, and I realised the answer might lead to Eko.

"Because we weren't alone," I said. "I didn't want an audience."

"You waited until you were alone?"

"*Aap.* When the men pulled ahead, like they usually do on the beach, I decided to do it then, today."

"You could have done it earlier," he said. "Why didn't you?"

"I wasn't finished with your books," I said, hiding my smile behind a sip of water.

Frode's laugh was contagious, and I spluttered water onto the table. It was my turn to wipe it clean.

"Ah, Inniki," he said. "What I could have done a week ago…"

The dull look in Frode's eyes was difficult to interpret, but my stomach churned with the thought that if I had punched poor Heidi the very first time she had hit me, I might have been with Eko already.

"Where is he, Frode?"

"He's on a ship," he said. "At least we think so. He left Halifax, Nova Scotia, two days ago. We think he's on his way to Greenland with a boat full of narcotics. The Americans have been tracking his movements in Canada, and they are ready to intercept him." Frode paused to take my hand. "I'm telling you this, Inniki, because I want you on that American ship. I need to know what's going on. I need to know what Eko is up to."

"And you think he'll tell me?"

"Ah, Inniki," Frode said. "I know he will."

Chapter 9

Frode spent most of the flight from Denmark to Canada cultivating a deep frown on his forehead. He didn't fly well, he told me, but that wasn't exactly true. He had hopped out of the American helicopter that landed in Thule with barely a second thought, hardly the manner of a man with a fear of flying. As for me, I *really* didn't fly well and the thunderstorms in Toronto, followed by the turbulence on landing in Halifax had not helped. I forgot all about Frode's frown when the American Coast Guard officer met us at the bottom of the stairs of the Halifax flight. He greeted Frode with a handshake and offered to take my bag, before leading us across the apron to a small Jeep.

"The helicopter will fly you out to the *Northwind*," he said, as he followed the markings towards a red and white helicopter parked just a short ride away from the terminal building. The rotors were already spinning, and the downdraught caught my hair, whirling it around my head until I clapped it beneath my hands and pressed my hair to my cheeks.

Frode paused at the foot of the short flight of steps leading inside the helicopter. I waited as he asked the Coast Guard officer about the length of the flight.

"That all depends, sir," he shouted. "The *Northwind* is in pursuit of a foreign vessel. They're keeping out of sight, just below the horizon, but at the first sign of trouble, the Captain will order the helm to full throttle."

"What's that?" Frode said, raising his voice to compete with the rotors.

"It's a chase, sir. When the Captain thinks it's time, he'll step on the gas." The officer nodded at the helicopter. "You could be in for a bumpy ride. Best get on board and let the crew tuck you in." He shook Frode's hand and passed my holdall to a crewman waiting by the door. "Good luck."

I climbed into the helicopter and took the headphones one of the crew gave me, flattening my hair behind my ears as I pressed them onto my head. The crewman reached out and twisted the microphone to a position in front of my lips. He reached for the jack at the end of a rubber-coated wire and pressed it into an adaptor above my seat. I smiled as he talked me through the seat belt, and the bucket seats. He gave Frode the same talk as he helped him into his seat.

"You look nervous, ma'am," the crewman said.

"I don't like flying," I said.

"Oh, this ain't like a plane. It's a whole other thing. You'll be fine." He raised his thumb. "You'll love it."

I raised my own thumb as the crewman sat down, and then turned to talk to Frode, waiting until he was settled in his seat before fiddling with the microphone in front of my lips.

"He said it will be better than the plane," I said.

"It will be. The wind doesn't affect them in quite the same way as a fixed-wing aircraft." Frode smiled as I frowned. "You flew from Thule," he said. "That wasn't so bad."

I nodded once and then thought of Eko and his love

of airplanes, the boyish shine to his face when he pressed his nose to the glass to stare at the propellers. He had worn the same look on the helicopter flight from Thule. I wished I could share his fascination and glee, but when the crewman retracted the steps and closed the door, I reached for Frode's hand and grabbed it.

The rotor noise changed pitch and the helicopter creaked as the pilot applied more power, lifting the aircraft until it barely rested on its wheels. The helicopter taxied to the runway like it was running on tiptoe, and I held my breath, letting it out in a shuddered gasp as we lifted into the air. I saw the airport buildings shrink below us, and then the pilot banked towards the sea. The buildings and trees shrank out of view to be replaced with the steely surface of the North Atlantic Ocean.

Frode patted my hand and I relaxed my grip on his fingers, nodding when he asked if I was all right, and again when he tried to convince me it was a much smoother ride than in an airplane. I pressed my hands into my lap and closed my eyes, trying my best to ignore the constant shake of the helicopter's fuselage, and the whine of its rotors. I allowed myself a small smile, feeling it tease my lips as I recalled words like *fuselage*, *pitch* and *taxiing along the apron*. I thought of the words in English, cursing Frode quietly for his homework, and wondering what books, if any, he might have brought with him. Having left most of my belongings in Copenhagen, and a few more at the training camp on the west coast of Denmark, I worried that I would be bored on a ship at sea, regardless of the mission.

My *mission* was Eko. It had been from the moment Frode waited for me outside the movie theatre. Whereas Frode had decided to invest time and effort into training me for the mission, it was my transformation from a city girl to a Greenlander that seemed to please him the most. While I often caught him looking at me, I never felt concerned, he simply didn't look at me in that way, unlike the furtive glances and lingering stares the other men gave me. Those looks could best be described as *hungry*. I opened my eyes and picked at the scabs on my knuckles, amazing myself at the sudden feeling of confidence that I could quash even the strongest appetites if I had too. Something else for which I had Frode to thank.

The remainder of the flight was as gentle as I supposed a shuddering can of metal beating through the air could be. I relaxed for a moment, stirring when the crewman got out of his seat to point at the red and white hull of the United States Coast Guard Cutter *Northwind*, just visible out of the helicopter's tiny windows. The pilot steered the helicopter into a tight banking turn to line up with the landing pad taking up the rear of the ship's deck.

"Frode," I said, shaking his arm to wake him. "This is it."

The pilot hovered the helicopter several feet above the landing pad. The crewman explained that he was anticipating the roll of the ship, and that we should be prepared for a sudden jolt. He got back in his seat and tightened the belt across his lap, gesturing for me to do the same. My stomach rolled as the ship rolled, and I closed my eyes. I pressed my hand to my mouth, cursing Frode for his platitudes, that helicopters were smooth rides. I flicked my eyes open at the sudden tug of my stomach, as if I was being stretched from the waist, down and up, and then the pilot slammed the helicopter down onto the landing pad, cutting the engines and applying the rotor brake as a small team of men swarmed around the helicopter to tie it down.

"We made it," Frode said, unbuckling his belt as the crewman staggered towards us.

It was suddenly a lot easier to appreciate why flying was a much better alternative to sailing. The helicopter pitched and rolled with the movement of the ship, and I clutched at Frode's elbow as we followed the crewman to the door. The fresh North Atlantic breeze was welcome, but it wasn't enough to the stem the churning in my stomach and I vomited onto the landing pad. The wind caught my hair, twisting it into the spit and vomit on my lips and chin. Frode took my arm, guiding me off the landing pad, past a smaller powerboat to the nearest door. I reached for the railing and he helped me to the side of the ship, holding my hair as I threw up into the ocean.

"*This* is your *attaché*?" a man said, as he joined us at the railing. "There's too many women on this boat already, Freddy."

"Inniki is the *only* woman on this ship," Frode said.

"Exactly," the man said. He prodded two stiff fingers into my shoulder. "What kind of a name is *Inniki*?"

I wiped my lips and said, "I'm Greenlandic."

"And what's that supposed to be?"

"I'm from Greenland." I frowned, and the sudden confusion settled my stomach for a moment. Long enough to get a good look, a lasting image, of a powerful man, perhaps ten years younger than Frode. His long brown fringe flickered in the wind, flashing past his eyes, forcing him to press thick fingers through his hair so that he could give me a hard stare. The look in his steel-blue eyes wasn't *hungry*, but more *predatory*. His look softened, and I felt a shift in his demeanour, as if I might provide an amusing distraction, just as long as I didn't get in his way.

"You look like a Comanche to me." He turned to Frode and said "We've got a briefing in five minutes. Get your squaw cleaned up if you want her to sit in." He snorted once before turning away and striding across the deck to the door. I heard it slam behind him just as the deck rolled and I grabbed the railings to vomit for the third time.

"That," Frode said, as I took a long, ragged breath and leaned against the rails, "was Roy Fitzpatrick. People call him *Fitz*." Frode nodded towards the door, as if we could see Fitzpatrick waiting by it. "He's with the Bureau of Narcotics and Dangerous Drugs, the BNDD. This is his operation."

"And I'm going to be attached to him?"

"You'll be my *attaché*. Basically, reporting to me, telling me everything that happens."

"And if I see Eko?" I said. The thought gave me a little burst of strength and I straightened my legs, nodding when Frode suggested we go inside.

"Then I expect you to do whatever the situation requires to protect him."

"Protect him?"

Frode opened the door, swinging it towards me. He waited for me to step over the deep lip and into the ship. Frode shut the door behind us. "There's a reason I sent you to a training camp, Inniki. Now, admittedly," he said, frowning as he led us in search of the briefing room, "it would have been better if you'd had more time to train. But circumstances must, as they say." Frode stopped beside two Coast Guard seamen standing either side of a door. The taller of the two men opened the door and gestured for us to go inside.

The air was thick with cigarette smoke, and I pressed my hands to my stomach, choosing to stand next to the door, instead of taking one of the empty seats at the table. Frode sat down as Fitzpatrick paused to acknowledge our arrival.

"You've all heard me say nice things about our Danish colleague, Freddy Worsaae." He waited for the other six men and the Captain of the *Northwind* to chuckle. "But you haven't met his squaw. I forget her name. But I wouldn't worry about it. You'll forget her as soon as we're done here."

"Ah," Frode said. "If I might."

"Might *what*?" Fitzpatrick said.

"I expect Inniki Rasmussen – that's her name – to accompany the strike team when you intercept the *Southern Star*. It is, after all, our intelligence that has helped the BNDD this far. You might remember that it was us who found the ship. I think that gives me the right to place an agent on your team."

"An agent?" Fitzpatrick laughed. I felt my stomach churn under his stare. He hooked the thumb of one hand into the broad leather belt at his waist and reached for his coffee mug with the other. He continued to stare until he had emptied his mug. "I might need something stronger," he said, to the Captain.

"I have something you might like in my quarters," the Captain said.

"Roy?" Frode said. "You haven't answered my question."

"Well, shit, you noticed."

"I did."

"Then I'll keep this simple. We'll put her on the

boat," he said, looking at me. "But she'll keep her head down and her mouth shut. Breathing is optional, so long as she does it quietly. And," he said, jabbing his finger towards me, "make sure you've emptied your fucking stomach before we leave." Fitzpatrick clapped his hands together. "Five minutes, gentlemen. Let's do this."

Frode waited for the men to leave the room, before pushing back his chair to join me at the door. I pressed my teeth into my bottom lip, shaking my head slowly as he started to speak.

"It'll be all right," he said.

"*Naamik*. It won't."

"They are just men. Loud and brash. No worse than Heidi. You remember how you dealt with her?"

"You want me to fight them?" I laughed, but my breath caught in my throat.

"No, Inniki," Frode said. "I want you to protect Eko. Now go," he said, peeling me away from the bulkhead and guiding me out of the door. "You must get ready. Can you feel it? The deck is shuddering. The Captain has increased speed."

Chapter 10

I kept my head down and my mouth shut, but mostly just to stay out of the wind, and to stop myself from choking on the fumes from the fuel a seaman spilled on the floor in his haste to begin the pursuit. Fitzpatrick – *Fitz* – to those closest to him, berated the man for his stupidity, and in that moment, I was forgotten. I tugged at the straps of the heavy, US Army issue flak jacket, and twisted my hair into a knot. Kunuk would be pleased, it nearly reached my bottom when it was flat and wet after a shower.

From my position at the back of the patrol boat, hidden from Fitzpatrick's view, and my every movement concealed by the noise of the engines, I had a perfect opportunity to study the leader of the BNDD and his partner, Mike Perkins. Perkins called Fitzpatrick *Fitz*, ending almost every sentence with an *ain't that right, Fitz?* I whispered the refrain, drawing the *z* into an *s*. Soft, like the northern Inuit dialect that Nassaannguaq and Eko shared. There was no place for soft consonants on the patrol boat. The crew held onto the railings, and the helmsman held onto the wheel, as the hull of the boat slapped and slammed the surface of the sea, racing towards the rust-stained hull of the *Southern Star*. Perkins was the first to spot the smaller boats being lowered down the starboard side of the lumbering ship. He let the heavy naval binoculars hang from the thick strap around his neck and pointed.

"They're running," he shouted, grasping the rail as the helmsman increased speed.

"Call the *Northwind*," Fitzpatrick said, grabbing one of the seamen. "Tell them to haul ass and board that freighter." He shoved the seaman towards the radio and stalked to the bow to stand beside Perkins.

"We're in it now," Perkins yelled. "Ain't that right, Fitz?"

"Yeah," Fitzpatrick said. "We most definitely are." He tugged at the strap around Perkins' neck and lifted the binoculars over his head. I crept forward as Fitzpatrick scanned the sea and watched the smaller speedboats drift away from the freighter. "I thought I told you to stay out of my way," he said, lowering the binoculars, but keeping his eyes fixed straight ahead.

"I'm here for a reason," I said.

"Do you hear that?" Fitzpatrick slapped Perkins on the arm. "I could swear I heard something I wasn't meant to."

"Yeah, there was something," Perkins said. He sneered as he stared at me, past Fitzpatrick's shoulder. "But it's gone now. It won't happen again."

"That's right," Fitzpatrick said. "I told that Danish prick we didn't need any tourists."

"That's right, Fitz. You told him."

I had heard something too, something Perkins told one of the Coast Guard officers while they were collecting their gear for the pursuit. He said something about Fitzpatrick being a *career-maker*, that if a guy did a few operations with *Fitz*, then he could practically choose his next assignment. But according to Perkins, Fitzpatrick was headed for even grander heights; he'd been given the nod to head up a department under the new Drug Enforcement Agency, still in development, but *looking for good people*, as Perkins put it.

I didn't think Fitzpatrick was *good people*, but neither was I supposed to talk, or be seen. I retreated to the rear of the boat, choosing to remain hidden at the stern, waiting for the right moment.

"It seems you were right, Perkins," Fitzpatrick said. He glanced over his shoulder, and I felt his eyes bore into mine. "It won't happen again."

As he turned away, I thought of Heidi, nursing her broken jaw on the beach. I couldn't imagine ever breaking Fitzpatrick's jaw, but the idea kept me focused, and I ignored the slap of the hull on the steel surface of the sea, and the sneer on Perkins' face. Instead, I looked ahead, surprised at how far we had come in such a short space of time. The freighter was larger now, lumbering along the coast of Labrador, the so-called *Iceberg Alley*. Frode told me that the icebergs came from Greenland's glaciers, and as the helmsman heeled the boat onto the port side to arc around the bow of the *Southern Star*, I saw the first bergs ahead of us, and the freighter's small speedboats weaving towards them.

"They're slipping away," Fitzpatrick said, grabbing the rail with one hand, as he removed the binoculars from his neck. He thrust them into Perkins' chest and pointed at the seaman standing in the bow of the boat pointing out growlers of ice. "Where's the 60?" Fitzpatrick said.

"Sir?"

"The M60 machine gun, you idiot." Fitzpatrick pointed at the empty weapons mount at the very tip of the bow. "Get it up and start shooting. We have to knock out their motors before they give us the slip."

"They'll never cross the ocean, Fitz," Perkins said, as two of the Coast Guard crew brought out the machine gun and fixed it to the bow.

"They won't have to," Fitzpatrick said. "They just need to get to the coast of Labrador. I won't let that happen."

The *tack, tack, tack* of the machine gun focused Fitzpatrick's attention on the bow of the boat, and I slid along the railings as we sped past the freighter. I looked for Eko at the freighter's railings, but saw only a few tiny men, too high up and far away to recognise. But if it had been Eko, I knew I would have recognised him instantly. Of course, that meant that he was either somewhere inside the freighter, or on one of the two boats disappearing behind the first of the icebergs. I watched as the tracer bullets from the machine gun, spun green tracer fire after the slower of the two speedboats, splintering the edge of the wall of ice close to the surface of the sea. Smoke pillowed out from behind the iceberg just a few seconds later, followed by a whoop from Fitzpatrick and a thunderous clap of his hand on the seaman's shoulder.

"Nice shootin', kid," he said. "We've got 'em now."

Perkins stuffed the binoculars inside a storage box and pulled the pistol from the holster at his belt. Fitzpatrick did the same. The two men checked the magazines, and then Fitzpatrick signalled for the helmsman to slow down. I gripped the rail as the bow of the patrol boat dipped, pushing a wave of grey water ahead of it.

"Slowly now," Fitzpatrick said.

Smoke drifted around the corner of the iceberg. The seaman fed a new belt of ammunition into the machine gun and turned the gun to the right as the helmsman took a lazy corner around the wall of ice.

I heard the sound of rotors and turned to see the black speck of the *Northwind*'s helicopter as it flew low towards the freighter. Fitzpatrick snapped his fingers at the crew and told them to stay focused. Beyond the sound of the helicopter, I thought I could hear the first speedboat powering away from the coast. I imagined it hiding behind the icebergs and wondered if Eko was onboard that boat, or the one smoking beside the iceberg.

The two men on the speedboat ducked as soon as we drifted into view. I grabbed the rail and leaned over the side, convinced that I had seen Eko before he disappeared behind the cloud of oily black smoke.

"Fitzpatrick unhooked a bullhorn from the side of the boat and pressed it to his lips. "This is the United States Coast Guard. Stand up and put your hands in the air."

"Fitz?" Perkins said. "What if they're armed?"

"Then they'll be sorry," Fitzpatrick said.

"Ain't that right." Perkins laughed, as he straightened his arms and pointed the barrel of his pistol towards the speedboat.

Eko was the first to stand up, and I rushed to the bow of the boat, his name tumbling from my lips. "Eko," I said. "That's our agent. It's Eko."

Fitzpatrick pushed me to one side. "Stay down."

But I couldn't. Eko was on that boat. I slid back a step, and pulled myself up, leaning against the railing, using all the willpower I had in a feeble attempt not to wave. Frode would have laughed, or despaired, but the smile on my face, and the warmth coursing through my body, made up for a month of sand and blisters in the training camp.

"Eko," I whispered.

The man next to Eko didn't raise his arms. He pulled a weapon into his shoulder and fired two bullets at our boat. Fitzpatrick order the seaman to open fire with the machine gun. Perkins stepped up to the railing, firing his pistol until the magazine was empty. He changed magazines, pulling one from his pocket as the machine gun fell silent and the seaman fed a new belt of ammunition into the feed tray above the trigger.

I screamed Eko's name as he ducked behind the outboard engines. There was a splash as the man with the rifle tumbled into the water. Fitzpatrick slapped me on the cheek, spinning me away from the railing. He ordered the helmsman to increase speed, gripping the railing with one hand as he sighted his pistol with the other. The seaman with the machine gun leaned into the butt stock, staring over the front sight as we closed on the speedboat.

I pulled myself up for a second time and saw Eko clawing at the side of the boat, waving his arm and shouting.

"He's with us," I said, as I ran to the bow. I slapped at Perkins' arm, tugging his sleeve until he lowered his pistol. "He's undercover. Why won't you listen?"

"Perkins," Fitzpatrick said. "Shut her up."

"Got it," Perkins said, as he twisted to grab at my hair. I leaned back, out of reach, and then twisted around him, grabbing his belt and spinning him onto the deck.

"Stupid squaw," he yelled, spitting blood as he slammed his chin onto the binocular chest.

I left Perkins on the floor, determined to reach the machine gunner in the bow, before he had another chance to fire.

"He's with us," I said, repeating it over and over,

until the seaman just stared at me. I pressed my hands on his arm, holding it as Perkins clawed his way to his feet and tried to pull me away from the bow. I kicked him in the shins, and again between the legs, just as Eko stood up. The speedboat spun around, pushed by a shallow wave, and the smoke from the ruptured motors cleared. Eko raised his hands above his head and shouted across the sea, his words travelling on the chill air peeling off the iceberg.

"I'm unarmed. I give up."

"Jump in the water, and we'll pick you up," Fitzpatrick said.

Eko looked down at the water and shook his head. "It's too cold. I'll drown."

"Your friend had a rifle. I don't know what you've got," Fitzpatrick said. "Get in the water."

"It's Eko," I said, reaching for Fitzpatrick's arm.

He jerked his wrist and slammed the side of the pistol into my head. I slumped against the railings, grabbing for the seaman as Fitzpatrick took aim.

"I won't tell you again," he said. "Jump."

The seaman helped me to my feet, and I reached for the railing. I wiped blood from my eye and turned my head as the knot holding my hair in a loose ponytail unravelled.

"Eko," I said, and then again, louder.

"Inniki?" Eko stepped onto the rear seat and waved at a plume of smoke as it drifted towards him. "What are you doing here?"

"I've been asking myself the exact same question," Fitzpatrick said. He spat into the sea, and then gripped his pistol in two hands. Fitzpatrick fired. The bullet slammed into Eko's body, spinning him into the back of the speedboat and out of sight.

"You bastard." I pushed off the side of the boat and threw my first and last fist at the side of Fitzpatrick's head.

Chapter 11

Eko's blood pumped through my fingers as I pressed my palm to the bullet hole in his side. The Coast Guard seaman from the bow, the one who had been busy with the machine gun, kneeled by my side, pleading with me to move my hand so that he could inspect Eko's wound.

"But if I move my hand," I said, "he'll lose even more blood."

"I'm a corpsman, ma'am, let me do my job."

"He'll die."

"No, not if you move aside."

"Just move," Fitzpatrick said. He dug his thick fingers into the neck of my flak jacket and yanked me away from Eko's body. "And stay there," he said, pressing me against the side of the boat with the toe of his boot.

Perkins glared at me across the deck, but I only had eyes for Eko, the blood thumping out of his side, pooling beneath the bandage the seaman bound around his wound. Eko groaned as the seaman rolled him onto his side to examine the exit wound.

"It's a through-and-through," he said. "I just need to pack the wound, stop the blood." He looked up at Fitzpatrick. "But we need to get back to the *Northwind*, and fast."

"Yeah, all right," Fitzpatrick said, waving at the

helmsman and spinning his fingers in the air, ordering him to pull away from the speedboat and go back to the Coast Guard ship. "It looks like it was a decoy, anyway. There's no drugs on this boat." He spat onto the deck. "Nothing at all."

"Maybe the helicopter crew will find more when they stop the other boat, Fitz," Perkins said. He grasped the railing as the helmsman increased speed. "Or maybe we'll find something on the freighter."

"We'd better," Fitzpatrick said. He shot a look at me, and then found a seat at the rear of the patrol boat.

The bow of the *Northwind* shone brightly on the horizon as the sun caught the red paint and the white stripes. Eko's blood was just as bright, and I crawled across the deck to take his hand. The seaman nodded as I approached, moving to one side to tidy away the paper bandage wrappings soaking up Eko's blood.

"He'll be all right, if we get back to the ship," he said.

"You're sure?"

The seaman shrugged. "I'm just a medic, not a doctor. We won't know for sure until they get a look at him." He placed his palm on the deck for balance as the helmsman bounced the patrol boat over a shallow wave. "Who is he, anyway?" he asked, after a furtive glance at Fitzpatrick. The big American smoked at the rear of the boat, and the seaman turned his head towards me.

"He's a friend," I said, and squeezed Eko's hand. His eyes were closed, but he rolled his head to one side, and I pressed my hand on his cheek.

"But from where? I mean he looks like an American Indian." The seaman lowered his voice as he glanced at my face. "You both do."

I didn't think about it, but I understood that for most people outside of Denmark, Greenland was that convenient white space on the map that often contained the text and symbols that needed to be put somewhere, without obscuring the rest of the world. On some maps it was omitted all together, just merged into the ice at the North Pole. Seen from an outsider's point of view, we had no real resources to speak of, nothing of interest to foreign investors. Whenever money was mentioned in relation to Greenland, it was usually a Danish politician concerned at how much it cost Denmark to keep Greenland as a part of its empire. We were a colony, and the capital of Godthåb was considered just another Danish provincial town. And yet, we had our uses.

"We're Greenlandic," I said, brushing my fingers through Eko's hair. "Like the Eskimo in Alaska."

"I've seen them," the seaman said. "They live in…"

"Igloos?" I felt the deck dip beneath me, as the helmsman slowed alongside the *Northwind*. "That's right," I said, with a flat smile. "We live in igloos."

"Get him up," Fitzpatrick said. He grabbed a line thrown by a seaman at the temporary dock floating by the side of the *Northwind*. He wound it around the stern cleat in a figure-eight. Perkins did the same with a rope at the bow, as the seamen from the patrol boat and two more from the *Northwind*, slid Eko onto a canvas stretcher and carried him up the steps leading to the *Northwind*'s deck. "Not you," Fitzpatrick said, as I moved to follow them. "You come with Perkins and me."

He pressed a hand on my shoulder and guided me up the stairs. Frode met us on the deck and opened his mouth to speak.

"Wait," Fitzpatrick said. He changed his grip from

my shoulder and tucked his thick fingers inside the neck of the flak jacket, pinching my hair under his stubby fingertips. He nodded at the freighter tied to the *Northwind*'s port side. "Go check it out, Perkins. See what they found. Then meet us in the briefing room."

"Right, Fitz."

As soon as Perkins was gone, Fitzpatrick opened the door and pushed me inside the ship, raising his finger as Frode started to protest.

"If she was an American I would have her in the brig for insubordination and striking two officers." He pushed me along the corridor. "I thought I made it clear – simple instructions. Keep quiet and keep out of the way. But did she? No, she fucking didn't."

"Whatever it is that Inniki did…" Frode started to say.

"No excuses," Fitzpatrick said. He opened the door to the briefing room and shoved me inside. He moved back to let Frode step over the lip of the door and into the room. "But as it is," he said, slamming the door and sealing the three of us inside the room, "I couldn't care less about your *attaché*," he said. "No, what really bothers me, is the fact that I ordered a Coast Guard Icebreaker to sail all the way into the North Atlantic based on a tip from you, Freddy."

"My name is *Frode*…"

"I don't *care* what your name is. What I care about is explaining this fuck-up to my superiors." Fitzpatrick leaned against the bulkhead and lit a cigarette. "You've got until I've finished this cigarette to tell me why there was nothing on those speedboats, and why your man tried to run, anyway."

"Eko was under…"

"Undercover?" Fitzpatrick blew a cloud of smoke at Frode's face. "He was so deep undercover, I had to shoot him."

"No, you didn't," I said.

"Inniki," Frode said, gesturing for me to take it easy with a wave of his hand.

"Let her speak," Fitzpatrick said. "This is her chance. At least until I've finished my cigarette."

"He was ready to give up."

"I gave him his chance. He refused."

"You told him to jump in the water."

Fitzpatrick shrugged. "We would have picked him up."

"No Greenlander jumps in the sea," I said. I thought of Kunuk. "They'll drown."

Frode gripped the back of a chair and pulled it away from the table. "Why did you tell him to jump?" he asked as he sat down.

"They were armed. I wasn't taking any chances." Fitzpatrick extinguished his half-finished cigarette in a cold cup of coffee. "You don't last as long as I have in this business by taking chances. His pal had already shot at us, I wasn't going to wait for yours to do the same."

"But he's working for us," I said.

"Is he?" Fitzpatrick turned his back on me and filled the coffee machine with fresh grounds from a tin in the cupboard. He talked as he worked. "So, we got a tip that there was a shipment of heroin coming out of the Golden Triangle. It was a from a reliable source – one of *our* undercover guys got it from an informant. There's been a steady trade of junk coming out of Thailand for over a year now. It's a legit business down there, propping up small villages and communities. Now, I don't much care about the *whos* and *whats* of the business, only the *how*, like how do they move it, and how do I stop it. When you told me how they were moving it," he said to Frode. "Then I just had to figure out how to stop it." He gestured at the bulkheads as he turned to lean on the counter. "This is the *how*. But I'm guessing that the Captain is going to tell me that the freighter is clean. I'll ask him to have his men check it again. He won't like it, but he'll do it. Perkins will be up all night, but I know we're not gonna find anything. It just don't smell right. Which brings us back to *how*. As in, how did this get so messed up? How did they know we were gonna stop them?" The coffee machine spluttered, and Fitzpatrick stared at Frode. "Did your man grass on us, Freddy?"

"I don't know what you mean."

"Did he rat us out? Is he playing both sides, or maybe just the one?"

"Eko is a good man," Frode said.

"I'm sure he is, but that doesn't tell me *how* they got tipped off then dumped all their junk into the ocean. Maybe it's floating somewhere, ready to be picked up. Who knows? But the truth of it is, your man chose to run, and that don't look good."

Frode glanced at me and then nodded when Fitzpatrick poured him a mug of coffee. "What you need to understand about Eko, is that he is thorough," Frode said, cradling the mug between his hands. "So thorough that even I have questioned his loyalties, from time to time."

"Which only makes me more suspicious," Fitzpatrick said. He glanced at me as he sipped his coffee. "And then there's you," he said.

"Inniki has had no contact with Eko for over a

month."

"That you know of," Fitzpatrick said.

"She was at a training camp," Frode said. "Remote. No communications without the knowledge of the camp instructors."

"Is that where you learned to fight?" Fitzpatrick asked. He looked at Frode. "She put Perkins on the deck with little more than a few kicks."

"He was going to shoot Eko," I said, looking at Frode.

"And then I did," Fitzpatrick said. "It'll take more than a swift kick in the balls to put me down." His eyes flickered between *hungry* and *predatory* as he stared at me. "But then, this gets us nowhere." He slid his mug onto the counter. "I've got the freighter locked down. The helicopter stopped the second speedboat, and the freighter's crew is either locked in the brig, dead, or recovering in sick bay. What I need to know, within the next twelve hours, is, what your friend can give me. Because right now, I've got nothing. And I don't like having nothing."

"Eko is recovering in your sick bay," Frode said.

"And he has twelve hours to do so. We're sailing for Dartmouth, and I want a plan to present to my boss before we arrive. If it doesn't include Echo…"

"Eko," I said.

Fitzpatrick shrugged. "I don't care what his name is, just what he can deliver. If the answer is nothing, he can rot in prison together with the freighter crew. But," he said, with a look at Frode, "if he is as *thorough* as you say, then he might still be useful. Because as it stands, this drug trafficking crew just got busted, which leaves your friend with an interesting opportunity to prove his loyalty to *his* friends back in Thailand. And *that* gives us the chance to put a man right in the heart of their operation. Now *that* gives me hope. It also gives me the *how* that I need to strike a serious blow against this operation. Give me the chance to do that and we can all start over." He looked at me and winked. "We might even become friends."

"We don't know if Eko is going to recover in just twelve hours," Frode said.

"Well, ain't that a shame," Fitzpatrick said, as he walked towards the door. "Because that's all the time he's got."

Chapter 12

Frode excused himself and said he would meet me in the sick bay. I wandered the corridors until a seaman pointed me in the right direction, down a flight of stairs and onto the lower deck of the *Northwind*. I smelled the sick bay before I saw it and steeled myself for the sight of Eko in a hospital bed. There had been no word about him since we had returned from the pursuit, and I could only hope that the corpsman had been right in his assessment – that in the right hands, Eko would live. But I already knew that he would. Ever since he survived the polar bear's attack in the graveyard, I knew it would take more than a simple bullet to kill Eko Simigaq. He was, after all, an *angakkoq*. He had familiars now, helping spirits.

But there was no-one to help me when I rounded the corner and walked straight into Perkins. He had chosen his spot well, in perhaps the darkest part of the corridor, furthest from the bulkhead lights and the stairs to the decks above and below.

"You're not very smart, are you? Walking the corridors alone. You should be more careful, seeing as you're the only woman aboard the ship," he said, as he peeled out of the shadows behind the pipes bolted to the bulkhead. His pistol was in the holster at his belt, but his hands were gloved; the leather creaked as he curled his fingers into fists.

In my mind, at least, it was no different from when I was alone on the beach with Heidi. There were no instructors to intervene, and no spectators to interrupt. I turned as if to run, and when I heard Perkins approach me from behind, I bent my arm and slammed my elbow into his nose. He was bleeding when I turned around and scraped the sole of my boot down his shin. Blood sputtered from his lips as he cursed and spat my name.

I stepped backwards, letting him stagger towards me as I checked my breathing. The scabs on my knuckles split as I formed my own small fists, punching Perkins once in his ear, and again in his nose. I hit him three times in his face, stronger each time, wilder. When he reached for his gun, I kicked him in the knee, hissing as he buckled to the deck. I hit him again on the back of his head and stabbed my elbow into the crown of his head. Perkins slumped to the floor, and I spat on his back.

My hair clung to my face, and to Perkins' blood that spotted my cheeks and my chin. I wiped the blood away with the back of my hand, curious that my mind was empty, that I was running on instinct alone – the need to react, and quickly. To remove a threat. Perhaps that was another quality that Frode had seen in me – another story perhaps, from my childhood. I could only remember the times I had bitten someone. But that primeval state of mind was, on reflection, true to who I was – a wild child of the north, closer to the land than people. Or at least, with a better understanding of the land. It was all so confusing. I stepped over Perkins' body, keen to be gone before he regained consciousness, or someone found him. They would carry him to the sick bay. I had to get there first.

"Inniki."

Frode's voice stopped me in my tracks, and I turned as he walked towards me. He paused beside Perkins, bending over to turn the man's head to one side, letting his blood and saliva drool onto the deck. Frode wiped his hands on a handkerchief he tugged from his pocket and stepped around Perkins.

"What happened?"

"He was going to attack me," I said. "So, I struck first."

"This doesn't help us very much, Inniki."

"I know, but he deserved it."

"I think you've made an enemy."

I lifted my chin and then reached for Frode's handkerchief. I wiped my hands as we walked along the corridor to the sick bay.

The *Northwind*'s medical officer turned as we entered the room. He studied my face for a moment, glanced at my hands, and then picked up a chart from his desk. "This way," he said, leading us to a bed positioned against the far bulkhead. The doctor stopped beside Eko's bed and traced his fingers along the first few lines of the top page. "He had us worried for a while," he said. "His vitals were all over the place. But then he stabilised, *before* we administered morphine. I think we could have sewn him up without any drugs. He simply didn't react."

"He was unconscious?" Frode asked. He nodded to me as I stepped around him to hold Eko's hand.

"On the contrary, he watched us the whole time. He just didn't react. It was as if he was controlling the pain somehow. I've never seen anything quite like it."

"And will he be all right?"

I knew the answer before I heard it. I could see it in Eko's smile, and the soft light shining in his deep brown eyes. His beard seemed wispier than I remembered, as if it had been thinned, just like his hollow cheeks drawing his face to his chin. Eko squeezed my fingers, and then tugged his other hand towards me, stopping at the end of the handcuff chain securing him to the bed.

"He will make a full recovery," the doctor said. "But I can't release him without the Captain's permission. He'll have to remain here until he is fit enough to move him to the brig."

"Thank you, doctor," Frode said.

"There is one other thing," the doctor said. "Perhaps you can explain it. But when we examined him, we found deep scarring on his back and side. The wounds are relatively fresh – still a deep healing red. I've been on a few Arctic trips with the *Northwind*, and we've stopped at several settlements in Canada and Alaska."

"Yes?"

"Well, I've seen such wounds a few times before. They look like they were made by polar bear claws."

"That's right," Frode said. "They were."

"Really?" The doctor clutched the chart to his chest and looked at Eko. "That is quite remarkable, because every time I saw such marks, they were on a dead body. If you're saying this man survived a bear attack…"

"I am."

"Then a bullet through his side really is quite inconsequential."

"Yes, doctor," Frode said. He smiled at Eko as he caught his eye. "There is one other thing you could help with, doctor. If you have time?"

"Of course."

"There is a man in the corridor. It looks like he has had a fall. I'm afraid he might require some medical attention."

The doctor glanced at the blood on my fingers and the spots on my cheeks.

"Of course," he said. "I'll go right away."

Frode waited for him to leave and then sat down at the foot of Eko's bed.

"You gave us quite a scare," he said.

"*Aap.*" Eko gave my fingers another squeeze. "But Inniki was there."

"It's my job," I said, as I brushed Eko's hair to one side.

"I'd like to add that I was the one who gave her that job," Frode said. "I'm just saying, that I put the two of you together."

"*Qujanaq,*" Eko said. "Thank you both."

Frode stood up and crossed the deck to a basin. He filled a paper cup with water and gave it to Eko. I helped him sit up to drink, careful not to let go of him. I never wanted to let go again.

"Unfortunately," Frode said, "we can't let you rest too long. Fitzpatrick needs some answers."

"Who's he?"

"He's the man who shot you."

"Ah," Eko said. "Him." He looked at me and lifted his free hand to brush the hair from the side of my face. He pressed his fingers lightly to my temple, tracing the bruise on my skin. "He's the one who hit you," he said.

"*Aap.*"

"I remember. Just before he shot me, he hit you."

"I'm all right, Eko."

Eko let his hand fall. He pinched the tips of my hair between his fingers and pressed them to his nose. "You smell of Greenland," he said.

"Salt from the sea," I said.

"And blood," Eko said, wrinkling his nose.

"Not mine."

Eko frowned and reached for my hand. His lips parted with a question, but Frode cut him short.

"We really are running out of time, Eko. Fitzpatrick has given us an ultimatum. He wants you to go back, undercover, working for the BNDD."

"What?"

"The Bureau of Narcotics and Dangerous Drugs," I said, with a smile for Frode. "I was paying attention."

"Yes, of course you were," Frode said. He turned to Eko. "Fitzpatrick and his Bureau are concerned about your status. I told them that you were thorough, and that you were deep undercover."

"I was."

Frode sighed, and I noticed his shoulders relax, just a little. It occurred to me that he really had been in doubt, whereas I didn't think I could ever doubt Eko. *Ever.*

"That's good to hear. But would you be willing to go back? Can you?"

"I'd say he has to," Fitzpatrick said as he entered the sick bay. Two seamen and the doctor helped Perkins into a seat by the doctor's desk, as Fitzpatrick walked across the deck to lean against the bulkhead at the foot of Eko's bed. "This all looks very cosy, but I think you're all missing the point. He," he said, stabbing two thick fingers at Eko, "doesn't have a choice. And neither do you." Fitzpatrick looked at me and then turned to stab the same fingers at Perkins slumped in the doctor's chair. "His nose is broken, and he has a concussion." He waved his fingers in front of his eyes. "Can't focus."

"He attacked me," I said.

"Maybe. But without witnesses, all you've got is trouble." Fitzpatrick turned to Frode. "I don't think much of your people, Freddy. I already shot one, don't make me shoot another." He looked at Eko as the handcuff rattled along the bed's metal railing. "Stand down, Chief," he said. "You're in enough trouble."

Fitzpatrick fished into his shirt pocket and pulled out a packet of cigarettes. He tapped one into his hand and tossed the empty packet onto the sheet at the end of Eko's bed. He smoked for a moment, looking at each of us in turn.

"The way I see it," he said, lifting his chin and blowing a cloud of smoke above our heads. "Is that you, Chief..." He pointed the tip of the cigarette at Eko. "Owe me a drug bust, of the biggest order. I want it, and you're going to give it to me. He's going to sign you over to me," he said, with a nod towards Frode. "And you, my little Comanche squaw, Eskimo... whatever you are – you're going to get off my ship, and out of my country. I don't ever want to see you again." He raised his hand as Frode began to protest. "She gets another twelve hours to leave. I'm not a monster. She'll get a last farewell to our friend the Chief, and then she leaves." He looked at Frode. "You'll escort her home."

"These are my people..."

"In *my* country," Fitzpatrick said. He nodded at Perkins. "Breaking my laws. You'll escort her home, and then we can talk about how to put our friend here back in play."

"I won't work without her," Eko said, squeezing my hand.

"Fine. Then I'll just sling the both of you in jail. I'll just have to find another way into the Golden Triangle."

He nodded at Perkins as the doctor escorted him out of the sick bay.

Frode gestured for Fitzpatrick to join him in the corridor. I watched them leave, my mind racing with thoughts of leaving the country, leaving Eko.

"That was him," Eko said. "The one who hit you."

"*Aap*," I said, as I plucked at Eko's fingers. "But I'm all right. Really."

I waited for Eko to say something, but he stared right past me. The gentle light that danced in his eyes when I first held his hand was gone, replaced with a flint-like hardness aimed like the tip of a hunter's harpoon straight at Fitzpatrick's head.

Chapter 13

I sat on Eko's bed as we waited for Frode, locking my fingers within his, studying his face, smiling as his eyes softened when he looked at me. Eko's hair was longer than it had been in Greenland, but without the sealskin cord holding it flat around his forehead, it was messy and free, like the feeling I had when I caught his eye. In that moment we were free, but it was complicated. Fitzpatrick's raised voice in the corridor, the handcuff around Eko's wrist, and Perkin's muttered curses from the opposite end of the sick bay – these things complicated matters, it made them messy.

"What do you think they are talking about?" I said.

"Does it matter?"

"*Aap*. It's our future."

"It's mine, Inniki. You must go back to Greenland. Stay there."

"*Naamik*." I tugged at his fingers. "I won't leave you."

"You don't have a choice," he said, looking up as Frode entered the room.

"He's right," Frode said, as he walked across the deck to Eko's bed. "But she has been granted a stay of execution, as it were. Fitzpatrick has agreed that Inniki can stay with me in Dartmouth, just until we know you have safely arrived in Thailand."

"Thailand?" I gripped Eko's hand. Thailand seemed so far away.

"Yes, that's the deal," Frode said. "Fitzpatrick wants him to go back in. He expects it. And in return, he'll make all of this go away," Frode said, with a wave that included Perkins as he limped out of the sick bay. "But I'll need to confirm that you accept. So, Eko. Are you willing to go back?"

"*Aap*," he said. "But it won't be easy. And I'll need a boat."

"Why?"

Eko let go of my hand to sit up in the bed. He beckoned for us to lean closer. "We dumped the shipment as soon as we saw the Coast Guard ship on the horizon. It is attached with a hook and cable to an iceberg." Eko grinned. "Think like a Greenlander, eh?"

"You hooked a tonne of heroin to an iceberg?"

"Not a tonne," Eko said. "More like one thousand pounds. It was a test run. I marked the iceberg with a cross of paint, close to the surface of the sea."

"Eko," Frode whispered. "How do you expect to find one iceberg in the North Atlantic?"

"This ship has a helicopter. The icebergs are moving towards Labrador. But this iceberg has an arch. It is very distinctive."

"And you marked it."

"In case it rolled or calved." Eko paused as he adjusted his position, wincing as he touched the tips of his fingers to the bandage wrapped tightly around his chest. "I need to recover the shipment," he said. "That will be my ticket back to the Golden Triangle. If we don't find the drugs, then I cannot guarantee they'll let me back in." Eko pressed his finger into Frode's chest. "The heroin is one hundred percent, ready to be cut. You must persuade the Captain of the ship to go and look for it. But not Fitzpatrick. He will take it…"

"And use it in a PR stunt," Frode said. "All right, I'll see what I can do."

"But I will still need a boat."

"Why?"

"To deliver the shipment."

"Eko…"

"It's the only way," he said, shaking his head."If I deliver, especially when they hear about what happened, then I will be in a much stronger position. I can help you, Frode. It makes sense. I just need to deliver the drugs. Then I'll go back to Thailand…"

"You've been there already?" I asked.

"*Aap*," Eko said, with a glance at Frode. "I helped them plan the route."

"And you were taking the drugs to Greenland?"

"*Naamik*, not Greenland. But in Greenland, they will be put on an empty container ship returning to Denmark, then on to other places in Europe. It was a test run. No-one expects anything to come out of Greenland. That's why it would work. It's what I promised the leader of the village in Thailand."

"What village?"

"It's close to the Burmese border."

Frode patted his pockets and pulled out a notebook. "Tell me again," he said. "From the beginning."

According to Eko, the drugs were already in America, but the route to Europe had been disrupted by an aggressive investigation coordinated by Interpol. The corner of Frode's mouth curled. After a quick look at me, he nodded for Eko to continue.

"Because the route to America was still open, I suggested we take a small amount of the American shipment and see if we could get it to Greenland, across the North Atlantic." The handcuff rattled around the metal railing as Eko shifted position. "If I could do that, then I would be given responsibility for that route. I would move further up the chain of command."

"That's quick work," Frode said.

"I can be very persuasive."

"You're also right. We've been focused on stopping drugs coming from the south. No-one thought to look north. This is good intelligence, Eko. I can use it."

"But not yet," he said. "Find me the drugs, let me take them to Greenland and I will prove the route is viable." Eko placed his hand on top of Frode's notepad. "You must trust me. This is what it will take. I have the contacts in Greenland – they were easy to make. I will give them to you, once I am back in Thailand. Fitzpatrick wants a bust to prove how powerful he is. But he doesn't understand. This is a business sanctioned by the local government, just like other crops. Opium is the lifeblood of the area. It's like fishing and hunting for the small settlements in Greenland. Without this crop, these villages will die, and the people will suffer."

"But we have to stop it, Eko," Frode said. "Or *our* villages will die, and *our* people will suffer. You do understand?"

"I understand. But if we can control the flow, thin it out, then there will be less suffering. Do *you* understand that?"

"Yes, but Fitzpatrick will want the location of that village. That's what he expects you to deliver. And, to be honest, Eko, I expect it too."

"It is just one village," Eko said. "There are many, all of which are involved in this business, farming the opium is important to the area. Destroying one village will make little difference."

"But it will send a message."

"If he wants to send a message, he can write a letter," Eko said. "I will deliver it for him. But if he wants to know how things are done, and how to stop it, that will take time." Eko reached for my hand. "What do you think, Inniki?"

"Me? I don't think about it. My role is simple. I'm here for you." I nodded at Frode. "He wanted me to help convince you to say yes. I did that. And now... Now I don't know what I'm supposed to do."

"Perhaps," Frode said, "you might like to get some rest, Inniki. You haven't slept since we left Copenhagen. And with all that has happened, you must be exhausted. I'll finish debriefing Eko, and then we can decide what your role will be after that."

"You want me to leave?"

"I want you to rest," he said. "Both of you."

He was right, I hadn't slept since Denmark. The fresh North Atlantic air had kept me awake, that and the threat to Eko's life. That had been enough to stop me from sleeping and to keep my seasickness at bay. But now that Eko was safe, and while the ship sailed a smooth course, sleep sounded like a good idea.

"You can rest in my quarters," Frode said. "The Captain assigned me a cabin while you were chasing Eko." Frode gestured at the handcuffs securing Eko to the bed. "I will find a key so that you can rest too. And then, when we arrive in Dartmouth, I will make sure there is time for you to recover, properly, before you leave."

"We can't wait too long," Eko said.

"Yes, of course. But at least a day or two. I will arrange it."

Frode gave me the key to his cabin, pressing it into my hand as I slipped off the edge of Eko's bed. I tucked it into my pocket, grasped Eko's hand one last time, and then walked to the door.

"Inniki," Eko said.

"*Aap*?"

"Remember Thule. Remember who you are."

"I know who I am," I said. I straightened my hair, smoothing it between my fingers, and curling it into one long length to one side of my face, down my chest, and past my waist. Kunuk could sit on it now. Now I was a true Greenlander. I had purged the city from body inch by inch. I smiled at Eko, saw the light dance in his eyes, and then turned to step out of the room.

Fitzpatrick was waiting in the corridor. My breath caught in my throat as he pushed away from the bulkhead and straightened his jacket.

"Cosy little chat, eh?" he said. "Got everything straightened out?"

"I didn't think I was supposed to talk to you."

"Well, shit, you're right about that. But then I think we should perhaps talk, just a little, so that *we* can get things straight. Maybe we can start over?"

Fitzpatrick curled his thick fingers around my elbow and tugged me along the corridor. We passed a group of seamen, each of whom stared at me, that familiar hunger flashing in their eyes. Fitzpatrick led me up the stairs and back to the briefing room, pushing me towards a chair as he turned to shut the door.

"There's fresh coffee," he said, pointing at the

machine on the counter. "I can sort out some food too."

"What do you want?"

"You're not frightened, are you?" he said, as he pulled out a chair and sat down. "I can see that. But then, after what you did to Perkins, I know you're not helpless. Freddy knows that too." He gestured at the chair, lighting a cigarette as I sat down. "What interests me, though," he said, puffing out a cloud of smoke as he tucked the packet of cigarettes back inside his short pocket, "is what you're really doing."

"I'm Frode's *attaché*."

"Right." Fitzpatrick picked a flake of tobacco from his lip. "Do you even know what that means?"

"I do the things he can't do."

"Like go on a small boat at sea, chasing drug traffickers?"

"Something like that."

"Or is it because you're banging our friend, the Chief? See, I think you're here to keep the Greenlander on a leash. That's the only reason I can see. You're not police. You're not some kind of special agent."

"I'm an *attaché*," I said.

"Sure. You can call it that." Fitzpatrick stood up. His cigarette burned in the ashtray as he poured two mugs of coffee. "You're not hungry?" he asked, as he placed one of the mugs in front of me. "I can get us some sandwiches."

I *was* hungry, but I was also wary, blowing on the coffee as I wrapped my fingers around the mug. Fitzpatrick was trying a new tack, and I struggled to anticipate what he wanted.

"You've got guts. I admire that," he said, as he sat down. "Between you and me, I even admire the way you handled Perkins. I mean, Christ, if he can't handle a girl... Well, shit, I don't know how useful he is anymore." Fitzpatrick plucked his cigarette from the ashtray. He stared through the smoke as he knocked the ash off the tip with a flick of his thumb at the unfiltered end. "You, on the other hand. I have a use for you."

"I thought you were sending me back to Denmark."

"Freddy convinced me otherwise."

"I work for Frode."

"Right. You're his *attaché*. Well, the thing is, this is an American ship, in American waters, on an American operation. Right now, Freddy works for me. So, you work for me too. As of now, you're *my attaché*. You understand?"

Fitzpatrick blew another cloud of smoke across the table. I coughed and waved it from my face. He leaned back in his chair, one hand curled around the coffee mug, the other pinching the cigarette to his lips. It seemed that I had advanced from an irritating bureaucratic compromise to something more, and that my behaviour was now tolerated, perhaps even appreciated in that I had become *useful*.

"What do you want me to do?"

"What you've been doing from day one," he said. "I want you to spy on your friend, Eko." Fitzpatrick grinned behind another cloud of smoke. He lifted his head at the sound of the helicopter powering up and taking off from the landing pad, and then stubbed out his cigarette. "Time to go to work," he said, and gestured at the door.

Chapter 14

"He wants me to spy on you," I said, as we watched the helicopter lower its cargo onto the landing pad. Eko leaned against the railing and I leaned against him, my fingers curled into his, as the crew of the *Northwind* secured the tightly-wrapped narcotics and prepared the landing pad to receive the helicopter. Eko had that boyish look in his eye as the downdraught from the rotors whipped at our hair. "Did you hear what I said?"

"What did you say?" Eko turned away from the helicopter and brushed my hair against the side of my cheek.

"Fitzpatrick wants me to spy on you."

"Inniki," Eko said, "*I* want you to spy on me. Just thinking about you looking at me…" I felt my blood flush my cheeks, colouring my skin with heat. "Inniki?"

"*Aap?*"

"We're nearly in Dartmouth." Eko pointed past the bow of the ship at the harbour buildings in the distance. "Frode said he will put us up in a room, in the city. Just for a night, before I leave."

I gripped Eko's fingers and looked through the strands of our hair tangled between our faces, and deep into his eyes.

"One night, Inniki," he said. "Would you spend it with me?"

I tried to speak, but the blood in my cheeks and the thump of my heart, pressed every word I knew down into my stomach. I raised my eyebrows instead, the silent Greenlandic *yes*. Eko tried to tame my hair with another brush of his hand against my cheek. I felt the tingle of electricity, a pulse of every thought I had had about Eko, every emotion – the whole range, as they charged between my cheek and the tip of his fingers.

"*Aap*," I whispered, knowing that he couldn't hear me, as the helicopter settled on the landing pad, and the arrival of Fitzpatrick and Perkins forced any further thoughts to the back of my mind.

Perkins glared at me from behind Fitzpatrick, as the two men approached the railing. The helicopter powered down and the pilot applied the rotor brake as the crew chocked the wheels and attached the tie-downs.

"Those are my drugs, Chief," Fitzpatrick said, stabbing his fingers at the cargo net and its contents dripping onto the deck.

"I need them," Eko said. "If you want me to go back in…"

Fitzpatrick stopped him with a wave of his hand. "Freddy told me, already. I think it's a crock of shit, but I'm going to let it pass. After I take a cut." Fitzpatrick nodded at the seamen waiting beside the cargo net. "I'll find a shitty little boat and I'll even help you load that crap in there, but I take half."

"Half?" Eko let go of my hand and took a step forwards, stopping when Fitzpatrick slapped his palm into Eko's chest. Perkins' hand hovered above the grip of the pistol holstered at his side. "I can't do this with *half*."

"You'll have to," Fitzpatrick said. He narrowed his eyes as Eko pushed against his palm, curious perhaps at

Eko's resistance, or just amused that he was stronger than Fitzpatrick thought he should be after taking a bullet in his side. "Besides," he said, lowering his hand. "You're a resourceful man, Chief. I'm sure you can figure something out."

"I'll have to, or I'll be dead," Eko said, staring at Fitzpatrick.

"Those are the breaks," Fitzpatrick said. He waved for the seamen to continue. Eko flinched at the sound of their knives sawing through the oilcloth and plastic wrapping to get at the heroin. "There's a small trawler in the harbour. You'll take that on your little trip across the Atlantic."

"Is it seaworthy?" Eko asked. He flicked his head to stare at Perkins when the man laughed. A stream of blood slipped out from beneath the bandage covering Perkins' nose.

"Sure," Fitzpatrick said. "Just don't get into trouble." He pointed his finger at me, and said, "Now, why don't you two go and have some fun, while Perkins and I do all the hard work."

"You'll load the trawler?"

"That's what I said, Chief." Fitzpatrick looked at me and smiled. "I always do what I say. If I've agreed something, it's as good as done, if you know what I mean?"

"Yes," I said.

"Good." Fitzpatrick gripped Eko by the shoulder and turned him towards the bow. "We'll be docking in just a few minutes. Why don't you get ready to go ashore? Make the most of your time here in Dartmouth." He relaxed his grip as Eko turned to face him.

"Where will I find you?"

"Me? You don't *find* me, Chief."

"Not unless you can find *The Salt Licker*," Perkins said. He started to laugh, only to stop when Fitzpatrick slapped at his arm and pointed at the seaman separating the parcels of heroin.

"Go bring me a sample," Fitzpatrick said. He turned back to Eko. "You'll get instructions about how to contact me when you get on the trawler. I don't have to remind you how important it is that you contact me, do I? Because," he said, with a glance at me, "I would hate to have to remind you. That would just be bad for business, and it would make you *my* business." He leaned in close to Eko's ear, but his words were pitched for both of us. "If you cross me, or even think about crossing me, I'll have to reach out through our little *attaché*, and then it will be up to her to get you to communicate…"

"If you touch her…" Eko said.

His face changed with those four words, his eyes changing colour from soft brown to hard black, growing smaller as his skin paled, and for just a moment, I caught the shadow of a bear, could even smell its musky damp fur. Fitzpatrick must have smelled it too. He wrinkled his nose and moved back.

"Well, shit, Chief," he said. "If I didn't know better, I might say you just threatened me. Did you?"

"*Aap.*"

"And what's that supposed to mean?"

"It means *yes*," I said.

I curled my fingers around Eko's arm and tugged him away from Fitzpatrick. We walked past the landing pad, along the port side of the *Northwind*. The Dartmouth gulls and seabirds cried and called above us, shrill and loud, but not loud enough to obscure Fitzpatrick's last words.

"Remember what I said, Chief. You cross me... There'll be consequences."

Eko stiffened for a moment, and then exhaled. His shoulders sagged and I felt his arm brush mine as we stopped beside three seamen preparing the gangway for use once the *Northwind* tied up at the docks. Eko beckoned to one of them with a wave.

"What can I do for you, sir?" the seaman said.

"Can you recommend a bar around here?"

"In town, or..." The young man frowned.

"Close to the docks," Eko said, as he turned to look at me. "Frode has us booked into rooms near the ship."

"Well, the closest bar is just around that corner," he said, pointing past the bow at a row of warehouses. "But it's more of a dive, really." He glanced at me. "I wouldn't take a lady there, that's for sure."

"But you would go there?"

"Hell yeah, sir. It's where we all go if we're in Dartmouth. And if the Captain gives us shore leave, of course." He nodded towards the landing deck behind us. "Even the Feds go there," he said, "if that changes your mind."

"Thank you," Eko said.

"Eko?" I said. "What are you doing?"

He shook his head and said nothing more until the *Northwind* pulled alongside the docks and the seamen lowered the gangway. Frode called from the railings for us to wait, as we walked onto the docks.

"You forgot your bag, Inniki," he said, struggling to carry two holdalls down the gangway. "Just because *he* has no luggage," Frode said, pressing my holdall into Eko's hand.

I reached for my bag but Eko pulled it out of reach.

"You've been shot," I said. "Let me carry it."

"I am healed," he said, and started walking. Frode stretched his legs to keep up.

"I apologise now if the rooms are a little shabby. We had to stay close to the docks – one of Fitzpatrick's numerous conditions."

"He's taken half the shipment," Eko said.

"Yes," Frode said. "There was nothing I could do."

"And the crew of the freighter?"

"Will be processed. The Captain of the *Northwind* sent them on ahead with his first officer and a detachment of seamen, while we searched for your iceberg. I could tell that he was quite impressed with your deception, although he would never admit it, of course. I think he even wanted to fly with the helicopter, just to see it for himself."

I smiled as we walked along the dock, Frode panting alongside us, praising Eko for this and that the closer we got to the hotel. He pointed at a narrow door squeezed between dirty timbers.

"This is it," Frode said. "Now, before we go in, I want you to remember that we are probably being watched. Fitzpatrick told me to use this hotel," he said, his lips curling as he looked at the door and the salt-stained windows of the rooms above it. "So, imagine that everything we do or say will be seen and heard."

"Everything?" Eko said.

I felt that same pulse as he squeezed my hand.

"Yes," Frode said, eyes narrowing as he looked at Eko, before glancing at me. "We have three rooms. I thought that would be best." He caught my eye for a second, and then shook his head. "This way. I'll get the keys."

Eko paused at the door, his gaze fixed on a neon sign advertising beer above a long low window of a bar at the end of the docks.

"Eko?" I said, tugging him into the hotel. "You need to rest."

"*Aap*," he said, and followed me inside.

The rooms were small, with barely enough room to walk around the bed to the washbasin in the corner. There was a shared bathroom and toilet at the end of the short hall by the stairs. The ceiling fan in each room pushed warm air into the corners, I stared at it as I flopped onto Eko's bed.

"I haven't slept for days," I said. The mattress squeaked as Eko slipped onto the bed beside me.

"Do you want to?"

"Maybe…" I said. My tongue clung to the roof of my mouth, as I tried to swallow.

"Inniki."

"*Aap*?"

"Do you want me?"

I swallowed, unsticking my tongue from mouth, drawing in the warm air as my heart started to beat faster. I could feel my blood in my veins, throbbing at my neck, pulsing at the very tips of my fingers.

"Yes," I breathed.

"*Yes*?" Eko teased my hair between his fingers. "We've been in America for two minutes, and you've forgotten your Greenlandic, already?"

"Yes," I said, reaching for his face. I pressed my fingers to his jaw, felt the wisps of his thin black beard beneath my fingers. "Teach me."

Eko kissed my fingers and lifted his leg to sit astride

me, pressing his knees against my hips. I stared into his eyes as he unsnapped the top three buttons of his shirt and pulled it over his head. His face was hidden for a moment and I stared at the bandage covering the bullet wound in his side. I ran my fingers over his torso and found the raised red ridges of thick skin, the healing tissue that would soon become scars tracing the mark of the polar bear. Eko tossed his shirt onto the floor and reached for my hand. He kissed the tips of my fingers, pressed his fingers within mine, arcing his back to bend over and kiss my lips. I pressed my teeth into his bottom lip, and then stopped when he winced.

"I'm sorry," I said. "I didn't think it would hurt."

"It doesn't." Eko collapsed onto his side, pulling me on top of him. "It's not you." He dipped his head to look at the bandage, pressing his fingers to a small spot of blood seeping through the soft cotton threads.

"You're still hurt," I said. "We can wait."

"*Naamik*," Eko shook his head. "I don't want to wait. Not a moment longer." He hooked his thumbs into the belt loops above my waist and settled me over his hips. Eko let go of my trousers and tugged at the hem of my t-shirt. "Maybe you can teach me, instead?"

I slapped at Eko's fingers and gripped the bottom of my t-shirt. I let my hair tickle his chin for a second and then I pulled my t-shirt up and over my head, covering my eyes as the collar caught around my chin. I felt Eko's hands press through the cups of my bra, felt his fingers searching for my nipples as I hooked my thumbs under the collar and tugged it free of my head.

"Inniki," Eko whispered, as I looked down at him.

"*Aap?*"

"Teach me."

Chapter 15

Eko's chest was smooth, his skin dark, save for the angry red claw marks scratched across his side, and the white bandage spotted with blood. I ran my finger around his nipples until he opened his eyes. He turned his head and smiled, creasing one side of his mouth. The black polar bear eyes had softened, sparkling in the ships' light shining in from the docks.

"Tell me about the bear," I said.

"What about it?"

"Why you let it attack you. Why Nassaannguaq called it. Why you slept by the side of a grave – whose was it?"

"That's a lot of questions."

"*Aap*," I said. "Tell me about all of them."

"Okay," he said, as he rolled onto his side. I hooked my leg over his hip, smoothing my calf against the tight curve of his buttocks. "It was my father's grave. His name was Ukatu. He was an *angakkoq* – a shaman."

"He's the reason you became a shaman?"

"*Naamik*," Eko said. He pressed his hand on my thigh, running his fingers up and down. A frown deepened on his forehead, until he shook it off. "Maybe he's why I became a shaman, but not the only reason. Many shamans are chosen, selected by an older shaman.

He or she will teach them all they know, to make sure they learn all the familiars and helping spirits, to learn how to ward off evil, to heal the sick. That kind of thing."

"*That kind of thing*?" I said, grabbing his fingers as his touch began to tickle.

"*Aap*," he said. "There is a lot to learn. But first one has to die, which is why Nassaannguaq called the ice bear." Eko pinched the raised skin of the claw marks. "It takes a powerful animal to lead you to the otherworld. Once you are dead, the shaman can bring you back, counting your bones, teaching you the names."

"But you didn't die," I said.

"Didn't I?"

"I was there. I saw you. You let the bear strike you twice. And then you fell."

"Dead," Eko said. "I died then."

I propped my elbow on the pillow and rested my head on my palm, staring at Eko, looking at the curl of his lip, or the light that danced in his eyes. But his lips didn't move, and his eyes shone no brighter than they did before. He was serious.

"You said your father was one reason," I said. "What was the other?"

"A shaman has powerful allies – familiars such as animals, like the bear, and helping spirits." Eko pressed his lips into a flat smile. "My reasons for becoming a shaman are not completely altruistic, I also wanted power."

"Power?"

"Imagine having the strength of a polar bear, the speed of a hare, the cunning of a fox. I can swim as fast as the *aarluuk*, the killer whale. I can stay warm with the fat of a seal. These are just the familiars. There are spirits too. You know them. But perhaps you have forgotten?"

"Tell me."

"There are many, but *Inuarakasik* is only small. He won't take too long." Eko tugged at the ends of my hair, brushing my breasts with the tips, covering my nipples. "He is small, human-like. He helped the great shaman *Aattaaritaa*. At least he tried to."

"What happened?"

"Well," Eko said, as he slipped his hand onto my ribs. I could feel the heat of his palm burning through my skin. "*Aattaaritaa* was worried that the world was going to end. The Danish missionaries had convinced him that he was going to go to hell and take his people with him. They told him that he should be baptised, and in that way, he could save them. But *Inuarakasik* didn't believe him."

"He didn't?"

"*Naamik.*"

"Eko," I said, twisting his nipple between my finger and thumb. "Why are you laughing? Tell the story."

"Ow," he said. "Okay."

I let go of Eko's nipple, curled my hand around his neck and kissed his lips. I tasted earth, blood and fire. I could smell the salt of Greenland's sea in his beard, and I wondered if this was love? Eko kissed me back, wiped a drop of saliva from my lips, and pressed me back onto the pillow.

"The story," I said, as he slipped his body onto mine. "*Inuarakasik*," I said, raising my voice as Eko slipped his hand between my thighs.

"He was small," Eko said, as he brushed the hair between my legs. "But he told *Aattaaritaa*, that if the world did come to an end, he would just go down there and fix it."

"Down there?"

"*Aap*," Eko said. "Down here."

I let Eko and his helping spirits fix the world, breathing in the musk of his sweat, feeling it bead and slip on my skin, as he poured his energy, all the elements of fire and water, earth and wind, into my body. I don't know how often I called out, and how many times his spirits answered, but I knew then that it was love, and that I would never be the same again. I was bound to Eko as he was to the spirit world of his father and all the shamans before him.

I slept for some time, only half aware of the guitar twang of Americana, drifting through the window, stirred around the room by the almost useless ceiling fan. The tunes caught in my ear and I opened my eyes. I saw Eko's shadow at the end of the bed. He stood to pull on his jeans, pressing bare feet into his boots, bending to tie the laces.

"Eko?" I propped myself onto my elbows. "Where are you going?"

"*Inuarakasik* and I have a little job to do."

"What's that?"

Eko tugged his t-shirt over his chest, and I saw the briefest crease of his cheek as he winced and smoothed the t-shirt over his bandage. He walked around the bed, smiled at me, and bent down to kiss me on the lips.

"There are some fires that need putting out."

"What fires?"

"In here," he said, slapping his palm against his chest.

"I don't understand."

"You don't have to, Inniki. It's okay."

"But you're going?"

"I'll be back."

"I want to know where, or... Why do you have to go?"

Eko sat on the side of the bed and curled his fingers through my hair. "You remember the story about *Aattaaritaa*?"

"*Aap.*"

"He didn't listen to *Inuarakasik*. He turned his back on the spirit world and became a Christian." Eko's teeth flashed in the dark as he smiled. "I will always listen to the spirits, and my familiars. And sometimes I will help them, just as they help me. I have asked *Inuarakasik* to help me sort out a problem, and he has agreed. But I must go now. Before it's too late." He smoothed his hand on my cheek and stood up.

"Eko?"

"Promise me you will not follow."

"What?"

"Don't follow me, Inniki."

Eko opened the door and slipped out of the room. I searched for my clothes as soon as I heard him tramp down the stairs. I pulled on my jeans and slipped around the bed to watch him leave the hotel and walk towards the bar at the end of the dock, skirting around a pair of drunken sailors talking to a woman in the shadows. I pulled on my t-shirt, tugged my hair out of the collar and let it hang loose down my back. I slipped on my shoes – barefoot, like Eko – and tied my laces.

"Frode wants me to watch Eko," I whispered into the gloom of the hotel room. "Fitzpatrick wants me to spy on him. But I'll follow him because I love him."

I opened the door and stepped out of the room. I had no idea what Eko's spirits were telling him, but I decided that he wasn't mad, or ill, he was... I searched for the word as I ran down the stairs, crashing through the hotel door and onto the docks.

Driven.

That was the best word I could come up with. *Stupid* was the next that came to mind, as I saw Eko stop outside the bar at the end of the street. The Neon sign buzzed in the heat of the Dartmouth night, encouraging all passersby with the promise of cheap beer inside *The Salt Licker.*

I ignored the sailors and the woman in the shadows, didn't even hear the whistle and shouts they called out after me. I stopped outside the bar and reached for the door, pressing my palm against the warm brass plate above the lock. I could almost feel the charge of energy building as I pushed it open. That's when I saw Eko stalk between the tables towards the bar, a trail of energy and ill wind in his wake.

"Well, shit," Fitzpatrick said, as Eko tapped him on the shoulder. "Shouldn't you be sleeping, Chief? Big day tomorrow."

I walked to the far side of the bar, heart thumping, but at least wary of getting involved. Eko's words were soft, but strong enough to drift along the bar to my ears.

"You struck Inniki with a pistol," he said. "I've come to make that right."

"What?" Fitzpatrick snorted. "What the fuck? Is this some kind of honour thing? Did I *dishonour* your lady? Is that what this is?"

"This has nothing to do with honour," Eko said. "It's simpler than that." He reached for Fitzpatrick's beer, lifted it to his lips and finished it. "Now," he said, slapping the glass onto the bar. "We fight."

I didn't count the number of men sitting at the tables around the bar, but they were three-deep when they stood to form a ring around Eko and Fitzpatrick. I heard the grunts of the first few blows, heard the crash of a table as Fitzpatrick toppled over it, and the splintering of a chair as Eko flung it at the wall, clearing a path to Fitzpatrick. Someone put another coin in the jukebox and the men in the bar cheered, staggering forwards and backwards in a perimeter around Fitzpatrick and Eko.

"Do you like *Oney*?"

It took a moment for me to realise the question was meant for me. I turned my head away from the fight, and felt my heart skip a beat as I stared into Perkins' beer-tinged face.

"It's Johnny Cash," he said, nodding at the jukebox. "But maybe they don't have music where you come from?" Perkins leaned against the bar, and said, "Where was that again?"

"Greenland," I said. I took a step away from the bar and bumped into a chair.

"No," Perkins said. "I don't think so." He pointed at the men ringing the fight. "It looks like it's the night for settling scores, and you and me," he said, pressing the tips of his fingers to his swollen nose. "We have some scores to settle. Don't you think?"

"*Naamik*," I said, as I slipped around the chair and headed for the door.

Perkins followed, caressing his nose with one hand as he clenched a fist with the other. I bumped against the door, found the handle, and pulled it open. The crashes and curses of Eko's fight slipped away as I turned and ran along the dock towards the hotel.

"Hey, no running away," Perkins said. His words

were slurred with beer and whisky, sour like his breath.

I glanced over my shoulder before bumping into one of the two men outside the hotel.

"Hey there," the man said, curling his arm around my waist. "What's the hurry?"

"Let me go," I said, squirming as he tried to close his arms around me.

"Just hold her there, friend," Perkins said, as he stumbled towards me. "She owes me money, and a good time."

"That right?"

The man laughed and I smelled more sour breath than I had the stomach for. I felt the bile burn its way up from my stomach, and, as the man locked his arms around me, I vomited onto his hands and his shoes.

"Goddammit," he said, relaxing his grip just enough for me to slip out of his arms and make a run for the hotel.

"I don't think so," Perkins said. He pulled his pistol from his holster and cocked it. "I don't think so at all. "We have scores to settle, and we're gonna settle them right now."

Chapter 16

There was a moment when I considered running, just as far as I could, for as long as I could. The thought brought me back to the Danish beach, the fight with Heidi, the nights spent reading Frode's English books, the days spent puking on the hard canvas floor of the boxing ring, wiping sweat from my eyes and blood from my mouth. Frode had put me in that camp for a reason. I had suffered too much to throw it all away for a drunk American Federal Agent.

"All right," I said.

I reached behind my head to tuck my hair inside the collar of my t-shirt. It clung to the sweat on my back, but the weight of it tugged it down towards my waist. I thought about Kunuk as I lowered my hands to my sides. He would always try and pin me down. But Perkins' hair was too short to grab and his body too bulky for me to wrestle onto the dock. I spread my feet as he pulled off his windbreaker jacket.

"Hey, are you a cop?" the man asked. He took a step back, tugging the woman with him. "Vice?"

"Maybe," Perkins said. "Why don't you piss off and leave us alone."

The man tugged his friend and the woman further along the dock, glancing over his shoulder until he decided they had moved far enough away. The woman disappeared into the shadows, while the two men turned to watch.

"Fitz says you could be useful," Perkins said, as he tossed his jacket onto the ground. "He said I should forget about you. But I can't, see." He lifted his chin and traced his finger along a blue bruise stretched along his jaw. It turned black as he started to circle around me, cutting the light from the lamp on the dockside, his body falling into shadow. "He said you were going to spy on your Eskimo lover. That you were going to keep us informed. I think that's a crock of shit. I don't think you're going to tell us a damn thing."

"But Fitzpatrick is your boss," I said, as I turned to face him. He kept moving, forcing me to turn. I wanted to keep him at an angle, keeping my shoulder between us.

"So?"

"So, shouldn't you do what he says?"

Perkins laughed and I took a step backwards. I glanced at the black water between the boats moored alongside the dock. It was about eight feet from the dock to the water, but the railings of the nearest boat were only about four feet higher than the dock. I edged nearer to the side of a trawler moored close by.

"Sure, Fritz is my boss, and you should always listen to your superiors," Perkins said. He pointed his finger at me, wagging it in an arc from one side to the other. "Only you're not very good at that, are you?"

"You're not my superior," I said. "Not my boss."

"Maybe not. But tonight, I think you're gonna do exactly as I say."

Perkins holstered his pistol and lunged at me with both hands. I twisted away from him and ran to the railings of the shallow draught trawler. I felt the crust of rusting iron on my palms as I reached for the top railing and pulled myself up and over the side. Perkins swore as I thumped onto the deck. He clambered over the side of the trawler. I heard him land on the deck as I reached the opposite side.

There was a boat hook clipped to the bulkhead beside the wheelhouse door and I grabbed it, tugging it free of the rubber clamps and swinging it at Perkins' head as he ran across the deck towards me. The metal hook caught him on the side of his head, and he pitched onto the deck.

We were alone on the deck and I could feel a familiar sense of release, a wild energy – raw and uninhibited. The men on the dock were out of sight, hidden by the wheelhouse. The sodium lamps of the neighbouring ships cast yellow arcs of light across their decks, but not far enough to light the deck of the trawler. It was just like the Danish beach. We were alone and invisible in plain sight.

"Fuck," Perkins said, as he rolled onto his side.

He pulled his pistol free, raising it in one hand as he pushed himself off the deck with the other. I raised the boat hook, holding it like a spear in two hands with the blunt end aimed at Perkins' belly.

"I could shoot you," he said. "Self-defence. I'd be well within my rights. You take one more step, I'll put you down. Fitz can go fuck himself. You need to be taught. You *need* putting down. It just ain't right…"

I stepped to one side. The muscles in my arms trembled, and I could feel the pulse of blood in my head, my chest – I felt it in my fingers as I gripped the boat hook. Perkins slipped his thumb onto the hammer and cocked the pistol.

"You're supposed to know your place," he said. "Never in my life, and I mean *never* has a broad had the fucking nerve to hit me. Never." He waved the pistol as he reached for the railing behind him. "I told Fitz, but he just fucking laughed. He said you was just different. That you weren't from round here – some other fucking country. Well," he said, filling his lungs as he straightened. "I'm sending you home tonight in a fucking casket."

Heidi had tried to do the same – to send me home. Whatever Frode's orders might have been, she tried her hardest to make me quit, to give up and roll over, like a dog at her feet. I'd seen plenty of Greenland dogs roll over at the feet of the alpha male, submissive, ready to be subdued. But I'd seen those same dogs attack the dogs beneath them. Maintaining the hierarchy was a full-time job. The alpha's job was tougher still. The dog that rolled over at his feet one day, might be the one to bite him in the neck two days, or perhaps even a week later, whenever the opportunity presented itself.

But some dogs never learned. They never came to anything, never gained a higher status in the hierarchy. Perkins would never rise above Fitzpatrick, even I could see that. But so long as he thought he could beat me, he would wait for that one opportunity, and I could never rest.

I wanted to rest.

Perhaps that was what guided my hands that night? I just wanted him to stop, so that I could rest. Not just for one night, but every night.

He frowned as I stepped towards him. I heard the squeal of his soles on the deck as he shifted his feet, his sharp intake of breath, and the dry scratch of his fingers around the grip of his pistol as he took aim.

I hit him in the chest first, stabbing the rounded end

of the boat hook into his sternum. He staggered back against the railing, and I whipped the boat hook around to slap his pistol into the water.

"Inniki."

Some part of me might have heard my name, might even have registered that it was Frode's voice. He shouted again, but I ignored him, choosing instead to focus on Perkins as he splayed his fingers and grabbed for the boat hook. After I slapped the pistol into the water, my return swing caught Perkins' arm, cracking against his elbow. He swore once, spitting onto the deck, before I twisted the boat hook and drove the end into his groin.

"Inniki, stop."

This time I heard Frode, as he clambered over the railing and lowered himself to the deck. I tossed the boat hook to one side as Perkins crumpled onto his knees.

"Step away from him, Inniki."

I pressed my fingers between Perkins' teeth, deep into his mouth until he gagged, and then I jabbed my thumb into the soft skin beneath his jaw. He tried to bite my fingers, but I pushed them further into his mouth, ramming my knuckles against his teeth. I twisted his head to one side and bent down to whisper in his bloody ear.

"Know your place," I said.

Perkins gagged once more on my fingers. I tightened my grip, pulled him forwards and then slapped the back of his head against the railings, slipping my fingers out of his mouth as he slumped to the deck.

"Inniki," Frode said. "What have you done?"

"He doesn't like me," I said. I clamped my arms around my stomach to stop them shaking.

"I know, but…"

"He was just going to continue. Like Heidi did," I said, wiping my fingers on my jeans.

"Inniki, you're a guest in this country, and he is a Federal Agent."

"He's a shit."

"Yes," Frode said. "But, regardless, he's your colleague. You have to work with him."

"No, I don't."

"Technically…"

"Frode," I said, as I twisted towards him. "Why am I here?"

"You're my *attaché*, Inniki. You know that."

"*Naamik.*" I shook my head, stopping him short as he started to speak. "More than that, or *other* that that. Why am I really here? Why did you send me to that camp? What do you want from me?"

"I need you, Inniki."

"But what for?" I pointed at Perkins as he curled into a ball beneath the railings. "You didn't bring me here to work with *them*. It can't *just* be about Eko? Is it?"

"You're right," Frode said. "There's a bigger picture. But you're not ready yet." He gestured at Perkins. "They're not ready for you either."

"Then what do I do? Fitzpatrick wants me to spy on Eko. You want me to control Eko. But tomorrow, when Eko is gone, I can't do either of those things."

"That's correct."

Frode brushed past me to pick up the boat hook. He turned the hook in the low light to study the blood smeared along one side. Then he tossed it over the side of the trawler, cursing under his breath as it floated and bumped against the hull. Frode sighed as he turned, and then he took my arm, his fingers pressed gently around my elbow as he guided me across the deck. He gestured at the dock and then waited for me to climb over the railings. He followed a moment later, casting one last glance at Perkins, before dropping down to the dock.

"Come with me," he said. "There's an all-night diner around the corner. "Not that way," he said, as I started walking back towards the bar. "We'll let Eko and Fitzpatrick work out their differences. They'll be halfway through a bottle of Bourbon by now. At least, I hope so. Whatever their grievance was about…"

"Me," I said. "They were fighting about me."

Frode nodded. "That makes sense for all the wrong reasons. But that," he said, pointing over his shoulder at the trawler, "was far too personal."

"He just wouldn't stop," I said.

"No," Frode said. "I can see that."

We walked past the front of the hotel. Frode lengthened his stride, as if the extra speed might increase the distance between us and the trawler. It did, but only so far as the entrance to the diner. Frode stopped at the door and reached for the brass handle.

"I'll tell you everything you need to know," he said, as he opened the door. "But first, let me order breakfast. There's a washroom at the back. Clean up while I order."

Frode pointed out the washroom as soon as we entered the diner. I walked past the counter, ignoring the stares of the fishermen. They clustered around sturdy tables like barnacles, legs sprawled like long lines, feet tucked into slime-scaled rubber boots. It was too early in the morning for wolf whistles, but despite the heaps of egg and bacon on their plates, they still looked hungry. I opened the washroom door and slipped inside, locking the door behind me.

There was blood on my shirt, and my fingers shone with translucent fish scales. They must have rubbed off the boat hook as I swung it. I gripped the sides of the washbasin and pressed my forehead against the pitted surface of the mirror. My breath misted the glass as it shuddered out of my lungs. I had put Perkins in his place, established my position in the hierarchy. And now it was Frode's turn to put me in *my* place, just as soon as I walked out of the washroom.

Chapter 17

The diner had two booths. The first was occupied with two fishermen sprawled one on each bench. Frode waited in the second. The coffee steamed from the mugs as I slid onto the bench opposite Frode. He pushed a plate of bright yellow eggs, sausage and bacon across the table towards me, herding the salt and pepper with one hand, pressing the knife and fork into my hand with the other.

"Eat," he said. "You must be hungry."

I added more salt before I realised none was necessary, then I worked my way through the eggs, stopping between mouthfuls to brush my hair out of my food as Frode talked.

"You won't remember," he said, "but this isn't the first breakfast we've eaten together." He smiled as I looked up, and then continued. "You were thirteen. It was shortly after the incident when you bit another boy – when you bit *two* boys, actually."

"I don't remember," I said, wiping my lips with the back of my hand. I didn't realise how hungry I was. And how tired.

"That would be the drugs. A sedative, regularly administered at the institution. They brought you there directly from school. Clara called me and asked me to come. I was outside Copenhagen, in Jutland, otherwise I would have been there sooner."

I rested my fork on the side of the plate and leaned back. I curled my finger through the handle of the mug but left it there on the table. Frode was adding another piece to the story of my life, just as Eko had done when he took me back to Greenland.

"Clara was a good friend," Frode said. "She understood the little I could tell her of my work, and I listened to her stories about you." Frode reached across the table and pressed his hand on top of mine. "I've known you for longer than you can possibly know. But you won't remember much about that breakfast. They had you doped to the eyeballs. Clara sat beside you," he said, nodding to my right as if she was sitting next to me in the booth. "She held your head back while I tried to feed you. The orderlies had given up. I had to send one of them away. You scratched his face the night before, which was probably why they had given you far too much."

"Why was I sedated?"

"Simply put? Because you were a danger to the other children, the orderlies at the institution, and possibly to yourself. Although I never believed it. Of course, I'd seen what you could do when provoked, just like you did tonight, but you displayed no signs of self-harm, of any kind." Frode laughed as he pulled back his hand. "No, you'd never harm yourself, or anyone you loved. Quite the opposite."

Frode sipped his coffee in silence, watching me across the table for at least a minute, maybe longer.

"What happened after breakfast?" I asked.

"Well, I'd never seen anything like it. My work has taken me to many countries, to many places, including institutions – prisons and the like. But I'd never been to an orphanage or anywhere they kept children."

"Kept?"

"That's what I thought, anyway. I called in a few favours and promised many more in return, but I got you out of there, and I helped Clara to bring you up. From afar, of course. You never met me again, but I saw you often. When you were little I would look in after you had gone to bed, and then Clara would tell me about you over a glass of wine, perhaps once a month. You could say I was your patron, Inniki."

"Why?"

"Why?" Frode looked away for a moment, glancing at the door as another trawler crew entered the diner. He nodded at them, and said, "It'll be busy now until the first boats start to leave."

"Frode," I said. "Why did you help me?"

He turned his head and smiled, but his eyes were dull, looking through me, rather than at me. I wondered if he was looking at a younger me, the sedated version at another breakfast table, ten years earlier.

"It was for Clara," he said. "She wanted children, but her husband died before she became pregnant. She never remarried, never even had a boyfriend. And," he said, lowering his voice to a whisper, "she never wanted me. I think I reminded her of Andreas."

"Her husband?"

"Yes. We worked together. There was an accident." Frode frowned. "I was driving. It was wet, and I drove too fast. We were undercover, but I didn't pay attention to the road, or the conditions. I drove around a bend – too fast. We hit a tree. Andreas died before they could cut him free of the wreckage." Frode placed his elbow on the table and rested his chin in his fingers, pinching at his bottom lips as he spoke. "I don't think Clara ever forgave me. Why should she? Anyway, once the case was closed, our relationship changed. I thought I could replace Andreas, to fill that part of her life. But then she went to Greenland, and she found you. You made her so happy, Inniki."

I remembered the fights, how I slammed my bedroom door. I blamed Clara for my life in Denmark, trapped in a strange country with its strange ways. I never fit in, and I blamed her. It was difficult to imagine how I might have made her happy.

"So, I did what I could to help. I provided money when Clara got sick. I even found you a job."

"At the office?"

"Yes," he said. "You never wondered why they took you back every time you quit?"

"I was fired, Frode."

"And yet, within a week, they called to ask you back." The light returned to his eyes as he smiled. "Strange, eh?"

"I was a lousy secretary."

"Yes."

I tugged the mug towards me and wrapped my hands around the sides. Frode had been looking out for me for so long, without my knowledge, but I had the feeling that it was more of an investment than it was charity.

"Why?"

"Because, Inniki, I saw something in you that I admired. They said you were a troublemaker, that you started fights. Well, I remember the school playground of my youth. Rarely did someone start a fight without a trigger. Boys and girls become bullies to satisfy a deeper need that their parents can't fill. You didn't have any parents, and your brother – your only sibling – drowned when skipping across the ice floes. I know," he said, reaching for my hand. "Clara told me. But what the teachers and social workers called *problem behaviour* I called *self-preservation*. You're a fighter, Inniki. You won't back down. But neither will you pick a fight you can't win. You choose them, choosing when to strike, and when to play the victim. But when you do strike, you strike hard, and once only." Frode squeezed my hand and then let go. "That's the good kind of rage," he said. "If applied properly."

"Which is why you sent me to the camp?"

"Yes."

"And Eko?"

"Eko?" Frode paused as the waitress came to our table and refilled our mugs with fresh coffee. He nodded his thanks, waiting until she moved on to another table before continuing. "He sees the vulnerable side of you. That's why he picked the fight tonight with Fitzpatrick. He's looking out for you. Which is what I need him to do. I won't lie, Inniki. I need Eko to want to come back. I need him to need you. We're sending him so deep into the heart of the drug trade that he'll start to forget why he's actually doing what he's doing. And we need him to forget – it's what he forgets that will keep him alive. He'll adapt and blend in. But every now and again, we'll need to bring him out, and that's why I need you. That's why *he* needs you."

"You're talking about love," I said. "You want him to love me."

"Yes," Frode whispered.

"You're using me to control him." I gripped the coffee mug, wondering what Frode would do if I threw it at him. I could feel the heat rising in my cheeks, but there was something else, something that tempered my anger, holding it in check.

"But you've always known that," Frode said. "Haven't you?"

"*Aap*," I said, because he was right.

It was also what I wanted. Knowing that Eko loved me, knowing that I wanted him to love me, was what made the training camp bearable. It made Fitzpatrick and Perkins bearable. It also made everything suddenly worthwhile. I didn't care about the mission, stopping the drugs, or severing the trafficking routes into America or Europe. I only cared about Eko.

"He makes me feel complete, somehow," I said. "Like he has given me back my culture, given me roots. He makes me feel whole."

"And you'd do anything for him."

"Yes," I whispered. "Anything."

Frode nodded slowly. He took a long breath followed by an even longer exhale, as if he was purging something from his body. "Then Clara, God rest her soul, will never forgive me – in this life or the next."

"Why?"

"Because I have succeeded. When I take Eko from you, you will do whatever I ask just to see him again."

"Yes."

"And when I need to meet with Eko, all I ever have to do is promise him that you will be there, and he will come." Frode was silent for a moment, and then he shuffled off the bench and stood up. He placed two ten-dollar bills on the table and tucked them under the edge of his plate. He nodded at the door. "I'm going to check on the boat and make sure they've put at least half of the cargo onboard. You can stay here if you want," he said, gesturing at the money. "I've left more than enough for waffles and a tip. Or you might want to go back to the hotel. It's the last time you'll see Eko before he leaves later this morning."

"And what happens to me when he does? Where do I go?"

"I'm going to put you close to him, Inniki, as close as I can. But it won't be easy. I'll tell you more as soon as he's gone."

I caught Frode's eye, holding his gaze until he turned away. I watched him walk to the door. He waved his thanks to the waitress and then stepped outside onto the docks. Frode's shadow passed the greasy window, and I waited until he was gone, before slipping out of the booth and walking to the door.

It was all I could to stop myself from running.

The hotel was unlocked, and the night auditor barely looked up from the TV screen as I rushed past the front desk. I took the stairs two at a time, caught my breath outside the door to our room, laughing at how thorough Frode had been – paying for two rooms when he knew he wanted only one. He had to keep up the appearances, to make it all seem so natural – to let love take its course. I turned the door handle and slipped inside the room.

I half expected to see Eko stretched out on the bed, and imagined curling onto his body, teasing him awake, and making the most of the last few hours. The thought made me giggle. I tugged off my boots and looked around the room. The dawn light revealed crumpled sheets but no sign of Eko.

I slumped onto the bed, stretching my fingers and gripping the sheets, pulling them towards me as I remembered the position of our bodies, the earthy, salty, musky smell of Eko's body.

"He's gone," I whispered, catching the first sob in my throat, biting my lip to stem the flow of tears. I had no idea when we would see each other again – *if* we would ever see each other again. Frode's work was complete, and without Eko I could never be whole. I would do whatever Frode asked me, without hesitation, just to see Eko one more time. So deep was my sudden feeling of sorrow, so intense it felt as if my ribs were being crushed until they cracked. But then I heard the guest from the next room banging on the door of the shared bathroom at the end of the short hall.

"Come on, man, you've been in there an hour already." His voice barrelled through the thin walls.

I pushed off the bed and reached for the door, pulling it open as I wiped a tear from each cheek. The man looked at me as I stepped out into the hall.

"Your boyfriend's hogging the bathroom. I gotta get to work. You gonna go in there? Get him out?"

"Yes," I said, padding barefoot down the hall. "You're sure it's him?"

"Foreign, like you," the man said. "Black hair. Yeah, I seen you and him in the bar. He had a hell of a fight, had quite a skinful after, but that's not why he's in there."

"I don't understand," I said.

The man pulled back his shirt sleeve and tapped two fingers on the vein in the crook of his elbow. "The Fed gave him something after they made up. I think your fella's getting high, miss. Way high, I reckon."

Chapter 18

I pushed the door open, leaning into it as it caught on the toe of Eko's shoe. I had to kneel and pull the shoe out from beneath the lip of the door before I could get into the bathroom. Eko was slumped over the toilet bowl, the ends of his hair dipping into the water as he cradled the bowl with one arm. His other arm was hidden. I lifted his head and rolled him away from the toilet to lean him against the bathtub.

"Eko?"

He rolled his head, pressing his chin to his chest as he slumped to one side. I saw his arm then, the bright spot of fresh blood where he had pushed the needle into his vein, just below the belt he had wrapped around his arm. Eko's familiar earthy smell was gone, replaced with something darker and ranker, it twitched in my nose as I tried to lift him onto his feet.

"Come on," I said, choking back a tear and gritting my teeth. I just needed to get him back to our room. I called out to the man in the hall, "Can you help me?"

The man nodded and stepped around me, the tail of his bathrobe snaked across my back. He tucked one hand under Eko's arm, waited for me to do the same, and then started to lift.

"I have a cousin," the man said, grunting once as we caught the full weight of Eko's body. "He was a good kid, doing well at college, and then he just got in with the wrong crowd. Broke my sister's heart to see him like that. Like your friend here."

I shifted my grip and tucked my shoulder under Eko's right arm, grabbing his belt with my left hand. We dragged him along the hall to the room and the man pushed the door open with his foot, grunting one last time as we stumbled inside. We dumped Eko on the bed, and the man retreated to the hall.

"Thank you," I said.

He stood there for a moment, looking at Eko, before catching my eye. "Best to get out now," he said. "Just grab your things and go, honey. Better for both of you. Don't let him drag you down."

"I won't," I said, but whether I wouldn't leave, or whether I wouldn't let Eko drag me down was unclear, both for me and the stranger in the hall.

"Okay then."

The man nodded once and then walked back down the hall. I heard him enter the bathroom, locking the door behind him. The pipes ticked and knocked as he ran the shower and I closed the bedroom door.

A strand of Eko's hair rested over his nose, the ends flickering with each breath. I looked at his bare feet, thought about his shoes in the bathroom. There would be time to get them before Eko was supposed to sail, although the light outside suggested that it was already morning. I sighed as I slipped onto the bed, holding Eko's hand as I wiped another tear from my cheek.

He was so strong, the other Eko, not this lifeless body – I didn't recognise *him*. He smelled strange too, like sour saliva. I could smell it on my skin as I rubbed my face. It was pervasive, unpleasant, not Eko.

The man said Fitzpatrick had given Eko something, and I thought about the sample Perkins had taken from the shipment of drugs on the landing pad of the *Northwind*. It made sense, somehow, that Fitzpatrick would poison Eko with the same product he expected him to deliver across the Atlantic. One last sucker punch to remind Eko who was in charge. But I failed to understand why Eko would do it.

He was strong. This wasn't my Eko.

Eko rolled his head onto one side and opened his eyes. I wiped the hair from his face.

"Inniki," he said. "You found me."

"*Aap.*"

"I knew you would." Eko closed his eyes again. "I was with the spirits."

"No," I said. "You were in the bathroom. I needed help to get you back to the room."

"I was on a journey. I was in the otherworld."

"*Naamik.*" I shook my head, pressed my knuckles to my nose, catching the sniffle before wiping my eyes. "No, you weren't Eko. You were high."

He squeezed my hand. "I'm sorry, it's hard for you to understand, but this way is easier than most." He turned his head and opened his eyes to look at the belt around his arm, and I let go of his hand to undo it. "It's easier than fighting a polar bear," he said, his lips creasing into a crooked smile.

"That's what you think?"

"It's what I know, Inniki." He rolled onto his side and I lay down next to him. "I am *angakkoq*, a shaman. I must travel to the otherworld. It is a passage – I cannot go there by normal means; I must find another path." He reached out to curl his finger along my jaw. "Tell me you understand."

"I don't like it," I said. "It doesn't matter if I understand."

"It does to me," he said.

"But you're a junkie, an addict."

"*Naamik*." Eko's smile faded as he shook his head. "I just use it, when I need to."

"For how long?"

"What?"

I pressed my fingers against the skin in the crook of his elbow. I could feel the tiny prick of raised blood beneath my finger. "How long have you been using heroin?"

"Just every now and again," he said. "When I need to visit with the spirits."

"In Greenland?"

"No. After."

I dipped my chin and pressed my forehead against his. My breath tickled his hair as I exhaled, and I curled my arm around his body.

"Okay," I said, convincing myself that it was all right, so long as he didn't get high in Greenland.

"You understand?"

"*Aap*," I said. "I forgive you."

"You *forgive me*?" Eko laughed. "I didn't ask for forgiveness." He pulled his head away from me. The smell of saliva returned, together with the look that turned his soft brown eyes into the black beads of the ice bear.

"Yes," I whispered. "I do."

Eko held my gaze for just a second, before rolling away from me, and sitting up on the bed. "I don't need your forgiveness, Inniki Rasmussen. I am *angakkoq*. I do what I must, when I must. You only need to understand – not forgive."

"Eko," I said, as I sat up. I reached for his shoulder, but he pulled away.

"Leave me," he said. "Take your things. Find Frode. I must go."

My breath caught in my throat and I pressed my hand against his arm. He brushed me away as he stood up.

"I have to get ready," he said. "You should leave."

"I don't want to go," I said. "Eko, don't tell me to leave."

Eko's eyes hardened as he channelled the strength of the bear. "Leave," he said, nodding at the door.

I clenched my fists, pressing my nails so hard into my palms that I knew, if I looked, there would be blood. Eko pointed at the door and I stood up. I could feel a pulse of fear and rejection throbbing just beneath the surface of the skin beneath my eye. My knee started to twitch, followed by something wild rising from my stomach, something raw, unrestrained. It was strong enough to match the bear, if only I could control it, but when I hurled my fist at Eko, he slipped easily to one side and I crashed into the hand basin. I tumbled onto the floor, twisting to get back on my feet. Eko caught me, pressing his palm against my chest, pushing me onto the floor. I bucked against his hand and he kneeled on my thighs, his hands against my shoulders. I could feel his fingers digging into my skin, as he pressed his forehead against mine.

"You must leave," he said, and I caught the sudden softness in his words. "You have to go. It is better this way."

"I don't want to," I said, my voice low, ragged and

breathy. "Don't make me."

"You must."

I reached for his hands, gripping them as I tapped my forehead against his. "*Naamik*."

"Inniki…"

"I won't go."

"*Aap*," he said. "You must."

"I might never see you again." I held my head tight against his, could feel my hair sticking to my lips, together with his. "Eko…"

"It's okay."

"No, it's not. What if…"

"Don't think about it," he said. "It's okay."

"You'll be gone. I won't see you." I pressed my hand to his cheek, slipped my fingers into his hair. "Fitzpatrick doesn't care about you, Eko. None of them do. They're just using you."

"I know."

"Then why are you doing this?"

Eko smiled. He lifted his head and kissed me on the lips. I smelled the earth, Greenland's grit and dust as he kissed my nose, my eyelids, my forehead.

"For Greenland," he said. "To keep her safe. To make the people strong again."

"And what about us?"

Eko pulled his head back and stood up. He laced his fingers within mine and tugged me to my feet. "We're connected, Inniki. We always will be, wherever we are." He brushed my hair to the sides, wiping away my tears with his thumb. His eyes were brown and soft once more. The bear was gone. "Listen to Frode. Do what he says, and we'll see each other again."

"You can't be sure."

"Yes, Inniki, I can." Eko stepped to one side to pick up my holdall. He took my hand and led me to the door. "Go now," he said. "I need to prepare for the crossing." I glanced at his arm and he shook his head. "*Naamik*, not like that."

"You'll be safe?"

"I have my friendly spirits," he said. "I'll be safe." He curled one hand around my neck and kissed me. His eyes shone as he pulled back to look at me. "And you will be too," he said. "You have a friendly spirit, Inniki. It watches over you. It keeps you safe, gives you strength when you need it." He cocked his head to one side, eyes narrowing, as he said, "Maybe you are *angakkoq*? Perhaps you should take the journey?"

"I don't fight polar bears," I said.

"No? I think you do. I think you already have."

I smelt the earth once more as Eko kissed my cheek and pressed my holdall into my hands.

"Go now," he said. "Until we meet again."

I was outside the room before I realised what was happening, that he had guided me into the hall and closed the door, softly but firmly. Separated by just a couple of inches of wood, I had never felt so alone.

And yet.

The day Kunuk died, when he slipped between the jagged floes of ice in the harbour – I had been alone then. Abandoned, just like I felt in the hall of the hotel on the Dartmouth docks.

I didn't hear Frode climb the stairs. I barely reacted as he said my name and pressed his hand to my arm.

"Inniki?"

I turned and frowned at him, just for a second, as if he was a stranger. Then I nodded at the door, and said,

"He needs to get ready. I have to leave. We have to go."

"You have your things?" Frode nodded at the holdall that I gripped in both hands.

"I'm ready," I said.

Frode gestured at the stairs. I glanced once at the door to Eko's room. For just a moment, if felt like a warm, dry wind was blowing along the short length of the hall. I closed my eyes, imagined it tickling my skin, sifting through my hair. I saw Eko, in the room, at the wheel of the trawler. I saw him crossing the Atlantic with his deadly cargo, his key to that other world, the *underworld* that Frode and Fitzpatrick expected him to enter, and to get lost in.

"He'll be all right," Frode said, as he tapped me on my arm.

The wind disappeared and I opened my eyes. I followed Frode down the stairs and out of the hotel. There was a taxi parked outside the entrance. Frode took my bag and opened the rear passenger door. I climbed inside as he put my holdall in the back. He got in beside me and leaned forwards to speak to the driver. I heard something about an *airport* and *as fast you can, we're running late*, but my thoughts were focused on the barefoot Greenlander in the bedroom, waving at me from the window.

I would do whatever it took to see him again, whatever Frode wanted me to. I wondered if such thoughts were rational, sane, or desperate. As the taxi pulled away from the hotel, I decided I didn't care.

Narkotika

III

Chapter 19

There was no-one to hold my hand on the flight, none of Eko's boyish excitement, or Frode's fatherly advice. I was alone in the smoky cabin, ringed by small Thailanders chatting at accelerated speeds, and American men conspicuous in their olive drab uniforms, and even more conspicuous without. They drank beer with whisky chasers and then fell asleep. The Thai passengers chatted into the night, shrieking and giggling as the aircraft shuddered in the occasional bout of turbulence.

I gripped the armrests and thought about Frode's last words and the furtive looks he had cast over my shoulders before I boarded the flight.

"I need to know how far you will go," he had said.

"How far away are you sending me?"

"That's not what I mean." He shifted on his feet, and then tugged me towards a pillar between two rows of seats in the waiting lounge. "I need to put you near Eko, as close as I can, but it won't be safe. You could also risk being seen by Perkins or Fitzpatrick."

"Where?"

"At an American Army camp in the jungle. You'll fly to Bangkok first. I'll have someone meet you there. They are going to put you on a plane to Chiang Rai, in the north of Thailand. From there, well... I still need to arrange it, but someone will drive you to the camp. They have to smuggle you inside."

"Inside an Army camp? Frode?"

"It's not as bad as it sounds. Well, actually it is. But with your dark skin and your long black hair, I think you'll pass for a local, especially at night."

"Frode…"

He lifted his hand to cut me off. "There's a young man at the camp, a Captain. His name is Miller. I trust him, Inniki. He's a good man. He knows you're coming. He'll take care of you."

"And what do you want me to do at the camp?"

"Watch, listen, learn and wait," Frode said. "I'll contact you when the time is right. Then you'll see Eko again. I'll need you to be ready to travel in the jungle. Miller knows this. He'll keep you safe."

"He's American?"

"Yes, but the good kind." Frode smiled. "He's on our side, Inniki."

"And Fitzpatrick isn't? Is that why we took a taxi? Does he know where you're sending me?"

"No," Frode said. He took my arm and steered me towards the large plate glass windows of the waiting lounge of Logan International Airport. He waited for an elderly couple to move and then continued, pulling me close and lowering his voice. "I've learned a few things since we've been in port. The Captain of the *Northwind* expressed some concerns, and I pretended not to understand. He let slip far more than I think he was supposed to. And now I'm telling you."

"Telling me what?"

"Fitzpatrick wants to locate this particular village, the one Eko's drugs came from. He thinks that by sending Eko back, he'll be able to track him all the way to the village. Once the location is established, he'll strike…"

"From the Army camp?"

"Yes. There are some very young, very disillusioned American soldiers there. They're still struggling to accept the end of the Vietnam War. And now they've been hired by the CIA, and indirectly by the BNDD."

"Fitzpatrick?"

"Yes. He intends to wipe out that village, Inniki. Do you understand what I'm saying?"

"Lots of people will be killed," I said.

"Yes, including some that we know, and love."

"Eko."

Frode nodded. "As soon as he contacts us, Fitzpatrick will organise the strike. It's up to you to convince Eko to leave."

"He doesn't know about the strike?"

"No, and I couldn't tell him, even if I wanted to. If Fitzpatrick thought Eko knew, he would cut his losses and get rid of him. He can't risk compromising the mission or warning the villagers. They would move production somewhere else – perhaps even deeper into the jungle, or across the border into Burma. I learned that it has taken a long time for the Americans to secure the assistance of the Thai government. There's a lot at stake, Inniki."

"It's all for show?"

"For the American people? Yes."

"And Eko?"

Frode laughed, but his eyes were dull and serious. "I can't imagine Eko leaving people he cares for, can you?"

"He cares for them?"

"Yes, like he cares for the villagers in Greenland. He is, in many ways, a remarkable man. Quick to adapt, quick to be accepted, and quick to love. But he does nothing without passion and sincerity. It is one of his most admirable qualities and one of his greatest weaknesses. He has been to the village only a few times, but if he thought the villagers were in danger, he would fight to protect them. It's up to you to stop him."

"And you think I can?"

"I know how he feels about you, Inniki. If anyone can, you can." Frode looked up as they called my flight. "I'll have an evacuation plan ready for you. Miller will guide you through the jungle." He looked at his watch, swore and then checked the boarding card in his jacket pocket. "I have to go back to Copenhagen. Are you ready?"

"I don't know."

Frode smiled, as if he hadn't heard me. "Tickets?"

"Here," I said, and showed them to him. The passengers began to walk past the assistant at the gate behind us. "Frode…"

"I know it's a lot to take in," he said, touching my arm and gesturing for us to walk to the gate. "But I wouldn't ask this of you if it wasn't important."

"You're using me."

"Yes," he said. "To save a life."

"But why? Why is Eko so important?"

Frode stopped and sighed. The assistant waved and pointed at the ticket in my hand.

"He's my son," he said.

"No. He can't be. His father is buried in…"

"Thule? A local hunter. I paid him to look after Eko and his mother. I was young. I was drunk. I was in Greenland." Frode took my hand. "I used to think Greenlandic women cast spells, but they are just so very different from other women, from the women I knew in the West. Even Clara – although I loved her, in my own way, she..." Frode let go of my hand. "I was silly. I fell in love for one night. And now, this is my penance, to protect those I love, in any way I can. Yes," he said. "You are part of that plan. I always knew he would love you. I just had to put you together."

"And now you control both of us," I said, stepping away.

"I didn't plan this," Frode said, as I walked to the gate.

I handed the assistant my ticket and showed her my passport, turning to Frode when the woman wished me an enjoyable flight.

"Yes, you did," I said. "Right from the start."

Frode had effectively removed all my options, the only path was straight ahead, onto the flight, and on to Thailand.

"Remember to take salt," Frode called, as I walked through the gate. "Not just water."

The plane shuddered through another bout of turbulence and I opened my eyes. I sipped at the water in the glass on the tray table. The second flight was shorter, but hotter, as if the humidity from the air pressing down on the airport had boarded the flight along with the passengers. It hadn't left, and the tiny jets of air above my seat did little more than remind me of what it might feel like to be cool, one coin-sized patch of skin at a time.

We landed in Chiang Rai a few hours later, and I tugged the scrap of paper I had been given in Bangkok out of my pocket. It was greasy in the hot, wet air that greeted us as we climbed down the stairs from the aircraft and onto the cracked concrete apron. I tugged my damp hair from my forehead and waved my ticket at my face. The card sagged in the heat, and I knew just how it felt. A man waved at me from behind a rope tethered as a guide to funnel the passengers into the airport. He lifted the rope as I approached and beckoned for me to duck beneath it.

"Freddy?" he said.

"What?"

"Freddy send you?"

"Yes," I said. I looked at the note in my hand. "Thaksin?"

"Good, good," he said, and nodded. "Come."

"What about my bag?"

"Later. Come now. It is long drive."

I followed Thaksin around the side of the airport building to the back of an American Army Jeep.

"Clothes in back," he said, as he climbed behind the wheel.

"Should I change?"

"*Chi*. Change now."

Thaksin unlocked a padlock threaded through the steering wheel and bolted to the floor. He let it drop into the footwell between the seats as I swapped my damp t-shirt for a loose black cotton shirt. I caught Thaksin looking at me in the rear-view mirror and he turned away. I swapped my jeans for the long black pyjamas. I felt cooler already. When I sat down next to Thaksin, he pressed a conical rice hat into my hands.

"For the heat, and to hide your face," he said. "If we stop, if there are soldiers, you say not a thing. Let me talk. Let me drive. I will get you there."

"To the camp?" I said, as I pulled the hat onto my

head, tucking my hair beneath it, away from my neck.

"*Chi*," he said, and started the engine with a press of a button to the right of the steering wheel.

The potholes in the road were worse than the turbulence in the air. Thaksin slung the Jeep around the smaller ones, before, bouncing through those that stretched across the road. As the road started to climb into the jungle, and the vegetation grew thicker, Thaksin reached behind my seat and pulled something into his lap.

"For you," he said, as he pressed the barrel of a rifle into my hands. "It is semi-automatic SKS *Chicom* rifle." Thaksin grinned, the failing light caught his teeth, flashing white in the gloom of the jungle. "There are many from the war," he said. "This one yours now. Keep it safe."

I tugged the rifle into my lap, and then turned it, stuffing it down by my side, out of sight.

"No," Thaksin said. "Keep it up. We almost there. You just another fighter for the camp. I have your papers." He patted his shirt pocket. "Just don't speak."

There were lights strung between the trees on one side of the dirt road. Thaksin slowed the Jeep to a stop and flashed his lights twice. Ahead of us, almost hidden by the vegetation, two men waved us forwards with the flash of a lantern. Thaksin waved at them as we passed, before stopping again at a checkpoint. One end of a metal barrier rested on an oil drum full of stones. I stared at it as Thaksin talked, thrusting the papers from his pocket at a young Thai soldier standing on our side of the barrier. The soldier nodded and waved to a second man and a boy standing close by. The boy ran to the opposite end of the barrier and leaped up to sit on a wide plank strapped to the end. The barrier squealed on its pivot as the boy's weight pressed the end down and we drove beneath it. The boy grinned and saluted as we passed.

Compared to the Danish training camp on the beach, the American Army camp looked like a rustic building site, with half-finished wooden huts and thick grass roofs dotted about the packed red earth.

Thaksin pointed up at the sky, and said, "From the air it looks like any other village."

Small cooking fires burned outside many of the huts, the embers glowing and reflecting in the groups of men and women sitting on their heels, preparing food and chatting as we drove past. Thaksin stopped outside a larger hut with thick mud walls and an overhanging roof of grass. He pointed to the bench by the side of the door.

"Take your rifle. Wait on that bench," he said.

"For how long?" I asked as I stepped out of the Jeep.

Thaksin shrugged. He turned the wheel and spun the Jeep away from the hut.

"Hey," I said, reaching out as I remembered my clothes in the back of the Jeep.

It was too late.

I spat the cloud of dust from the Jeep's wheels and watched as Thaksin sped through the camp. He was gone in less than a minute, and I was alone, again.

Chapter 20

If I didn't move, I didn't sweat. At least that was my reasoning, but the sweat trickled down my sides, between my breasts, collecting in the folds of my black shirt, beading along the strap of the coolie hat on my head. The sweat stains were lost in the black fabric of my pyjamas, and the dark that descended on the camp. It really did look like a village. But there were fences in the surrounding tree line, and the road through the village widened in places, running straight and smooth on hard-packed red earth that could accommodate helicopters and light cargo aircraft. I had seen pictures of the American Army bases in Vietnam. They were surrounded with large broad swathes of open ground. This camp felt more claustrophobic less combat effective. Such thoughts amused me until the mosquitoes found me.

There are plenty of mosquitoes in Greenland, which often surprises people. Wolves in the north will lie on patches on ice where it is too cool for mosquitoes. I didn't know what to do in Thailand. The heat, the humidity and the bugs, were all beginning to take their toll, and I could feel the stress of travel and my worry about Eko growing on my mind. I twitched at every mosquito buzz, slapping at my skin and drawing the attention of an older woman and her young son. She called out, and when I didn't respond, she sent her son to fetch me. He tugged at my hand and pulled me across the red earth to a small cooking fire. The old woman greeted me and pressed a handful of fresh leaves onto the fire. She grinned at me through the thick smoke that billowed out and around a black pot suspended over the fire from a tiny tripod. I choked in the smoke, and so did the mosquitoes, leaving me alone for the first time since I had arrived.

The woman chatted and I smiled, shrugging my shoulders each time I thought she asked me a question. The boy rocked on his heels, pointing at my hair, and nodding when the woman said something. He disappeared inside the small wooden hut behind them, returning with a worn rice hat that was broader and less pointed than my own. He gave it to the old woman, and she sent him back inside the hut with a light tap on his bottom.

As soon as he was gone, the woman stood up and removed my hat. She chatted as she fixed my hair, smoothing wrinkled fingers through the knots. I closed my eyes, letting her tug at my hair. The boy returned with a small brush and then the woman really got to work, swapping her words for tuts, tugs and the occasional sigh. She removed the knots and brushed my hair all the way down to my waist. She said something to the boy, and he pulled a leather cord from his pocket. The woman pulled my hair away from my face and bunched it in a tight tail she tied at the base of my skull, wrapping the cord around my hair and pinching it with a knot. She walked around me and crouched in front of me, pressing the rough skin of her thumbs to the skin either side of my eyes. She smiled with uneven teeth, cackling through the gaps as she reached for the worn hat and pressed it lightly onto my head. She clicked her tongue and pointed at the bench by the hut. The boy jogged to the bench and returned with the rifle. He laid it on the ground by my side and the woman patted the stock.

The smoke thinned and I heard the first buzz of the mosquitoes, as they returned to plague me. But the smoky taste of my skin seemed to put them off, and I smiled at the woman.

"It's better," I said, hoping she understood English.

The woman fired back a response that I did not understand. Then she patted the rifle again, lifting it and pressing it into my hands. I understood that she wanted me to keep it close, and mimed a few positions, before leaning it against a log within easy reach of my hand. The woman nodded, patted my knee, and poured soup from the pot into a smooth hardwood bowl. She pressed the bowl into my hands and mimicked the action of drinking from the side.

I spent the rest of the evening at the old woman's side, nodding when she offered me more soup, and again when she lifted a handful of green leaves and gestured at the fire. She fed the flames, fanned the smoke and chatted. She seemed content for me to listen. The boy drifted in and out of the hut. The last time I saw him was when he bent over to kiss the old woman on her head, before leaping out of the way as she tried to catch him in a hug. He called from the door, said something that might have been *goodnight* and then waved at me, before disappearing inside.

The woman and I sat in silence for at least another hour, before she too stood up, saying something as she gestured at the hut. She went inside, and I assumed they were going to sleep. I looked at the bench, barely visible in the shadows, before adding the last sticks to the fire. My legs ached from the crouching position, but it wasn't unfamiliar, Kunuk and I had sat like this for hours as kids, plucking crowberries with our grandmother, drawing circles in the dirt, and watching the *ammassat* swimming in thick steams in the rocky harbour. But my adult legs needed to stretch, and I stood up. I remembered the rifle, picked it up and slung it over my shoulder, before walking back to the bench.

I stopped halfway, turning to look at the sudden activity close to the camp entrance. Raised voices chattered through the night, highlighted with bobbing lanterns and black shapes flitting through the shadows. I tightened my grip on the rifle sling and walked towards the huts closest to the barrier. My sandals slapped on the earth and the mosquitoes returned, but the excited chatter near the gate sparked my curiosity and made the whine and bite of the mosquitoes almost bearable. I stopped beside the last hut between me and the barrier and watched as it was raised, and a group of men and women filed into the camp.

They wore black pyjamas like my own, only dirtier, streaked with mud, the cuffs of their trousers stiff above their naked ankles. They wore the same sandals, the same hats. The women wore their hair tied tight at the back of their heads. I was perhaps a little taller than they were, but not noticeably so. The women tumbled out of the column and into the arms of friends and family. The men did the same, and the column burst into a plume of unruly back feathers, flickering in the lantern light. As the soldiers dispersed, and the feathers settled into the arms of loved ones, there were just two people left, a short woman with her rice hat tipped back onto her shoulders, and a tall white man wearing tiger-striped fatigues.

The woman's hair shone with sweat in the lantern light. She had a pretty almond-shaped face tapering to a soft point at her chin, but the long scar on her cheek pulled her lip upwards in permanent sneer. Her eyes were bright and alert. They focused on me the second the column dispersed, and I forgot all about the mosquitoes as she stared at me.

She clicked her fingers at the man standing beside her, and he looked up, shifting the short-stock carbine in his grip, as he turned in my direction. His face was tinged with the crust of old camouflage paint, and it was difficult to say if he had a long face, or if it was rounder. But he was tall, and the light pack on his back was almost lost between his broad shoulders. He was taller than Eko, but the blue eyes that shone in the lantern light were just as keen as Eko's. He answered the woman, gesturing for her to grab a lantern, before they walked towards me.

Frode told me that Captain Miller would look after me, once I arrived at the camp. Thaksin had told me to wait, and I wondered if it was Miller I had been waiting for. The man stopped just a few feet in front of me. The woman walked on. She prowled around me, tugging at my shirt, tapping the stock of the rifle, before reaching up to flick the hat off my head. She lifted the lantern and held it high to shine on my face. The man spoke in Thai, and then switched to English just a second later.

"Do you have a name?" he asked, as he tucked the carbine into the crook of his arm.

"Frode Worsaae sent me," I said.

"That's not what I asked."

The woman tutted and pressed the lantern closer to my face. She flinched as I lifted my hand to wave her away. I saw the flash of a blade in her free hand, as she slid it out of the scabbard sewn into the strap of the satchel hanging from her shoulder.

"Tiên," the man said. "Put the knife away."

The woman sheathed the blade and took a step backwards. She placed the lantern on the ground and slid the rifle she carried on her back into her hands. She held it in a casual grip, but the intended effect was not lost on me.

"My name is Inniki," I said. "Frode sent me."

"I don't know anyone called *Frode*," the man said. "He must have sent you to the wrong place."

I thought for a moment, glancing at the woman as she tightened her grip on the rifle. "You might know him as Freddy," I said, thinking of the name Fitzpatrick used for Frode. I thought it might have a been slur, but then Danish names could be difficult to pronounce.

"I know lots of Freddys."

"But this one is Danish. Old and short." I paused at the twitch of a smile on the man's lips. "He looks gentle, but really…"

"He's a manipulative son of a bitch?"

"Yes," I said. "That's exactly what he is."

The man nodded at the woman and she slung the rifle once more. He reached out his hand, and said, "Captain James Miller."

"Inniki Rasmussen."

Miller gripped the magazine of his carbine and held it at his side as he walked. He flicked his head for me to follow and I walked beside him. The woman walked in front of us, carrying the lantern and leading the way.

"Her name is Tiên," Miller said. "It's a Vietnamese name, but she's one hundred percent Montagnard, from the mountains."

"And she works for the Americans?"

"She works with me," he said. "But yes, *we* work for the Americans. Is that why you're here?"

"I suppose so. It's not always clear."

Miller's webbing shifted as he laughed, and he unclipped it, dropping it onto the bench as we arrived at the hut where Thaksin had left me. Tiên hung the lantern above the bench, before slipping inside the hut. Miller sighed as he sat down. He rested the carbine in his lap. He hadn't let go of it once since I first saw him. He nodded at the seat next to him and I sat down.

"Freddy is a bit of a character. I'm sure he means well, but he's always so serious."

"Yes," I said. Just like I had noticed Miller had yet to let go of his carbine, I also noticed the way he looked at me, scrutinising, evaluating, he had worn the same look since we had met.

"He told you to look out for me?"

"He said you would help me."

"Hm." Miller tipped his head back against the wall of the hut. He closed his eyes for a moment. When he opened them again, his gaze was softer. The camouflage paint cracked around his lips as he smiled. "That wasn't exactly what he said, was it?"

"No." I returned Miller's smile. "He said you would look after me."

"Right," he said. "That sounds like Freddy." Miller stood up as Tiên came out of the hut. "We start tomorrow. Tiên will find you a place to sleep."

"She doesn't sleep here?" I asked, surprising myself that I was pleased to discover that they did not share living quarters.

"No," he said, pointing at a row of huts closer to the tree line. "And it's best you stay over there. More Americans arrive tomorrow. I don't know exactly what Freddy wants you to do, but I can see why he chose you. From now on, you are a Montagnard – a tall one. Tiên will help you blend in. Do what she says," Miller said. "Do *everything* she says, and you'll be just fine." He picked up his webbing and walked into the hut.

Chapter 21

Tiên woke me with a sharp jab of her toe in my ribs. I crawled off the bamboo mat and tugged my slippers onto my feet. For lack of anything else I had slept in the black pyjamas, with only the briefest of smiles at the thought that that was what they were meant for. Tiên beckoned from the doorway and I followed her through the camp to the river. The air was cooler there, and I lifted my head, turning into the light wind as it teased wayward strands of hair out of my ponytail. Tiên clapped her hands and pointed at the river. She kicked off her sandals, tugged her shirt over her head and pulled off her trousers. She folded both and placed them in a small square pile on top of her sandals. She nodded for me to do the same, and then stepped into the river.

I hadn't stripped in front of many women, but it wasn't my body I was nervous about revealing, it was my underwear. My panties and bra were dirty from travel, but it was the colour of them that made Tiên laugh. She hadn't said a word up until that point, and I was pleased to discover she was human. I placed my pink underwear on top of my piled clothes and then walked to the water's edge. The river was muddy brown, hiding my toes as it lapped over them. Tiên beckoned again, then splashed me with a swift strike of her palm against the surface of the water. I shrieked for a second, and then laughed. The water was warm.

Tiên waved me over to the flat rock she was sitting on, and I sat down beside her. The rock was smooth and warm on my bottom, and I ran my hands across my skin, scratching away the layer of sweat and grime with my fingernails. Tiên handed me a monkey knot of soft bamboo and nodded for me to use it. She sat beside me, smoothing wet hands through her black hair. Tiên turned her gaze on my body, tilting her head to one side and then looking at her chest as if comparing the size of our breasts. She had yet to speak, and in a moment of boldness, I pointed at the scar on her cheek. She opened her mouth and leaned towards me. There was a ragged chunk of flesh where her tongue should have been, and several of her back teeth were missing, while others were cracked and sharp. My breath caught in my throat as I realised that whoever had cut out her tongue had broken many of her teeth in the process. Tiên closed her mouth and then used her thumb to mime the action of someone slashing her cheek with a knife.

"I'm sorry," I said.

Tiên shrugged, and then held out her hand. I gave her the bamboo sponge and she slipped behind me to wash my back.

I watched the riverbank as Tiên scrubbed my skin clean. She stopped scrubbing at the same time as I saw him step out of the trees. Miller's chest was pale white, a stark contrast to the deep brown skin of his arms, face, and the V that stretched from his neck to his sternum. His hair was only slightly darker than his pink belly, a light red burned to a soft peach colour in the sun. He stopped at the river's edge, unbuttoned his tiger-striped fatigues and loosened the cord at his waist. He pulled his trousers off to reveal even more pale white skin. My breath caught in my throat for a second time, and Tiên's ragged breaths behind my back suggested she was looking in the same direction as I was. Like Tiên, Miller obviously didn't wear underpants.

I crossed my arms over my breasts as Miller waded into the water just a few yards downriver from our rock. He stopped when the water was at his knees, turned to catch my eye, and then dived into the river. I saw the white flash of his buttocks before they disappeared beneath the surface. Tiên made a sucking sound in her throat that could have been a giggle, and I turned around to smile.

"He's very white," I said.

Tiên's brown eyes widened and the sneer above her lip softened for a moment. She pressed the sponge into my hand and sat on the rock. I scrubbed her back as Miller surfaced downriver.

There had been men in my life before Eko, but only a few. The young Danish men I met during my late teens in Copenhagen typically shied away from me, often with quips and barbs aimed at my so-called *native* roots. Some invited me to dance at discos, only to comment about how much I had drunk even before I had started. *You are Greenlandic, after all*, they would say. Clara tried to soften the rejections, claiming that society was to blame, not me, that I shouldn't take it personally. But I did. Of course, I did. But Eko was different. He understood me, my culture, and my roots. But would he understand how I felt when looking at Miller's naked body in a river in northern Thailand? I wasn't so sure. Tiên pressed her knuckles into my thigh, frowning when I looked at her. I had stopped scrubbing.

We left Miller in the river and dressed on the bank. I bunched my underwear in my hands and carried them back to Tiên's hut. I tossed them on the bamboo mat and then followed her outside. She pointed at sticks and I fetched them. She clicked her fingers at the flames, and I fed them. When she made a clucking noise in her throat, I poured water from a jerry can into the pot above the flames. Tiên rolled a dough into flat circles. When the water boiled, she swapped the pot for a pan, cutting knobs of soft butter out of a wooden bowl, and frying the bread. She made the clucking noise and pointed at a wooden crate to the right of the door of her hut. She held up three fingers and I returned with three enamel mugs and three metal plates. Tiên pointed at the water and tossed me a metal box. She mimed taking three pinches of leaves from the box and I added them to the water. Tiên nodded and turned her attention back to the bread.

"Are you doing everything she tells you?"

I looked up as Miller approached the fire. He lifted his feet in what looked like deliberate movements, almost casual, practically silent. He sat on his heels on the other side of the cooking fire, nodding at Tiên, before looking at me.

"She hasn't *told* me to do anything," I said.

"No?" Miller pointed at the fire and the tea, the mugs and the plates that Tiên flipped the bread onto. "Sure looks like it." He took the plate that Tiên handed to him and nodded his thanks.

Tiên clicked her fingers and I poured the tea. We ate in silence, and when the first mosquitoes buzzed around our heads, Tiên added a handful of green leaves. I watched Miller through the smoke as he ate. Without the camouflage paint, his face was lean, young but with old eyes. I looked away as Tiên and Miller exchanged a glance, suddenly uncomfortable, as if I was intruding. But the moment passed, as did breakfast. As soon as the plates were cleaned, Tiên put the fire out. She grabbed her hat and her rifle and clicked her fingers for me to do the same.

"She'll need water," Miller said, as he stood up.

Tiên nodded and then ducked inside her hut. She returned with a broad canvas belt with two metal drinking bottles attached. The pouches between the bottles held ammunition for a rifle. Tiên pressed the belt into my hands and then pointed at a water barrel two huts further along from hers. When I returned Miller was gone. Tiên clipped the belt around my waist and then slung a bamboo tube around my shoulder, miming the action of eating with her fingers. She picked up Thaksin's rifle and gave it to me. I started to sling it over my shoulder, but she shook her head. She gripped her rifle in two hands and waited for me to do the same. Satisfied, Tiên led me between the huts to a trail at the opposite end of the camp from the entrance.

Miller was waiting beside a row of sandbags. He wore tightly-laced high-collared boots, and held his carbine by the magazine. There was no sling attached. The webbing on his chest held several bottles of water and a broad pouch across his belly with six magazines tucked inside and secured with button-down flaps. His olive drab shirt was dark with sweat, as was the bandana he had tied around his forehead.

"Freddy told me to look after you," he said, as we approached. "Well, it's gonna cost you about ten pounds in sweat. Be sure to drink, and when you drink, drain the bottle. I don't want to hear water sloshing around in half empty canteens."

"*Aap*," I said.

"What's that?"

"Yes."

"Okay then." Miller hiked his thumb over his shoulder towards the trail. "Tiên will lead. You'll follow about twenty yards behind her. No more. No less. If she goes slow, you slow down. If she runs, I expect you to keep up. Understand?"

"Yes."

"You watch her hands. If she holds one up, you stop, move into the side, and crouch. Wait for a signal from her. Move on if she tells you to."

"Okay."

"No speaking, no sighing, no farting. No sound whatsoever." Miller looked at my feet. "You might struggle to run in those. If so, kick 'em off and pick 'em up. The trail is packed hard, but don't step off it in bare feet."

He spun his finger in front of me and I turned around, jerking backwards as he tugged at my bottles and belt. I turned again when he tapped my shoulder.

"I don't know exactly what Freddy wants you to do, but if he put you here, then it has something to do with the jungle. You need to learn how to move in it. That's what this is about. We'll worry about the next step as soon as we know what it is."

"Okay," I said.

"One more thing," he said. "The Thai will know you're foreign just from the way you look and the way you move. Some of the Americans will too, up close. But at a distance you'll blend right in. Do what Tiên does, walk like she walks, and you'll be fine."

"You're the only American I've seen," I said.

"They're away on R&R in Bangkok. They'll be back tonight. Stay clear of them. Stick with Tiên. If you see me, pretend like you don't know me, and I'll do the same."

"Why?"

"Because those are Freddy's rules."

"I thought you didn't know why I was here."

"I don't, but you're not the first Greenlander he's sent me. There was a man here, a few months ago." Miller smiled. "Surprised? Don't be. There's always a bigger picture. Freddy makes sure of that."

"Do you remember his name?"

"Yes," Miller said. "I do." He pointed at the trail. "We're wasting daylight. Remember what I said and keep up with Tiên."

Tiên clicked her fingers and I turned around. She started to lope along the trail, and I lifted my foot to follow her.

"Wait," Miller said, gripping my shoulder with one hand. "Twenty yards, remember?"

"Yes," I said.

Miller's hand stayed on my shoulder until Tiên was far enough ahead. He let go, and I started to run. I thought of Eko for the first hundred yards, until the heat sapped at my strength, and the sandals slid beneath my soles. I paused to kick them off, then tucked them into my belt and continued. The rifle was heavy in my hands, the earth was hard beneath my feet, but it was the heat that I struggled with most, willing it into my lungs with noisy breaths.

All those miles I had run along the beach in Denmark, had done little to prepare me for the jungle. I soon forgot all about Eko, Miller's naked body, and my assignment. The only thing I thought about was Tiên, and when, if ever, she would stop.

Chapter 22

When Tiên did stop, when she finally raised her hand and ducked into the side of the trail, I almost ran past her. Miller hissed at me to stop running, and when I didn't, he closed the distance between us and pulled me to the ground just a few yards from where Tiên crouched, partly hidden by the sprawling jungle growth. Miller turned me onto my side, one hand pressed on my arm, the other wrapped around the grip of the rifle he tucked into his shoulder.

"Stay down," he whispered, pressing his lips to my ear. "Control your breathing."

I turned my head to see his face, watching as he flicked his gaze forwards and to both sides of the trail. He lifted his hand from my shoulder and curled his fingers around the rifle's hand guard. His eyes narrowed and he pressed his cheek close to the rear sight. He didn't move for at least a minute, he hardly breathed. Sweat rolled down his cheeks, adding to the dark stain growing on his collar.

Then, perhaps a minute later, he relaxed his grip on the rifle and lowered it. He tapped me on the shoulder and gestured for me to sit up. Tiên padded down the trail to join us, crouching by Miller's side as I pushed myself into a sitting position. Miller took a canteen from the pouch on his webbing, unscrewed the cap and pushed it into my hands.

"Drink it all," he said, as I pressed the mouth of the canteen to my lips.

The water was warm. It dribbled down my chin as I chugged at it. I lowered the canteen and stared at Tiên as she moved her fingers through a series of shapes and numbers. Miller nodded, asked once if she was sure, and then looked at me.

"Drink up," he said.

"What happened?"

"Finish the bottle, then I'll tell you."

I drained the last of the water inside the canteen, held it above my lips, and then screwed the cap back on. Miller took it from my hand and tucked it into his webbing. He tightened the cap with one more turn before he spoke.

"The camp is a secret, which means everyone in the local area knows about it," he said. I waited for him to smile, but he didn't. "We're close to the Burmese border, and the border with Laos. Both countries are interested in what the Americans are doing here, and they send out bandit patrols, just to keep an eye on us. The bandits are local mercenaries, paid for information, but they can't be traced to any one country. It makes them dangerous, as they know they are on their own. If we run into a patrol, and we can't talk our way out of it, the only thing left to do is fight. Tiên heard them long before their path crossed ours. They've gone now, heading back to their camp, and I think we should too." Miller peeled back the rubber cover hiding the face of his watch. "It's getting late and getting hot."

"*Getting* hot?" I said.

"That's right. It gets worse from now until sometime

early in the morning. I need to get you home."

"Home is a long way from here." I pictured the icebergs in the Tasiilaq harbour, the smaller growlers, and the chips of ice floating in the surf and washing onto the thin sandy beaches. The first layer of ice was always salty, smelling of brine and sea tang. But after that layer it was the purest kind of water, thousands of years old. The very thought of sucking a small piece of glacier ice from the sea was almost too much. I thought about crying but didn't think I could spare the water or the salt. What was it Frode had said?

Miller pulled a strip of tablets from his shirt pocket. He pressed one between my lips and handed me a second canteen.

"Salt tablet," he said, as I swallowed it with another mouthful of water. Miller took the canteen and shared it between the three of us. Tiên drank the least. She tapped Miller's knee and pointed down the trail. "Come on," he said, as he helped me onto my feet. "You did well for your first run. We'll take it slow on the way back." He took the empty canteen from Tiên and stuffed it into the webbing pouch. "I've got point, you walk twenty yards behind me. Tiên is tail-end-Charlie."

"What's that?"

"It means she comes last," he said. He nodded once at Tiên, flashed a brief smile at me, and then switched his grip on his carbine. Miller set off down the trail. Tiên tapped my shoulder when it was time for me to follow.

The walk back was gentler, and I had time to appreciate the shades of jungle greens and browns. There are no trees in Greenland, only bushes, stunted by the Arctic climate. There was nothing stunted about the jungle, but there was far more death and decay. The walk allowed me to smell the jungle, the rich humus, and the cloying and claggy perfumes of rotting fruit and vines. A bush in Greenland was stubborn. It might be small and thin, dry and brittle, but it was rarely dead, and it didn't rot. Here, in the jungle, on both sides of the path, death was everywhere, and it was wet. But there was life too, a chorus of noise, the beating of wings, the rustling of small animals, the crashing of bigger ones. I glimpsed rodents, jumped at the screech of monkeys, and walked straight into the back of Miller.

"Don't worry about the monkeys," he said.

"I didn't see you."

"I know. I saw *you*, Inniki." He waved at Tiên and then pointed along the path. "Almost home. You can walk by my side until we reach the camp."

I moved to sling my rifle over my shoulder, but Miller stopped me, hooking his finger around the sling.

"Best to keep it in your hands," he said, and let go.

"Why am I carrying I rifle?"

"In case you need it."

"And why would I need it?"

"That," Miller said, "is a question for our friend, Freddy."

We walked the next hundred yards in silence. Miller turned his head when a sound caught his interest, cocking his ear to listen, before giving the trail ahead his full attention.

"I once saw a clouded leopard," he said. "They have these huge incisors." He lifted one hand to his mouth and hooked two fingers in front of his top lip, lowering them when I smiled. "No-one believed me, but I know what I saw. You spend enough time in the jungle, and you get to see some things."

"And you've been in the jungle a lot?"

"Yep," he said. "Two tours in 'Nam, and then, once we started to pull out, I got picked for special duties at twice the government salary."

"You took this job for the money?"

"No." Miller paused to adjust his webbing before he answered. "I said *yes* to the job because I didn't know what else I was going to do. I got good at something, and I realised that it would take a while to get good at something else. I heard of guys back home in the World. They found it hard to find something – *anything* that they could do at the same level they did over here. Plus, there was all that crap about being called a rapist, a child-killer. We were just doing our jobs. We didn't do any of those things, leastways, no-one I knew did." Miller sighed and wiped the sweat from his eyes. "Anyway, I was good at finding things. I graduated from the Army's training school in Nha Trang, and they put me to work with the Lurps."

"What?"

"Long range reconnaissance patrols," Miller said. "Six-man teams, working behind enemy lines. I saw a lot of guys get torn up, but I always managed to come home in one piece. Not one scratch. Well, it got to the point where the other guys thought I jinxed the mission, that if I was on a mission, everyone but me would get hit. Stupid, but there's nothing like superstition to ruin a good team. My Commanding Officer transferred me to another unit, and I was sent to a Special Forces camp, which is where I met Tiên. We did the same work, but just the two of us, or me and a bunch of Montagnards. That's French for *mountaineer*. She's one of the mountain tribesmen – *people*. The Green Berets used them a lot, and the French used them before we did." Miller glanced over his shoulder to wave at Tiên. "She's lost more than I care to think about."

"But you do," I said. I could see it in his eyes.

"Yeah," he said. "I guess I do."

"And is that what you do here?" I asked. "Find things?"

"That's right. Whatever they tell me to."

"And what are you trying to find?"

"A village." Miller waved his hand in wide arc that moved from west to east. "There are villages all over this area. Tiny and remote, straddling the border. A lot of them are involved in growing opium. Some of them are processing it into heroin. That's what we're looking for. You see, we can't burn the fields, because it's a crop, and the growing of opium supports the villagers and the districts. But if we find a village that is refining the crop, then we can crush it with impunity. That's why we're here."

"But you can't find the village that is refining the opium?"

"We've found lots of villages doing the refining, but we can't find *the* village. There's one village that has got the brass... the *bosses*... all worked-up. It seems we need to be able to link the heroin being pushed on the street in the States with the product they have in the village. We're waiting on confirmation."

"Eko," I said.

"What's that?"

"My friend." The word *friend* tasted strange on my tongue. "He's the one they're using to make the link. You've met him, if he was the Greenlander they sent to you, the one before me."

"Don't connect too many dots, Inniki."

"Why?"

"It's best that you don't," Miller said, as we reached the camp. He looked up at the sound of something thwacking at the air in the distance. He lifted his hand and pointed to a distant spot in the hazy grey sky. "Helicopter," he said. "At least two."

"I can't see them."

"You will. They're about three minutes out." Miller waved for Tiên to hurry. "Follow Tiên back to her hut. Eat, drink and rest. Stay inside and out of sight."

"Where will you be?"

"With them," he said.

I stared at the spot he had pointed to and saw two dark shapes grow out of the low cloud.

"I see them," I said.

"And that's as close as I want you to get. Keep your head down, and out of sight."

Miller started to walk off the trail and into the camp. I reached for his arm and stopped him.

"Why are you doing this?"

"Doing what?"

"Working for Freddy, when you are working for the Americans. Are you a spy?"

"A spy?" Miller laughed. He looked at Tiên and she rolled her eyes. "No, I'm not a spy."

The air shuddered with the approaching thunder of the helicopters. I recognised the shapes as those they showed on television. They were the same kind that the Americans had in Greenland, Hueys, like the one Frode had flown to Thule in. The first helicopter flared as it approached the wide part of the dirt road running through the camp.

"What then?" I asked. "I think I have to know, if I'm going to trust you."

"Do you?"

"Yes," I said, raising my voice as the helicopter landed. "But I need to know."

"I'll let Freddy tell you one day," he said. "But, just to make you feel better, let's just say he helped me when no-one else would. I owe him for that." Miller glanced at Tiên and she reached out to take his hand. "We both do," he said.

There was a light in Tiên's eyes. It lit up her face and softened the scar on her cheek. She let go of Miller's hand, but the connection remained, and it occurred to me that it would always be there, that they would always be connected. It was enough, I felt, for me to trust Miller, *and* Tiên. Frode obviously did, but just how he managed to put all his pieces – his assets – in one place eluded me. But then I realised that not *all* the pieces were in one place. Not yet. Eko was still missing.

Chapter 23

Miller was gone for the rest of the day and into the night. The camp was louder, the smoke from the cooking fires thicker, and the mosquito bites sharper. It felt like the arrival of the Americans had amplified everything with a new and foreign intensity. When the first bulldozers arrived later in the day, the American engineers stripped the camp of its jungle roots and cleared a perimeter on all sides, starting with the swathe of vegetation from Tiên's hut to the river. We watched them all night, looking up periodically as we cleaned our rifles, tended to the cooking fire, collected water and made tea. The magical world that I had entered when walking the jungle path to the river earlier that same day was stripped bare, naked beneath the black sky, dazzled by the glare of the bulldozer lights. The noise was incessant, like fat metal mosquitoes, gnawing at the trees, felling them with a crack of woody fibres.

Tiên watched the bulldozers but made no sign that she wanted to comment. The light in her eyes dulled, and not even the flicker of the cooking fire flames could brighten them. Only Miller's return, long after midnight, could change the impassive set of her face. She turned her head as he approached, waited for him to sit cross-legged by the fire, and then poured him a mug of tea. He rested his carbine in his lap and reached for the mug, nodding his thanks as Tiên handed it to him.

Miller drank in silence, looking at us both through the campfire smoke, nodding for a second cup of tea, and then unlacing his boots. He removed them and his socks, setting them close to the fire as he wiggled his albino toes. He caught me smiling and shrugged.

"My body is like a strip of litmus paper," he said. "Changing colour every couple of inches."

I watched his face as he finished his tea, catching his eye as he lowered the cup from his lips. My heart was full of conflicting thoughts, as I stared at Miller. He was younger than Eko, and yet those eyes, wrinkled with war, made him seem older than Frode even. I looked away, glad of the dark to hide the flush of colour I felt rising up my neck.

Miller pressed his cup into the earth beside the fire, turning it as he looked over his shoulder at the bulldozers behind him. "I used to like this camp," he said. "Of all the Army camps I have lived on, this one was the most natural. I've had my best night's sleep here, but that's all gonna change. This," he said, gesturing at the razed ground between us and the river, "is what we do best. Tear up the countryside and flatten the earth. They'll string razor wire in three rows at first light, dig in a field of landmines, then put up watchtowers in each corner." Miller tipped his finger between the four corners of the camp. "Machine guns in low towers, sandbags and bunkers between them. It's straight out of the Vietnam textbook." He glanced at Tiên, and I saw the sneer twitch above her lip.

"Why?" I asked.

"Because they're gearing up for an operation, based on new intel." Miller hiked his thumb over his shoulder, pointing towards the river. "They want a clear field of fire in case of retaliation."

"From who?"

"The bandits and militias protecting the heroin. They have a lead on the village, the one they think is producing the drugs they picked up in the States."

"They know where it is?"

"Not an exact location, but they have a better idea." Miller looked at Tiên, and said, "We've been there before, but we turned around about three klicks too soon."

"Klicks?" I said.

"Kilometres, because of the scale of the maps," Miller said, turning to look at me. "Tiên and I have been looking for the village for a while now. We just finished with a long patrol when you arrived, now they want us to go out again, at first light." Miller reached for his socks and began pulling them over his toes. "You should get some sleep, Tiên," he said.

"What about me?"

"You'll stay here."

"I should come with you. That's what Frode would want."

"No," Miller said. "You'll flake out on the trail, and we can't carry you."

"I know I was slow and weak today," I said. "But I feel better already."

Tiên made a clucking sound in the back of her throat, and I turned to see her shake her head.

"No, really," I said. "I can do it." Miller ignored me as he pulled his boots. I stood up as he reached for his carbine. "If I stay here, they'll find me. The Americans. You told me to stay out of sight, but for how long?" I pointed at the bulldozers as they drove back inside the original perimeter of the camp. "Now I can't even walk to the river without someone watching me. How long do you think it will take them to find me? One day? Two? And how long will you be gone?"

"We're going on patrol, Inniki. This is not a training mission."

"I'm not *training*," I said. "Frode sent me here, on my *mission*. I need to come with you. I'm the only one who can identify Eko…"

"Not the only one," Miller said, confirming what I already thought to be true, that Eko had been here, and that Miller had taught him like he was teaching me.

"Okay, but I'm the only one he'll talk to. That's why Frode put me here. That's my only purpose. You have to let me do my job."

Miller gestured for me to sit with a wave of his hand. I sank to my heels and waited.

"Tiên?" he said.

Tiên stared at me for a full minute without blinking. She made two fists, then raised her index fingers, bumping them against each other, and then bobbing them through the air, side by side, in a slow arc in front of her body. Miller nodded.

"What did she say?"

"That she'll make sure you're tied at the hip. You'll stay with Tiên. I'll send one of the Thai Strikers in Tiên's place as lead scout. Tiên stays with you." Miller's webbing creaked softly as he stood up. He rested the carbine in the crook of his arm and looked down at me. "You're right about being discovered," he said. "The Americans in camp today might not know you, but we're getting some new meat at the end of the week. It seems the BNDD are calling the shots, and they are sending a couple of guys down here to oversee the op." Miller nodded towards the Americans' quarters. "It's those guys – the Feds – who worry me. They've seen too many war movies, and now they want to play soldier. Plus, from what you and Frode have told me, you probably know them."

My stomach cramped at the thought of Perkins. Perhaps I should have thrown him over the side of the fishing trawler, not just his pistol. But Frode had stopped me going too far, and he had promised that Miller would look after me. It seemed unlikely, but the truth of it was that I was safer on patrol with Miller and Tiên in bandit country, than I was hiding behind the razor wire of the American camp. The look on Miller's face suggested he thought the same thing.

"Get some sleep," he said. "We leave in a few hours."

The twenty Thai Strikers were all men. They wore tiger-striped fatigues like Miller did, beneath an assortment of webbing, pouches, small backpacks, bamboo tubes of sticky rice, bandoliers and long belts of bullets draped around their necks. They wore tightly-laced boots on their feet, and that was the only thing I had in common with them – Tiên had presented me with a pair of used boots and three pairs of black socks when she woke me that morning, digging her toe into my ribs with her customary greeting. She wore her sandals, favouring open feet to the pinched toes of the boots.

Tiên tapped my arm and made me bend over so that she could slip a satchel over my neck and shoulder. I tugged it into a position just past my hip, before slinging a rice tube over my other shoulder and picking up my coolie hat. Tiên handed me my rifle and we walked out to join the patrol. Miller and I were the tallest, but Tiên and I were the only ones dressed in black.

Miller nodded as we fell into line. He tucked a canvas map case into the space between his shirt and the ammunition pouch he wore across his stomach. The lead scout, the shortest of the Thai, nodded at a signal from Miller, and started to walk off the camp.

"Miller, wait up."

An American waved at Miller, as he jogged between the huts to walk by his side as the scout stepped onto the trail. I waited in the column as the Strikers followed the scout in staggered groups of ones and twos. The American had a loud voice, and even his whisper carried clearly along the column.

"When you find the village," the man said, "and if you see the target, you have a green light to take him out. Understood?"

"I thought this was just a recon mission?"

"Which it is, but this is coming down the chain, right from the top. You know Fitzpatrick?"

Tiên slapped at my thigh as I twisted my head towards Miller. She shook her head and pushed me towards the trail.

"I know of him," Miller said.

"Well, it seems he's got a real hard-on for this guy. Something about a double-cross? Maybe. It's not clear. But he's given the kill order."

"Let me find the village first," Miller said. He lowered his voice, and together with the increasing distance between us, his last words were masked.

"Good then," the American said.

Fitzpatrick had never trusted Eko. I understood that. But he needed him. As Frode had said, the BNDD desperately wanted a man on the inside of the drug trafficking ring they had intercepted, but clearly Eko was not their ideal undercover agent. It occurred to me that Fitzpatrick had never called Eko an *agent*, regardless of how many times Frode had reminded him of Eko's status, as a Danish undercover operative. Of course, he never mentioned the part about Eko being his son.

I stumbled on the path as I let my mind wander. Tiên slapped my leg and straightened me, turning my body, but not before I caught a glance of Miller's face, as he brought up the rear of the column. He caught my eye for a moment, before looking away, sweeping the trail or hiding his true purpose – it was difficult to know. With Tiên's help I fell in line, and as the scout picked up the pace, I thought less and less about Eko, and focused on keeping up, and not falling over in the heat.

We marched through the day, stopping for five minutes every hour – long enough to share a canteen of water and maybe a mouthful of rice. Tiên made me take off my boots. She smeared a rubbery sap on the irritated skin of my heels, encouraged me to dry between my toes, and then waited for me to lace up my boots as the column stretched and prepared to move. The Strikers spoke in hushed voices. Miller said nothing. He caught my eye once as the lead scout moved off down the trail, and once again his look was unfathomable. I drained the last of the Tiên's canteen, hefted my rifle, and then walked in front of her along the trail.

She tugged at my arm and forced me to crouch on the trail just a few minutes after the last break. She pressed her finger to her lips and tapped the rifle in my hands, nodding when I placed my finger on the safety lever on the right side of the trigger guard. Miller slid along the trail, passing me with barely a whisper of fabric. I turned my head as he continued along the column of Thai Strikers. He stopped to crouch beside the second man in the column, holding his carbine in a ready position.

My mouth felt dry as we waited, and I glanced at the canteen secured to Tiên's satchel. She followed my gaze and shook her head. I looked up as a breath of air twisted along the column. It was drier than the humid air of the jungle, and the familiar tang of Greenland that it carried made me frown. The Strikers must have felt it too. A second later, the jungle erupted with the crack of gunfire and the zip of bullets tearing at the broad leaves above our heads. Tiên shoved me to the ground and I tasted red earth on my tongue as she kneeled on my back and opened fire.

Chapter 24

With every squeeze of the trigger, Tiên pressed another breath out of my lungs as her knees rocked my back with the recoil. I gulped mouthfuls of air between bullets, as Tiên tracked her targets on the south side of the jungle trail. The rim of my coolie hat was caught on a branch that had fallen beneath a hail of bullets, wedging it to one side so that I could see the trail. I saw the snap and tear of leaves as a bullet ripped through the vegetation. But there was nothing to be seen, no sign of the bandits. Tiên focused on the leaves, aiming in the direction the incoming bullets had travelled from, burning through a strip of ammunition with smooth, calculated shots in rapid succession. I breathed when she reloaded and rocked when she recoiled. The bullets blistered along the side of the trail until one of them caught Tiên in the shoulder and lifted her off my back.

"Tiên."

I crawled towards her, as she pressed her hand to her shoulder, waving me back to the trail as she scrabbled in the undergrowth for her rifle.

"It's here," I said. I found Tiên's weapon and carried it to her in the crooks of my arms, dragging my own by the sling I hooked around my fingers. "You're hurt."

I pushed the rifles to one side and slid deeper into the undergrowth, twisting the satchel from my hip to my stomach. Tiên brushed me to one side as she reached for her rifle. The bullets zipped and zinged above our heads, thwacking into the trunks of the hardwood trees, splintering the heavy lianas hanging from the boughs. I tugged a bandage from my satchel, tipped my coolie hat behind my head and tried to press the bandage onto Tiên's shoulder.

She shook her head, rushing through a series of sucking and clucking sounds in her throat, as she fumbled to press new bullets into the rifle.

"You're bleeding," I said. "Let me help you."

Something heavy crashed through the vegetation and onto the trail. A small man thrust the barrel of his assault rifle through the trees, aiming at Tiên and me. Tiên paused, grabbed the barrel of her rifle, and swung it in an arc to knock the man's rifle to one side. He pulled the trigger and a stream of bullets ploughed into the soft earth, filling the hot, wet air with the sound of thunder and the smell of cordite. I dropped the bandage and pulled my rifle into my lap, fumbling with the safety as I pressed the stock into the earth between my legs, gripped the barrel with one hand and pulled the trigger with the other. The rifle jolted into the earth as the bullet blasted into the man's head. His body cartwheeled across the path, blood arcing from his head and splashing dark red on the bright green leaves.

Tiên tugged the rifle out of my hands, aimed at the man and put two more rounds into his body. She took a breath, lowered the rifle and nodded at me. Her hair was plastered to her forehead. She brushed it to one side with her sleeve, smearing her skin with a ruddy brown swathe of dirt.

"Okay," I said. "I'm okay." I took a second to focus,

ducked my head at another round of bullets that zinged into the trees above us, then searched for the bandage. I found the white cotton tail, speckled with dirt, and tugged it into my fingers. I kneeled beside Tiên as she reloaded both rifles, and wound the bandage around her shoulder, looping it around her neck to tie it in place. "There," I said, and leaned back onto my heels.

Tiên turned her head to look at the bandage. She winced as her shoulders started to shake. Tears streamed down her face, as the bandage slipped down her arm. I stared, open mouthed, until I realised, she was laughing.

"Well, I tried," I said.

Tiên wiped the tears from her cheek and then pressed her finger and thumb into a circle to flash me the OK sign. She reached for the bandage, tugged it off her arm, and tossed it to one side. Tiên pressed my rifle into my arms, nodded towards the trail, and then pointed at her back.

"Stay behind you?"

She nodded, and crawled forwards, onto the trail. Tiên paused by the side of the dead bandit. She slung her own rifle over her shoulder, letting it hang down her back as she picked up the man's AK47, and two magazines from the bandolier strapped across his bloody chest. Tiên scanned the trail as she checked the weapon, slapping a fresh magazine into the receiver, before crawling along the trail to where two Thai Strikers returned fire. I crawled behind her, pressing my fingers into the earth, and the sticky drops of Tiên's blood that she left on the trail.

The first Striker slapped his partner on the arm when he spotted us, lowering his weapon and beckoning for Tiên to crawl straight to him. He pulled a bandage from his webbing and dressed her wound, binding it tight around her shoulder. I watched from the trail, hugging my rifle to my chest, choosing to focus on the Striker helping Tiên, rather than let my thoughts wander to the dead man on the trail with one of my bullets in his head. Tiên clicked her fingers, pointed at a depression on the north side of the trail, and shoved me towards it. I crawled into the hole, felt the pool of stagnant water press into the knees of my pyjamas, and waited.

I heard Miller's voice. His American accent rumbling through a string of orders delivered in rapid Thai. I didn't understand what he was saying, but the Strikers responded with a renewed intensity of return fire, as Miller duckwalked along the trail towards us. He crouched beside Tiên, glanced at me, and then prodded the bandage around her shoulder. He nodded, slapped the Thai Striker on the arm and said something that made the man smile.

"You hurt?" he said, looking at me.

"What?"

"Inniki, are you hurt?"

"No."

"Then get over here and start shooting." Miller clicked his fingers and grabbed my sleeve as I crawled out of the depression. He pulled me to my knees, raised my arm and tucked the butt of my rifle into my shoulder. "Aim," he said. "Breath and squeeze."

I aimed into the trees and pulled the trigger.

"Aim. Breathe. Squeeze."

I fired again. Miller adjusted my aim with a gentle push of the rifle to one side. I felt the warm Greenland wind on my cheek, felt the tiny hairs on my skin begin to prickle, as the rifle jolted into my shoulder, and the rich smell of the jungle earth and the sweat of my body tickled the hairs inside my nose. I could smell Miller's body, Tiên's blood, and the Strikers' breath.

I could smell everything.

The leaves of the jungle snapped in the vacuum of my bullets. I saw the subtle variety of colours in the earth – not just red, but maroons, sumac and cinnamon. Specks of gunpowder grey and brimstone black filled the pores of my fingers and cheeks, I could taste it on my tongue. The jungle brimmed, looming large with every pull of the trigger. I giggled as I stopped to reload, my fingers fumbling with the bullets until Tiên steadied them. Miller nodded, cupped his hand around my neck and pressed his thumb against the side of my face.

"Keep shooting," he said, before he let go and scooted back along the trail, giving words of encouragement here, correcting arcs of fire there.

Miller disappeared just as Tiên finished reloading my rifle. She pointed, I aimed, breathed and squeezed. I grinned between each bullet, drunk on repetitive action, convinced that it was the right thing to do and the only thing that mattered in that moment. I burned through another load of bullets, paused to reload, and then lifted the rifle to my shoulder to begin again. Tiên stopped me with a hand on the barrel, shaking her head as she pressed my rifle downwards.

The Strikers had lowered their weapons too, and a wave of calm sank across the trail. The monkeys started to chatter as the gun smoke lifted, and the Strikers tidied up the ground around them, pressing used magazines into the pouches on their webbing, patting each other on the back, grinning in the aftermath of battle and the dense heat of the afternoon.

Tiên wasn't the only casualty. Miller supervised a team of two Strikers who worked quickly to stem the flow of blood from one man's groin, pressing slippery fingers inside a blood-soaked tear in the man's combat trousers. Miller pointed, repeating soft commands in Thai until the Strikers shook their heads and backed away.

"Inniki," Miller said, as he pressed his carbine into the hands of a striker and tore the wounded man's trousers wide open. "You've got small fingers. Help me."

Tiên took my rifle and crouched beside me as I kneeled on the trail.

"You need to find the femoral artery. If we don't clamp it, this man is going to bleed to death. Do you understand?"

"*Aap*," I said.

"I'll take that as a *yes*. Now," Miller took my hands and pressed my fingers into the wound high up in the man's thigh. "Don't look, just feel. Find the tube. And when you've got it," he said, taking a clamp from one of the Striker's bloody hands. "Don't let go."

The wounded man groaned until a Striker kneeled by his side and injected a syrette of morphine into his shoulder. I stuck my tongue between my teeth and dug into the man's flesh. I felt his blood pulse over my fingers.

"That's it," Miller said. "Work your fingers around it."

I thought of a scene from my childhood – a hunter on a sandy beach in Greenland, as he butchered a seal on the sand, paring the skin from the meat. There was blood. It fascinated me as a child, but it was not bloody, not like this. The artery slipped between my fingers, and I clenched my teeth, startling myself with a prick of my own blood on my tongue.

"Come on, Inniki," Miller said. "You had it. Get it again."

Miller held a pair of scissor-like clamps above my fingers. I nodded that I had a grip and I pulled at the artery between my fingers. Miller slid the clamp along my finger, bumping the flat nose over my knuckles, before clamping it around the artery.

"That's it," he said, clicking his fingers for the next clamp. "Get the other end."

The other end was easier, with only a dribble of blood slipping over my fingers. Miller grinned as he secured the second clamp, stepping back to let the Thai take over.

"Well done," he said, pulling me to my feet with a bloody hand.

I watched as the Strikers worked on their wounded brother. I brushed at a tear on my cheek and the smell of blood from my fingers, together with the jungle rush of combat just minutes earlier, jellied my knees. I started to crumple towards the floor, only to have Miller catch me in his arms, and help me sit down.

"Water," he said, holding out his hand. One of the men pressed a canteen into his fingers. Miller unscrewed the cap and held the bottle to my lips. The first mouthful dribbled over my chin as I choked. Miller waited, and then made me drink a second and a third time. "You did well," he said, screwing the cap back on the canteen. "And you probably saved Lek's life." Miller gestured at the Thai Strikers gathered around the wounded man. "They watched you. They won't forget what you did."

I looked up at the men standing around me. Some of them smiled, others caught my eye and nodded, Tiên reached out to pluck at the sleeve of my arm. Her face softened with a smile, and I looked past the scar on her cheek to see the light dancing in her eyes.

"You did well, Inniki," Miller said. "Now I want you to go back to the camp with these men. They're going to take their friend back to the camp doctor."

"Where are you going?" I asked, as the Strikers lifted the wounded man onto a foldable stretcher.

"There are blood trails leading into the jungle. We're going to follow them. Maybe we'll get lucky and take a prisoner who can tell us the location of the village."

"Eko's village?"

Miller bit at the corner of his lip. He looked me in the eye, and dipped his head, just once, briefly.

"Okay then," I said. I held out my hand and he pulled me to my feet. "I'm coming with you."

Chapter 25

Miller hesitated. I brushed my hair from my face and pushed my hat back onto my head. The rifle was slick with blood from my hands and I wiped it with my sleeve, glancing up at Miller from beneath my hat as he talked with Tiên. I don't know who was more unhappy – Miller because I was determined to stay on the patrol, or Tiên because he was sending her back to camp with the wounded Striker. Tiên made a huffing sound in her throat, crossed her arms across her chest and kicked at the loose earth on the side of the trail. She looked like a stubborn child, but for the ugly scar creasing her cheek.

Tiên looked at me, flashed a few quick signs with her fingers at Miller, and then shouldered her rifle. She carried the AK47 in her hands, with the extra magazine stuffed into the front pocket of her satchel. Tiên took my hand and squeezed it hard, as she looked into my eyes. She held it for a moment, then let go to brush her fingers through my hair. She turned away before I could say anything, falling into the small column of Strikers winding their way along the trail back to camp.

"She likes you, Inniki," Miller said.

"Is that what she was saying? When she was signing?"

"No. She told me to look after you, and what would happen to me if I didn't." Miller changed magazines, tapping the dirt out of a full magazine from his pouch, before slapping it into the carbine. "I don't like this, but I agree with Tiên that there is still too much activity at the camp – too many Americans." Miller tucked the carbine into the crook of his arm. "Frode should never have sent you."

"But he did," I said.

"Yes, he did."

The remaining Thai Strikers checked their weapons and tightened their webbing straps, watching Miller, waiting for the sign to move out. Miller pulled back the rubber cover of his watch and checked the time, the sun, and then the trail. When the lead scout returned from a brief reconnaissance, Miller organised the men into three groups of four, with me and the scout included in the last group.

"Stay right in front of me," he said. "If I can't reach you with my hand, I'll tell you to stop."

"Okay."

"Let the scout and the man in front of you lead the way. If they stop…"

"I stop."

"Exactly. But touch nothing and assume every step is booby-trapped."

"Booby-trapped?"

"If the bandits think they're going to die, or one of their men has died, they'll hide a grenade beneath a thigh, or under the stomach. When you roll the man over to check if he's dead, then you both are." Miller nodded towards the trail. "You can still catch Tiên."

I looked along the trail and then shook my head. The jungle was still preferable to bumping into Perkins or Fitzpatrick in the camp.

"I'll stay with you."

"And do exactly what I say."

"*Aap.*"

"See," Miller said, with a sigh, "I still have no idea what that means."

"It means *yes.*"

"All right. Well just say *yes* next time. There's not enough room in my head for more languages. I..."

Miller turned at a sound from the lead scout. He pulled me down to the ground and pressed his hand on my shoulder, as he snaked around me and into the jungle.

"Wait there," he whispered, before disappearing behind a curtain of broad leaves.

I could just hear the whisper of voices, and the metallic click of the Strikers flicking their rifles from *safe* to *semi* or full *auto*. Miller seemed to always have his rifle set to *semi*, even in camp. I wondered if he couldn't afford the second it took to fiddle with the switch, if that was something he had learned during the war in Vietnam.

I turned my head at the soft crack of a rotten branch behind me. Miller had sent the Strikers into the jungle in three lines like splayed fingers. I didn't remember anyone being behind us. I spun on my heels at the second crack of the branch, raising my head and lifting the rifle to my shoulder as a man burst onto the trail. He had a bayonet attached to the end of his assault rifle, and he thrust it towards me as he ran. I dipped to one side, felt the bayonet tear through the arm of my pyjamas, and the nick of steel as it sliced into my arm.

I thought about crying out but couldn't waste the energy or the breath. I swung my rifle around to face the man, only to feel it jolt in my hands as he batted it out of the way, drawing me inside the arc of his rifle swing, close to his body. I dropped my rifle, bunched my fist and struck the man in the stomach, then again in this sternum. He reeled and the angry lines on his face softened into creases of surprise. I surprised him a third time as I jerked my knee into his groin.

I found my voice as the man tumbled onto the trail, yelling Miller's name, as I pounced on the man, wrestling the rifle from his grasp. He twisted beneath me, curling his knee into my chest. I slapped at his hand as he reached for my throat, and then wrenched the rifle out of his grip with two hands. The man's finger slid along the wooden stock. I grabbed the barrel with one hand and gripped the magazine in the other, shoving the stock into the man's stomach with a scream. I heard the crack of his knuckles, and then smelled the fusty tang of fish on his breath as I forced the air from his lungs. He vomited onto his chin, just as Miller crashed through the leaves with a Striker on either side.

"Inniki," he yelled. "Roll off him."

I let go of the rifle and tumbled onto the trail. Miller leaped onto the man's chest, cracking one of the bandit's ribs as he landed on him. The man gulped enough air into his lungs to scream, before Miller slammed the butt of his carbine into the man's forehead. The man's eyes closed as his head slumped into the trail.

"He must have snuck around us while we were working on Lek." Miller caught his breath and stood up. He took a step back, letting the Thai Strikers pull the man to his feet. The bandit swayed between them as Miller bound the man's hands in front of him. "Are you all right, Inniki?" Miller asked, glancing over his shoulder as he tightened the knot.

"I'm fine."

"You're not hurt?"

"No. I'm okay."

"Your arm," Miller said, pulling a bandage from his webbing. He widened the slice of black cotton on my sleeve with a quick tearing action. "It's not too deep," he said.

"I moved..."

"Good," he said. Miller tore open a small packet and dumped sulfa powder on the wound, before binding my arm with the bandage. He turned around to look at the Strikers, nodding at the prisoner on the ground. "We'll take him back to camp with us. It's time to go home."

Miller whistled and the two other Striker groups returned to the trail, falling in either side of the bandit. The scout moved to the head of the column as I picked up my rifle.

"That's twice you've proved yourself today," Miller said. He reached out to brush dirt from my cheek, and I felt the rough touch of his finger. Miller caught my eye, and then dropped his hand. He looked at his fingers and shrugged. "They're not very clean," he said.

I slung my rifle over my shoulder, waited for Miller to say something more, and then, when he didn't, I fell into line behind him. We moved quickly down the trail and I imagined bumping into Tiên and the men with the stretcher around every corner. But they must have moved faster than I thought, because the next thing we saw was the new perimeter around the camp, a swathe of hewn earth. Teams of Thai soldiers supervised by Americans strung razor wire in lazy coils across the open ground. Miller moved to the head of the column, waved at the Americans, and then waited for them to guide us through the wire and into the camp.

"Prisoner?" one of the Americans said, when he saw the bandit.

"Yep."

"They'll want him in the new redoubt. Over there," he said, pointing at a low fortified building in the centre of the camp.

"That didn't take them long," Miller said.

"They just finished it."

Miller waved the Strikers on, pointing at the new structure as two men escorted the prisoner past him. Miller caught my eye, and looked away, saying nothing. I walked through the camp to Tiên's hut.

The camp was noisier than when we had left, with two radios competing for the humid air between the Americans' accommodations. Led Zeppelin blasted out of the speakers of one of the radios, and a familiar country and western song from the other. I paused as someone turned off the rock music and Johnny Cash plucked at his guitar, singing about *Oney*. I stopped by the door of Tiên's hut, clenched my bloody fingers as I recognised the song, and then pushed the image of Perkins from my mind. I leaned the rifle against the wall of the hut and collected water in the pot for boiling. Johnny Cash had finished singing by the time the water started to boil, but I could still see Perkins in the Dartmouth bar, and again, crumpled on the deck of the boat moored to the dock.

The blood on my skin was stubborn, like the image of Perkins. I worked on both, sitting on my heels, washing my fingers in warm water, then boiling more for tea. The water bubbled, masking Tiên's soft footsteps as she approached the campfire and crouched beside me.

"Hi," I said.

She smiled and nodded at the fresh bandage wrapped around her shoulder. She took the tin of tea leaves from my hand, fussing and clucking as she pointed at the flour for the bread. I rolled the dough as she oiled the pan. I sipped my tea as Tiên fried the bread, wincing every now and again as she twisted her shoulder.

"I can do it," I said, leaning forwards to help.

Tiên clucked, then hissed, and finally leaned back. She watched me spread the dough on the pan, catching my eye each time I looked up.

I paused at what sounded like a scream coming from the centre of the camp. Tiên flicked her eyes towards the new redoubt. She curled her fingers around her mug. Her knuckles paled at the second and third scream.

The screams continued into the late evening, longer and more drawn out, until they stopped completely. Tiên fed the campfire and I cleaned the dishes. When the dishes were stacked, Tiên clucked and swiped at my leg with the tips of the leaves in her hand. She nodded into the dark and I sat up as Miller joined us. He smiled at Tiên, said something about her shoulder, and then took a long look at the redoubt.

"That's the part I'll never get used to," he said.

"That man," I said, pointing at the redoubt – the fortified compound in the centre of the camp. "The prisoner. Did they hurt him?"

"Yes."

"Did you?"

"No," Miller said. He looked at Tiên. "I didn't."

She held his gaze for a moment and then nodded, a simple dip of her chin, but it was enough for Miller to relax, and he sagged beside the fire.

"It was one of the new arrivals," he said. "An

American. I've not seen him before, but he's with the BNDD. He and his boss must have flown in while we were on patrol. He's a nasty piece of work," Miller said, and I immediately thought of Perkins. "It looked like he enjoyed what he did, long after the prisoner told us what we wanted to know."

"He told you where Eko's village is?"

"Yes." Miller sipped at his tea. His face flickered with orange stripes as he looked at me through the fire. His fingers were still bloody, dirty and cracked, lit by the flames as he grasped the mug in his hand. "They're planning the operation right now."

"And Eko? Is he there?"

Miller shrugged. "We don't know yet. I leave tomorrow. Just me and a handful of scouts. We'll radio back once we've found the village, and that's when the show starts." He finished his tea and held the mug loosely in front of the flames, turning it to catch the light. "You'll stay here," he said, when he looked up. "Both of you."

I started to speak as Tiên shuffled forwards.

"No," he said. "Not this time." He looked at Tiên. "But I do need you to do something."

She rocked back onto her heels and waited.

"This new man, I don't like him," he said. "And he knows you, Inniki."

"Me?"

"When his boss, Fitzpatrick, talked about Eko, this other guy mentioned something about Eko's girlfriend, another *Eskimo* – that's what he called you."

"Perkins," I said.

"Yes, that's him. And he's dangerous, Inniki. Stay away from him."

Chapter 26

Miller was gone for almost six days. Tiên kept me busy washing clothes and collecting firewood. She sent me with the wives and the children, following a narrow path through the newly laid minefield to the river. We had to cross the river to collect wood from the far side of the bank, tossing logs and branches into the water, upstream of the camp, and letting them float to the clear-cut riverbank close to the camp. When we washed on the flat rock, I saw the flash of binocular glasses as the Americans in the low tower scanned the river. Tiên's eyes narrowed as I scrubbed her back. She stared at the tower, and I wondered what she would tell me if only she could speak.

Perkins found me late on the fifth day,

His voice, pitched that tiny bit higher than the other Americans in the camp, cut through the mist and cooking fires one morning. He followed a small group of men carrying a body between the razor wire to the river. There were two Americans with him, both armed with M16 assault rifles, while Perkins carried just a pistol holstered on his belt.

I took the pot off the fire and put it to one side. Tiên watched me as I stood up, adjusted the sandals I now favoured, and picked up my rifle. She shook her head, and then hissed when I didn't react.

"I'm just going to follow them," I said, slipping the coolie hat onto my head. I tugged my hair into two curtains of black strands, one to hide each side of my face.

Tiên stood up and scattered the ashes of the fire, letting the coals glow within the hollowed-out bowl in the earth. She took the AK47 from where it leaned against the side of her hut and slung it over her shoulder. She raised her stiff arm, bending and testing it, before removing the sling around her neck. She put her hat on and reached up to adjust mine. Tiên pointed at a spot two feet behind her, and I understood that that was the distance I should keep between us. She clicked her fingers at the large pot we used to boil rice, and I picked it up while she collected several smaller pots to carry. From a distance, we would look like any of the other women walking to the river to wash our pots. Some of them carried weapons too – it seemed that most people did in the jungle.

Tiên led the way and we snaked along the path to the river. Perkins and the Americans were another hundred yards downstream. They watched as the Thai soldiers tossed the body into the river. The body splashed into the brown water, then rolled, disappearing for a moment, before an elbow or knee, and then the back of the dead man's head, reappeared to break the surface. The body drifted away from the bank and the Thai returned to the camp. We picked our way to another flat rock, closer to the bank, often used to wash clothes. We crouched on our heels and cleaned the pots, as the Americans' voices drifted upriver on a warm but gentle wind.

"That one confirmed it," Perkins said, with a nod to the body floating downriver. "With the coordinates Miller radioed in last night, together with the description of the terrain, I don't think there's any doubt. Am I right?"

"Sure," the taller of the two Americans said. He scratched at the square patch of straggly beard covering his chin. "But given what we know, I just don't think an operation of the size you're suggesting…"

Perkins bristled, raising his voice to cut the other man off. "We're sending a message, Pete. Don't you understand? It needs to be big and bold."

"We tried big and bold," Pete said, pointing to the east. "Why don't you ask the Vietnamese if they got the *message*."

I tilted my head for a better look as Perkins laughed. "That's funny," he said. "But then, you've never worked with Fitz, have you?"

"This is the first time."

"And probably your last, if he ever heard you talking like that. Listen, you want a job when you get back home? If you do, then you'll get onboard and pretty fucking quick. Fitz doesn't have time for doubters, or slackers. If he says he wants to send a big fucking message, then that's what we do. It's what Washington wants, after all."

I dipped my head as Perkins glanced in my direction. Tiên shuffled around me, putting her body between his and mine.

"Anyway," he said, lowering his voice. "That's all there is to it. The Thai government have signed-off on the camp; they know what we're going to use it for. The heroin is cutting through their people too. We're doing everyone a favour here. So what if we make things go bang. The message is that the American government and its allies will not tolerate the harvesting, production and sale of heroin to the United States."

"Tell that to the CIA," Pete said.

"Yeah, okay," Perkins said. "But wait until it's been proved, right?"

"Right."

"Until then, I suppose we can release the last of the informants."

"You're gonna let them go?"

"I said *release* them," Perkins said. "I have no intention of letting them go. Just get them off the camp. Send them downriver."

"Where are you gonna be?"

"With Fitz in the redoubt. There's a few more details to be worked out." Perkins pointed at the grey clouds above the river. "Think they'll fly in this?"

"Air Cavalry can fly in anything."

"Ain't that right," Perkins said. He pulled a red bandana from his pocket and wiped his brow. "I'll see you back in camp."

I ducked my head as Perkins walked along the riverbank. He paused at the start of the worn trail leading back to the camp, close to where we kneeled by the river. Tiên looked up and smiled at him, while I kept my eyes locked on the water lapping over my toes. I heard Perkins curse, followed by something about a *hideous face*, and then he was gone.

We waited until the Americans were gone too, and then I tipped my hat back to look at Tiên. "I want to hear about the plan," I said.

She shook her head, jabbing her finger towards the camp. She flashed her fingers through a series of signs I didn't understand, and then finished by running a long thin finger across her neck. That I did understand.

"I'll be careful," I said.

Tiên stared at me, her pupils contracted to black points like bullet tips. Her eyes softened as she shrugged her shoulders, and then winced as the soft flesh of her wound stretched within the stitches.

"I'll see you back at the hut," I said, as I stood up.

I left Tiên at the river and hurried along the path to drop the pot off at her hut. I paused, wondering what to do with the rifle, before slipping it off my shoulder and leaning it against the hut wall. I set my hat firmly on my head and did the same trick with my hair to make a screen for my face.

It occurred to me that my previous role – to convince Eko to do what Frode asked of him – required little of me. I was supposed to be there, to look pretty, and to remind Eko of Greenland, to give him someone to care about. But Frode must have known that being pretty – or at least *acting* pretty would only get us so far. He had, of course, taken it one step further, by creating every opportunity for us to fall in love, to strengthen the bond, making it more difficult for Eko to break the rules and to disappear into the underworld. I was Eko's lifeline and Frode's insurance. But since I had arrived in the jungle, I had realised something else.

They both underestimated me.

I think it was Tiên who opened my eyes to my true strengths. I had grown used to the scar on her face, and the severed stump of her tongue in her mouth. We had seen each other naked, but it had nothing to do with the clothes we wore – or didn't wear. She had stripped me to the core with her eyes, those same eyes that Miller sought when he needed approval, acceptance, or maybe even forgiveness. Tiên was ten times stronger than I would ever be, and yet her vulnerability made her even stronger. Eko thought I was vulnerable, Frode counted on it, but Miller – the third man in my life – was the first to actively put me in harm's way. Although, I doubt he would have done it without Tiên's approval.

She had a lot to answer for.

I curbed the smile spreading across my lips and walked around Tiên's hut. It wasn't just the Americans bustling about the camp. The renewed activity had invigorated the Thai soldiers and their families. Weapons were being cleaned, rice cooked and cooled, stuffed into bamboo tubes and stacked ready for the next patrol. Some of the men walked around in underwear and sandals, as the blood and grit of the last patrol dripped out of the sleeves and legs of their fatigues, pooling on the red earth beneath the clothesline. I walked past, zigzagging between Jeeps and groups of men carrying crates of ammunition and weapons.

The redoubt had a low roof covered in heavy sandbags. The bench outside was almost taller than the building. An American lounged on it, reading a tattered paperback that he propped on his pink chest, oblivious to the chug and stutter of the generator. Like Miller, the man's upper body was a contrast of shades of brown, pink and white. He flicked at the lip of his boonie hat as I walked past, his eyes locking on me as I tried to affect a casual but determined pace.

"You're a little too tall to be Thai." The bench creaked as the man sat up. "And you understand English," he said, as I stopped.

"Yes."

"A little or a lot?"

"What?"

"How much English do you understand?"

"A little," I said, lowering my hat to cover my eyes.

"I haven't seen you with any of the families." The man tossed his book onto the bench as he stood up. He adjusted the pistol hanging in a canvas holster from the broad webbing belt around his waist. "Would you like a beer?"

"No," I said. "Thank you."

"Is that a *no* or a *thank you*?" He grinned when I looked at him.

There were more men inside the redoubt. My breath caught in my throat when I heard Perkins' voice, replying to Fitzpatrick's deeper commands, as they climbed the steps to the door.

"Do you want that beer?" the American said.

"I'll take a beer," Fitzpatrick said, grinning as he ducked beneath the fortified timber of the redoubt door. He stepped to one side and straightened his back. Perkins joined him as the American soldier opened a cooler next to the bench and pulled out four bottles. I thought about running, or even walking away, but it was too late.

"Four beers?" Fitzpatrick said.

"One for my new friend," the American said. He nodded at me as Fitzpatrick took a beer and handed another to Perkins.

"You've made a new friend," Fitzpatrick said. "Isn't that nice. Does she have a name?"

"We haven't got that far," the American said. He shrugged and held out the bottle for me to take. "I thought a beer might loosen her tongue."

"And more besides, I'm sure." Fitzpatrick laughed, as he popped the top of the beer.

I kept my eyes on the ground. The American held the

beer bottle at about waist height, pushing it towards my hand until I reached out to take it. The bottle was wet with lukewarm water. I took it and started pulling it towards me, but the soldier held onto it.

"Your name first," he said. "Then you get the beer."

"You don't need to buy her name, soldier," Fitzpatrick said. "We know her name, don't we Perkins?"

"We sure do, Fitz," Perkins said. He stepped between me and the soldier and raised the bottle in his hand, pushing the lip of my hat up. "Hello Inniki," he said. "Have you missed me?"

Chapter 27

The redoubt roof was low, piled high with timber, tin and sandbags. The walls were thick – packed with stamped earth pressed between wooden slats. The air was heavy, thrust around the room in arcs of hot waves from the fan spinning on the desk in the first of three rooms cut into the earth. Perkins pushed me towards the room on the left, the one with the single naked bulb hanging from the ceiling, and the wood pallet at the bottom of a square pit directly below it. Fitzpatrick pulled the thin chain by the side of the bulb to turn on the light, as Perkins shoved me into the pit.

"It's amazing how you keep turning up," Fitzpatrick said. He pulled a chair out from beneath a rough-hewn table, carried it to one side of the pit and sat down. Perkins stood beside him and glared at me, one hand on his pistol. His cheek muscles twitched, and his nostrils flared in the eerie light wobbling from the bulb as it spun above me. "I'm sure my good friend Freddy had something to do with it, but why don't you tell us how you got here, darlin'. And what up you're up to."

I shifted my feet on the pallet slats. There was something tacky beneath my sandals, seeping into the grain of the wood. I looked up at Perkins; my head was about the height of his waist. His toes shuffled at the edge of the pit, as if he was ready to jump in beside me, and that Fitzpatrick only had to say the word. That's what he was waiting for. One word from his boss was all that stood between me and the rage that welled up inside Perkins. I could see it spilling over in a thin sheen of spittle on his fat lips.

"We're waiting, Inniki," Fitzpatrick said.

"I'm here for Eko," I said.

"Of course you are, darlin'." Fitzpatrick looked at Perkins, slapping his thigh to get his attention.

"What's that, Fitz?" Perkins peeled his eyes away from me, but his cheek continued to twitch. I heard the snort of air in and out of his nostrils.

"She's here for the Chief. Like always." Fitzpatrick ran his stubby fingers through his thick hair. "I just don't get it. It's like this is Freddy's only play, the only trick up his sleeve. What do you say, Perkins?"

"I say that's about right, Fitz. He's only got one play," he said, as he turned to sneer at me. "And it's a lousy one at that."

Fitzpatrick rested his elbows on his thighs and leaned forwards. He squinted in the light, muttered something about changing the bulb, and then stared right at me.

"Freddy's using you," he said. "You must know that?"

"Yes," I said.

"Well, that's a start," Fitzpatrick said, with a nod. He pointed at my face, the tip of his finger just inches from my nose. "Shows you've got some smarts. But I still don't get why you're here." He lowered his finger and tugged a cigarette from the packet in his shirt pocket. The air thickened as he blew the first cloud of smoke at my face. "Maybe you're here to send a message to the Chief?"

"His name is *Eko*," I said.

Fitzpatrick stared at me as he took a long drag on his cigarette. The bright glow at the end reflected in his eyes, and I saw a demon, barely restrained, just beneath the surface. Perkins' demon was already out, pulling and tugging at his muscles as he shifted position, and then started to pace beside the pit, turning his head as he walked up and down, his eyes fixed on me. Perkins paced as Fitzpatrick talked.

"About six hours after leaving Dartmouth, your friend *Eko* turned off his radio. We tracked him for a while with a plane, until it needed to turn to refuel. Then he was gone. Freddy said Eko was going to meet a man in the port of some shitty little excuse for a town in Greenland, but of course, we heard nothing. So, your man, your *friend*, slipped away. He must have a network in Greenland – Freddy suggested as much. But he gave the Danes the slip." Fitzpatrick paused to finish his cigarette. He ground the butt beneath his heel. "My problem is, I didn't much believe anything Freddy told me before. And now," he said, pointing at me, "with you turning up in *my* camp. Well, shit, I don't believe *anything* Freddy tells me. Not anymore. Never again. Which puts us in a bit of a quandary, don't it?"

"I don't understand," I said.

"No?" Fitzpatrick lifted his head as Perkins turned at the end of the pit. "For fuck's sake, Perkins. Will you just stop?"

"Boss?"

"Stop pacing. Just fucking stop."

"Okay. All right." Perkins folded his arms across his chest and glared down at me. His knees twitched, tugging at the cuffs of his trousers.

"That's better," Fitzpatrick said. "Now, darlin', we have to decide what to do with you. I can't have anyone compromising this op. There's too much ridin' on it. Now that we have a lead on the Chief – a positive I.D. – we're going to take out his little operation."

"I don't understand," I said. Fitzpatrick's words made no sense. "Eko is working undercover. He's on our side."

"Our *side*? That's rich." Fitzpatrick laughed. "Oh, that's good. Let me stop you right there, before that frown on your pretty head gets any deeper. Eko has never been on our *side*. There is no *side* with him. He's in this for himself. It was Eko who established the route from American to Europe. Sailing across the Atlantic was his fucking brainchild. But it gets better, you see, he doesn't stop to deal or sell any drugs in Greenland. No, they're *his* people, you see. He doesn't give a flying fuck about the hundreds and thousands of Americans getting high and sick on junk. Just so long as the Eskimo are all right, so long as they don't get hooked, well, Eko's conscience is clean, eh? We know where his allegiances lie. That's for fucking sure."

"Ain't that right, Fitz," Perkins said. He shuffled his feet closer to the edge of the pit, until his toes were hanging over the edge.

"He's undercover," I whispered. I forgot about Perkins for a moment, as the image of Eko with the needle in his arm on the bathroom floor of the hotel, pushed its way into my mind. He said he used it to visit the otherworld. He had also said that he needed to protect his people, but there had to be more to it.

"You're wondering what his angle is. Eh? Darlin'. Well, it's simple. Eko's angle is *Eko*. It's all about him and the profits. It's all about money."

"I don't believe that."

"Really? Well, shit, I don't really care much about what you believe."

Fitzpatrick stood up. He grabbed the back of the chair and carried it back to the desk. I looked from him to Perkins, and then pressed my hand on the edge of the pit. Perkins lifted his heel to stamp on my fingers. He grinned as I pulled them away.

"It seems the two of you have some business together," Fitzpatrick said with a nod to Perkins. Perkins unbuckled his belt, sliding it slowly through the loops around his waist as Fitzpatrick walked to the door. "It's a shame, really, I think that young fella with the beer was hoping to have some fun with you tonight, darlin'. But after Perkins is done with you, I'm not sure he'll be too keen after all." Fitzpatrick nodded at Perkins. "As long as you like but keep it quiet."

Perkins grinned as Fitzpatrick stepped out of the room.

The sides of the pit were smooth. I lunged for the edge furthest from Perkins, but he reached it quickly, snapping the end of his belt on the earth like a whip.

"Not so easy, eh?" he said. "Now, hold out your hands."

"No."

"I said hold out your fucking hands." Perkins bent down and grabbed my hair, tugging me around the pit as I flailed at the sides with my arms. "Put your hands together and I'll stop," he said, as he pulled me in the opposite direction. I cried out and he wrenched at my hair, pulling one way and then the other until I held up my hands and pressed my wrists together. I felt the first flecks of Perkins' spittle on my face as he bent over my head to wrap his belt around my wrists. He pulled a small knife from his boot and cut a hole in the belt close to the buckle. Perkins tightened the belt, closed the buckle, and then tugged at the end of the belt like a leash. "That's better," he said.

I almost spat the word *fairer* at him, but I kept my mouth shut. My hair was stuck to my face with sweat, tears and the spit on my lips. Perkins pulled me around the pit, and I stumbled over the slats in the pallet, trying to keep up.

"I wondered what this would be like," he said. "This moment. I've had some time to think about it, after you left me on the deck of that trawler. You didn't hurt me as much as you might have thought, or even hoped, but when they found me, some of the men laughed. I didn't like that. No-one laughs at me," he said, with a sharp tug of the belt. "Do you understand? No-one. Anyway, I figured that I owed you the same kind of humiliation. Something I could enjoy."

Perkins clicked his fingers and grinned as two Americans ducked into the room. I recognised the one called Pete, and the other man from the riverbank. They nodded at Perkins and took a position on either side of the pit. I saw the hunger in their eyes, the same kind that I had seen before, but it was keener, heightened by the fact that they knew they were just about to eat.

"These men have been in the jungle far longer than you and me, Inniki," Perkins said. "You might say that they need this as much as I do. So," he said, with another tug on his belt. "We're going to take this slow, and do things…"

I didn't give him the chance to say *quietly*. I

screamed, for as loud and as long as I could, until Perkins tugged me into the side of the pit. Pete grabbed my hair, pulling it back and tipping my head as the other man stuffed Perkins' sweaty red bandana into my mouth. I gagged for air, snorting hair away from my nose, watching as the men hammered two thick wooden pegs into the ground at the opposite end of the pit, one at each corner. Pete took two lengths of rope, looping them around my ankles and tying them to the poles, as Perkins pulled my arms. The edge of the pit bit into my lower back, and I tried to scream as Pete jumped into the pit and fiddled with the buttons of his fly.

I didn't need Perkins running commentary to tell me what was about to happen. I didn't need the heat from his stale breath in my face to reveal how excited he was. The first touch of Pete's fingers on my thigh as he ripped my pyjamas was enough. I kicked and bucked within the limits of the ropes around my ankles. The second American ran around the pit to help Perkins stretch my arms. My muffled screams were all I had left, as the two men pulled me from above, and Pete, standing in the pit, wormed his way into position.

That's how she found us.

I didn't hear her, and nor did they.

I felt the weight of Pete's body between my legs as he slumped on top of me, pressing me down into the pit with his chest and head. I opened my eyes to see the machete in the top of his skull, the broad blade was buried at least an inch deep, killing him instantly. But the weight of his body pressed me deeper into the pit, as Perkins and the other American let go of the belt to deal with Tiên.

I knocked my head on the edge of the pit and slid

onto the pallet. My legs, stretched and tied above me, shook as I tried to push Pete's body off my chest. I caught a glimpse of Tiên as she leaped over the pit, grabbing the handle of the machete and ripping it free of Pete's head. Perkins cursed and I heard the first crack of his pistol, blinked in the flash of the blast, and sniffed at the cordite. I pulled the bandana from my mouth and strained at the belt looped around my wrists.

"Get the fucking bitch," Perkins said.

He fired again, and I heard the bullet thwack into the wooden slats holding back the earth of the redoubt. I twisted onto my side to see the second American stagger away from the pit with the machete buried in his belly. Tiên lunged into view, reaching for the handle of the blade. She gripped it once, and then reeled towards the wall as Perkins swung a chair at her. He stumbled past her and ran out of the room.

Tiên recovered, tossing the broken chair to one side. She stepped out of view and I heard the wet snick and a soft groan as she pulled the machete out of the man's belly. Tiên returned to the edge of the pit and sawed through the ropes around my ankles. She jumped into the pit, pulled Pete off my body and slid the machete between my wrists, sawing through the belt until my hands were free.

Tiên leaned forwards, pressed her hand to my cheek and looked into my eyes. Her pupils softened when I nodded that I was okay. It was only when we were out of the pit, that I saw she was bleeding. I reached for the tear in her shirt, but she slapped at my fingers, shook her head, and led me out of the room. Tiên's blood dripped all the way up the stairs and into the night.

Chapter 28

_____

The spotlights from the newly built watchtowers pinned us to the wall of the redoubt, as we stumbled over the top step and into the camp. Tiên sagged within my grasp, pressing her hand to her stomach. The bright yellow light revealed the blood pulsing through her fingers, and she stopped to lean against the wall.

"We have to go, Tiên," I said, gripping her body and pulling her away from the redoubt. I didn't know *where* we would go, but I latched onto the idea that we would be safe in her hut, away from the redoubt, hidden from the lights. Tiên groaned and I pulled her away from the wall.

"Inniki Rasmussen, stop right there."

Fitzpatrick's voice boomed through a loudspeaker, loud and commanding, clipped by the feedback. I held up my hand to shield my eyes from the light, blinking in the glare as the shadows of men with guns flickered past the spotlights. Beyond the bustle of the camp, I could hear a dull *whop whop whop* that could have been helicopters or the distant rumble of thunder. I ignored it and tightened my grip around Tiên's waist.

"Two men are dead, Inniki. Stop now and you might just save your own life."

"I was attacked," I said, stopping as Tiên reached out for the wall. She slid down the side, smearing the earth wall with blood, until she crumpled on the ground, head down, and her back against the wall.

"You killed two American soldiers," Fitzpatrick said.

"They tried to rape me," I shouted. "You know that. Perkins knows that."

Fitzpatrick stepped in front of the light. He tossed the handset for the loudspeaker to a soldier behind him and walked towards us. Fitzpatrick was flanked by three soldiers on either side, their weapons raised. Perkins followed two steps behind them.

"Perkins was lucky to escape with his life. Your attempt to murder him," he said, with a flick of his stubby finger at Tiên, "failed."

"Murder?"

"That's what you will be tried for."

Fitzpatrick turned his head at the sound of boots thumping across the packed earth between the huts and the redoubt. He reached for the pistol at his hip and pulled it free of the holster. Perkins pulled his own pistol and gripped it in two hands, as a small group of Thai Strikers led by one tall American, stepped into the light.

"Let them go," Miller said. His carbine was raised, with the stock firmly pressed into his shoulder.

"This doesn't concern you, Miller," Fitzpatrick said. "Don't tarnish your career by getting involved. Just back off and take your men with you."

The men either side of Fitzpatrick bristled as Miller took a step forward.

"My friend needs medical attention. I'm going to take her and Inniki to the camp doctor."

"No, you're going to lower your weapon and turn around."

Miller flicked the safety selector switch on his carbine to full *auto*. The Strikers beside him did the same, gritting their teeth as they made the decision to stand by the young American soldier.

"Stand down, Captain Miller," Fitzpatrick shouted. The pistol in his hand shook for a second, before he lowered his voice and tried again. "This is a Federal matter now, son. Beyond Army rules and regulations. You can still walk away."

"I'm not leaving without them," Miller said. He glanced at Tiên, and added, "She needs a doctor right now."

"And she'll get one, as soon as you back away."

Miller paused for a moment. A wave of calm passed across his face, just like I had seen in the middle of a battle, when he had to make life and death decisions in a matter of seconds. He lowered his rifle, pointing the barrel at the earth just a few feet in front of him.

"I'm going with her," he said. "Inniki comes with me."

"That ain't right, Fitz," Perkins said. "She tried to kill me."

Miller gestured at his men with a sharp nod of his head. "You know where we've been, and you're waiting on Intel. I've got it, but you'll get nothing from me until a doctor gets to work on Tiên, and Inniki is standing right beside me."

"That's insubordination, Captain," Fitzpatrick said. "It'll go on your record."

"My record?" Miller laughed. "Everything in this camp is *off the record*. You know that, because that's how you want it. Now get me the doctor, now, and we can settle this."

Fitzpatrick lowered his pistol and nodded at one of the American soldiers. The man ran off towards the camp hospital, a small rectangular hut with a reinforced roof and a low door just like the redoubt.

"James Miller," Fitzpatrick said, as he holstered his pistol. "Where's your family from?"

"They're Scots," Miller said, lowering his carbine.

"Irish," Fitzpatrick said, jabbing his thumb into his chest. He fished a packet of cigarettes out of his pocket and lit one. The flare of the lighter caught the rage tugging at the creases of Perkins' face. Fitzpatrick tucked the cigarette packet away and pressed his hand on Perkins' arm, lowering his pistol. "Wait in my hut," he said.

"Boss?"

"Just do it."

I caught Perkins' eye as he turned away, and then he stepped out of the spotlight and disappeared into the night. The doctor and two medics rushed between Fitzpatrick and Miller. I helped them lift Tiên onto the stretcher, and then walked with them to the camp hospital. Fitzpatrick followed, together with his small detachment of Americans. Miller caught my hand as he walked alongside us.

"Inniki?"

"I'm okay," I said. I let go of his hand to duck through the low door of the hospital. Miller moved to follow, but Fitzpatrick caught his shoulder and stopped him at the door. I slunk to the wall, and waited there, staying out of the doctor's way, and listening to the two Americans.

"That Greenlander is trouble," Fitzpatrick said. "They both are. My advice is to stay clear of her, because if you don't, bad things tend to happen. Just ask Perkins."

"Perkins?" Miller shifted his position for a better

view of Tiên. He watched as the doctor set up a drip, gave her a shot of morphine, and then got to work examining the wound in Tiên's stomach. Miller looked at me, nodded once, and then turned away. "I don't think Perkins needs any help to make trouble."

"Regardless," Fitzpatrick said. "I now have two dead Americans – killed by your Montagnard. How do you suppose I write that up?" Fitzpatrick paused to finish his cigarette. "It's her word against Perkins'," he said. "And we're a long way from home. Even further from hers." I heard the soft scratch of Fitzpatrick's shirt and imagined him pointing in my direction. "No," he said. "About the only thing that will redeem any of this, is a successful outcome to the mission. So, tell me Captain Miller, what do you know?"

"Here?"

"You're the one who didn't want to leave her side. And I want my Intel. So, yeah, *here*."

"All right."

The thunder I thought I had heard earlier, sharpened to the more familiar thud of rotor blades, beating the humid jungle air into submission as a flight of helicopters approached the camp. I heard little of what Miller said, until he raised his voice as the helicopters started to land.

"He's definitely there," Miller said.

"You're sure it was him?"

"He was here, at the camp, a little while ago. I got to know him then. I made a positive I.D. It's definitely Eko Simigaq, the Greenlander."

"And the village? How are the defences?"

"There's a lot of activity – lots of civilians. I would suggest a smaller operation from the jungle, not the air."

"Washington expects a punitive response, Captain. I

need bold, not subtle."

"Then you can expect casualties. On both sides. Also," Miller said, with a sigh. "There are women and children in the village. Lots of them."

"There are women and children in American too – lots of them. Heroin affects them too. There are casualties in every war; a drug war is no different."

"But you're sure about Eko? You really believe he's turned? As I understand it, there's only one person who can find out for certain." Miller ducked to point through the door. "And she's standing right there."

"Her usefulness ended the second those American boys died, Captain Miller. I suggest you start to accept that. Now," Fitzpatrick said, with a nod towards Tiên. "See to your woman – both of them. I'll leave a guard here, and there'll be another outside their hut. I expect you to be at the briefing later tonight, and ready to go before dawn. The cavalry has arrived, Captain. Everything else can wait."

I waited for Fitzpatrick's heavy footfalls to fade away, and then joined Miller at the door as he stooped to enter the tiny camp hospital. He took my hand and nodded at Tiên.

"The problem with Tiên," he said, as he swallowed. "Is that she does exactly what I ask her to."

"Yes," I said. "Those men were going to rape me. I think they would have killed me too. Tiên stopped them. She killed them."

"In Tiên's book, it's the same thing."

"I owe her my life."

"Yes," Miller said. "That makes two of us."

He let go of my hand, gave me his carbine and took a step closer to the stretcher laying on a raised platform in the middle of the room. He talked quietly with the doctor, nodding when the doctor pointed, and again when the two medics rolled Tiên gently onto her side, to show Miller the exit wound, now packed with gauze, soon to be stitched. Miller pressed his palm on Tiên's brow, smoothing her hair from her forehead. In the yellow light of the hospital lamp above the stretcher, Tiên's face looked warm. The morphine had softened her muscles, relaxed her cheeks, and almost flattened the ugly scar on her cheek. She looked so peaceful.

"But she needs a hospital," Miller said, as he joined me. "The doctor can stitch her up, but the chances of infection are high. It's only a few days since she was shot in the shoulder. She needs proper help. I need to get her out of here."

"Maybe I can help?"

I turned at the familiar voice that drifted through the door as Frode stepped inside the hospital.

"Is that Tiên?" he asked, peering around Miller's shoulder.

"Yes," he said. "What are you doing here?"

Frode smiled at me and gestured for us to follow him outside. "There's not much room in here. Let's talk outside." Frode said a few words to the guard outside the hospital, pulling an envelope from his pocket and encouraging the guard to look at the letter inside. "I realise you can't read it," Frode said. "But that's the official seal, right there. You might want to check with Fitzpatrick, but I can assure you that the Danish government won't let her run away." Frode pointed at me, as the guard nodded. "If you could just give us a little privacy, I can call you back when we're done." Frode smiled again as the guard suggested he would take a smoke break. "Thank you," Frode said.

"How did you get here?" Miller asked, as Frode tucked the letter inside his jacket.

"With this," he said, patting his pocket. "It's actually an invitation to the annual reception at the palace. But the royal seal is what gets people's attention."

"You bluffed your way here?"

"Well, I suppose I did," Frode said. "A friendly word with one of the pilots helped. I just needed a lift, I said."

"Together with a gunship." Miller laughed.

"They do seem rather keen," Frode said. The light dancing in his eyes paled as he looked at me. "What's going on, Inniki?"

"Perkins," I said.

Frode nodded. "I'm sorry about that. And Tiên?"

"Gut shot," Miller said. "I need to get her out of her. To a proper hospital. I don't suppose that letter can buy her a trip to Chiang Rai?"

"I'll see what I can do. I'm expecting Thaksin to arrive with my luggage later."

"Good luck," I said, thinking of the change of clothes I had in my holdall.

Frode frowned for a second, and then continued. "What I really want to know," he said, "is if Eko is at the village."

"Yes, he is," Miller said.

"And can we get to him?" Frode looked at me. "Can Inniki?"

"I really don't know," Miller said, and shook his head. "The briefing is tonight, and the helicopters leave before dawn. They're going to raise that village to the ground, and everyone in it. It's a classic search and destroy op."

"But you got a message to him? Like we agreed."

"I sent the message, but I don't know for sure if he got it."

Frode turned away to pace back and forth for a moment. He stopped after a few seconds, reaching out to place his hand on Miller's webbing. "Eko has been working on this for some time. He's already proven that he can get drugs across the Atlantic and into Europe. He has opened a new route, gained the trust of the traffickers, and worked his way higher and higher into their organisation. But I can't prove that without evidence. Fitzpatrick," Frode said, pointing towards the redoubt, "refuses to see the bigger picture. He thinks that *this* is as big as it gets. That by destroying one village with a massive show of force will stop the production of heroin entirely. He thinks he's cutting off the head of the snake, but he doesn't realise just how many snakes there are in the jungle. The only way we can change that, is if we can get to Eko, before Fitzpatrick kills him."

"And you're sure?" Miller said.

"About what?"

"Sure, that Eko hasn't turned? Fitzpatrick thinks he has."

"Well of course he thinks that. Thinking anything else would make all this," Frode said, sweeping his arm with an arc to encompass the camp, "completely unnecessary."

"All right," Miller said. "I'm all out of suggestions. What do *you* suggest we do?"

"The only thing we can do," Frode said. "We need to get Inniki onto one of those helicopters."

Chapter 29

They held the briefing in the middle of the camp, with seats for the pilots and squad leaders arranged in a semi-circle around a large map of the area. The Thai Strikers stood behind the seats, leaning forwards to listen but not necessarily understand what Fitzpatrick was saying. Fitzpatrick had assembled about fifty men for the operation, including those who would remain at the camp. Frode and I stood in the shadows behind the Strikers. The guard detail Fitzpatrick had assigned to watch over me stood to one side and smoked. Fitzpatrick jabbed his stubby fingers at the map as he talked.

"Four Hueys with five Strikers and one American in each will approach the village from the south. The Cobra gunship," Fitzpatrick said, nodding at the two pilots sitting to his left, "will fly ahead of the main group, and strafe the outskirts of the village, pushing the combatants inside the perimeter. This allows the ground troops to land in this clearing here," he said, stepping closer to the map to tap an area ringed with a thick red circle. "The Hueys will lift off and circle the camp in a high orbit while the Cobra remains on station to provide support as directed by ground troops."

Fitzpatrick gestured for Perkins to stand up and take over. I shrank behind Frode, as Perkins took his place in front of the group and scanned the rows of men.

"He can't see you, Inniki," Frode whispered.

Perkins tucked his thumbs into his belt and started to speak. "As most of you know, we're two men down. So, we've spread you guys between the ground troops," he said, looking at the American soldiers in the front row. "One American per group, apart from my team. We're going in "heavy" with three Americans, including myself, and four strikers. We have one job," Perkins said, holding up a finger. "We're going to find this man." He walked to the map and tapped a picture of Eko taped to an area below the village. "We find him, secure him, and bring him back. If we can't bring him back, we kill him on site. It's that simple. The other three ground teams will secure the village, and eliminate any and all threats, while locating the drugs. Document and then destroy with C4 explosive. We turn this village into splinters and dust. By this time tomorrow night, it will be but a memory, and you will have the thanks of the American people."

"They're going to kill Eko," I whispered, as I leaned close to Frode.

"I'm afraid so," he said.

When Perkins was finished, he waved Miller forwards, before sitting down in the front row. Miller talked about the terrain, the heights of the surrounding trees, the vegetation in the clearing, and the distances between the buildings. The pilots and squad leaders took notes. Miller paused to answer questions, expanding certain aspects with further details when required. I caught him looking towards the rear of the group, felt his eyes searching for Frode and me, and then his attention was drawn back to the group, and a single question that made everyone stop writing and listen.

"What kind of resistance can we expect?" one of the

Americans asked. "What strengths?"

Miller glanced at Fitzpatrick before replying. "We observed maybe sixty people in the village, over a period of six hours. There might be more. But it's unlikely. We were there in the late evening – too dark to work the fields."

"And their strengths? Are they armed?"

"I counted seven men, aged between seventeen and sixty. All of them had AK47 assault rifles. There were maybe thirty women and twenty children."

"*Seven* armed men?"

"And twenty children," Miller said.

The American scratched his head with the end of his pencil. "Well, I'm glad we've got the gunship."

The Americans laughed, all except Miller. He stared past the Strikers, caught my eye, and then looked away. Fitzpatrick stood up and nodded for Miller to go back to his seat.

"I'm sure Captain Miller will answer any other questions you might have. But let's get one thing straight. You've been chosen to do a very specific job, and you're getting well paid for it. This op is the result of a long period of investigation. We've tracked these drugs all the way to the streets of Boston, and Washington – the capital, boys. They sent this shit to fuck up our people. Now it's our turn. We're sending a message – clear and simple. The war in Vietnam is over, but *this* war is a war on drugs, and it starts at dawn. But we've learned from Vietnam, and we won't make the same mistakes. We're gonna do things our way, from day one. If we do it right, there might not be a day two." Fitzpatrick paused in anticipation of a response.

"Ain't that right, Fritz," Perkins said. The men either

side of him murmured, but the rest of the group said nothing.

"What? You don't think we can do this? Or is it because you don't think we should?" Fitzpatrick laughed. "You boys were picked because you spent most of the war on the wrong side of one border or another. But we're flying a different flag here. This op has been green-lit all the way from the top, together with the cooperation of the Thai government."

"It's not that, sir," one of the Americans said. "It's the seven guys and twenty kids…"

"You're worried about collateral damage? Tell that to the parents back home. It's their *kids* who are getting fucked up with junk in their veins. It ends now. We stop this. Grow a backbone and serve your country. That's what you're getting paid for." Fitzpatrick paused to check his watch. "All right, enough talk. You've got an hour to prep, and I want those birds in the air at zero-four-hundred hours. Let's get this done."

The Strikers clumped in a group as the Americans dispersed. Miller walked over to the Strikers and talked them through the operation, while Frode and I watched from the shadows. Fitzpatrick and Perkins talked with the helicopter pilots. I waited with Frode until Miller joined us.

"This is Somchai," Miller said, nodding at the tall Thai who walked beside him. "He's about your height, Inniki," he said, lowering his voice. I recognised him from the trail. He was the one who had bandaged Tiên's shoulder.

"I remember you," I said.

Somchai grinned, as Fitzpatrick called the soldier watching over me to the briefing area.

"Here's what we're going to do," Miller said. "Somchai is going to go with Tiên to the hospital at Chiang Rai. If that's still an option?"

"It is," Frode said. "Thaksin should arrive soon."

"Thank you," Miller said. "That's the second time I owe you."

"Nonsense," Frode said. "You don't owe me anything."

"Okay." Miller tucked his hands into his webbing and looked at me. "You'll wear Somchai's fatigues. But you'll need to cut your hair…"

"Yes," I said.

"I've got camo paint for your face. You'll join me in my stick…"

"Stick?"

"My group of Strikers," Miller said. "But I need you to stay right beside me and do exactly what I say."

"I can do that."

"Can you?" Miller's eyes hardened. "Because I told you to stay away from Perkins. But you didn't. You followed him down to the river."

"How do you know…"

"Because you and Tiên were seen. Now she's gut shot and I have to get her out of the country."

"I'll see to that," Frode said.

"Okay," Miller said. "But I need to know that she is going to do exactly what I tell her to." He turned and jabbed his finger into my sternum. "Inniki?"

"Yes," I said. "Whatever you tell me to." I stared into his eyes, and saw the hard edge begin to soften.

"Good," he said. "Because this is the plan. As soon as we're on the ground, you and me are going to find Eko."

"What about Perkins' team?" Frode asked.

"Sure, they can go look for him, but if Eko got my message, then he'll be in a hut to the north of the village."

"How sure are you?"

"We caught one of the kids from the village. I'm as sure as I can be," Miller said, with a glance over his shoulder. "I said nothing about the raid, which would be probably be interpreted as treason. Arranging a meet with Eko is bad enough." He looked at Frode. "I'm going out on a limb here, Freddy. Tell me I'm doing the right thing."

"You are." Frode took Miller's hand. "I promise you. If we can get Eko out, then…"

"That will be tricky," Miller said. "No matter what they said during the briefing, there's only one mission, and it ends with Eko in a body bag. Apparently, the BNDD don't like agents who are deep undercover. They don't trust them. Why should they?"

"But it takes time to build relationships," Frode said. "He needs time to earn their trust."

"Fitzpatrick doesn't have time," Miller said. "He's bucking for promotion, and he needs results. This," he said, with a wave at the camp, "has nothing to do with a war on drugs. It's all about power. If this is successful, Fitzpatrick is looking at a senior position within the BNDD and whatever comes after it. If Eko is where I told him to be, then I'll have made an enemy for life. I'm finished in the Army, maybe even my country…"

"We can use men like you," Frode said. "I can promise you that."

"Really, Freddy? You've got that kind of pull? No offense, but most people think Denmark is the capital of Sweden, or something like that. You're not exactly a world player."

"We might not be in the spotlight, but we have certain areas of influence, and we won't forget what you're doing here, tonight."

"I'm not doing it for me," Miller said. "Just get Tiên out of the country. Look after her, and we'll be even."

"You're a noble man, James," Frode said.

"Noble?" Miller laughed. "Well, I don't know about that."

I did. And it wasn't just his loyalty and the depth of his love for Tiên. You could see it in the eyes of the men who followed him and fought beside him. Miller carried a quiet confidence and a respect for other people and cultures. The humidity lifted for just a second as the warm familiar wind of Greenland licked at the beads of sweat in my hair and on my forehead. I imagined Miller in Greenland, and wondered if he would find peace there, as I did. This man who had known nothing but war, year after year, was in desperate need of peace, and I felt compelled to give it to him.

But the mission – Eko – came first.

"I'll need some scissors," I said, as fought the knot of fear in my stomach, attempting to distract it with the practicalities of preparing my disguise.

Miller teased a pair of bent-nosed scissors out of the medkit on his belt. He looked at my hair as he placed the scissors in my hand.

"I think you'll need this," he said, and tugged the knife from his webbing. Miller reached out to tip the hat from my head. He teased several long hairs into one strand and cut it away with the tip of his knife. Miller curled the length of hair around his finger and then tucked it into his shirt pocket. "For luck," he said, and handed me his knife.

I said nothing. The knot in my stomach twisted into something else, not unpleasant, but confused. There were things to be done, and no time for things unsaid. I didn't know if there would ever be time, or what I might say if there was. We each had our jobs to do, our *mission*. And mine was Eko.

"And there's Thaksin and his cousin," Frode said. He pointed at the headlights of two vehicles bouncing up the dirt road to the front gate. "I'd better get over there, and check-in with Fitzpatrick."

"Be sure to show him that letter," Miller said.

"Oh, I intend to." Frode looked at me for a moment, and then nodded at the scissors and the knife. "You're a brave young woman," he said. "And I am forever in your debt."

"There's a lot of that going around," Miller said. "Come on. We need to get moving."

Chapter 30

The first tears spilled from my eyes as I gripped my ponytail and sawed through it with Miller's knife. I stared into the cracked mirror that the Strikers had taped to a beam beneath the grass roof of an open-walled cooking shelter. They used it when smearing the camouflage paint across their cheeks, and now they sat in a circle and watched my transformation. The innocent Greenlandic girl disappeared with each saw of the knife, each snick of the scissors. I blinked through the tears and the sweat to stare into the mirror. I saw Kunuk shaking his head, pouting with the thought of just how long he would have to wait, before he could sit on my hair. I spoke to him in Greenlandic, drawing curious looks from the green and black striped faces sitting cross-legged, or lounging against small backpacks in front of me. I told Kunuk it was important. That it was a game we had to play. But as I cut the last errant tuft of hair from my fringe, I suddenly thought of Eko. It was for Eko, not Kunuk, that I grew my hair. He needed me to be Greenlandic. But to get to him, I had to become something and someone else. Kunuk's image disappeared and I stared into the mirror. Somchai stood next to me. He squeezed a gob of greasy war paint into the bay of his thumb and index finger. Then, with gentle dabs of light fingers, he painted my face.

Somchai erased Inniki with every brush of his fingers. I became that other person. I'm not sure who, only that it was necessary. I could have been Somchai, preparing to fly into battle. Or maybe Tiên, before a patrol, clucking and hissing at Miller, signing with rapid flicks of her fingers and twists of her wrists.

The paint was deep, pricking my thick Greenlandic eyebrows into stilts of caked hair. Somchai smeared it across my lips, and it seeped into my pores. I felt mosquito feet testing the depth, before whining away in the warm pre-dawn air. And then he was finished. Somchai stepped to one side, tugging me in front of the men. They dipped their heads, chattered to one another, pointing, approving. Somchai tucked the tube of paint into his pocket and removed the floppy boonie hat he wore on his head. When he tucked it onto my head, the men clapped, softly. Somchai grinned and slipped away.

"You look the part," Miller said, as he ducked under the grass roof. He took a moment to check my appearance, tugging at my arm to turn me one way, and then the other. I felt the light scratch of his fingers as he brushed hair from my neck, and the low electric pulse as his hand brushed mine. "Inniki," he said.

"No. Not Inniki. Not today."

Miller nodded. He clicked his fingers at one of the men and took the carbine from his hands. "When you hold the rifle, you hold it loose. I've watched you. With the carbine, you need to keep it tight. You need to look the part."

"I know," I said, as I took the carbine.

"I know you do, but it's the details." Miller fiddled with my webbing, adjusting pouches and tightening straps.

"What about the man guarding me?"

"I outrank him," Miller said. "I told him I was responsible for you. We've served together before. Luckily for us, he respects me more than he fears Fitzpatrick. You won't be missed. Not with all this activity. I told him I had you locked away for the op."

"And Frode?"

"You didn't hear the shouting?"

"No."

"He presented himself, and his letter, to Fitzpatrick. I left them arguing about the limits of international cooperation. They were still at it when I said goodbye to Tiên." Miller tugged one last strap, before looking into my eyes. "She's going to be all right, Inniki. Thaksin's cousin will drive her and Somchai to Chiang Rai."

I dipped my chin, and then reached up to brush at the tears streaming down my cheeks.

"Let me," Miller said. "You'll ruin your make-up."

Miller's touch was softer than before, as my tears beaded on the tip of his finger. He wiped them against his thumb. He stepped closer. I could feel his breath on my cheek, on the tip of my nose. I felt the light prick of stubble above his painted lip as he brushed my lips with his, before pulling away, slowly.

I swallowed, fighting the rapid thumps of my heart, drawing the warm air between us through the thin gap between my lips.

"She likes you," Miller said. "She wanted you to know that. She called you her *sister*. Her own sister was killed the night they removed her tongue."

I reached for Miller's hand and grasped his fingers.

"It's about a year and a half ago. I was on a recruitment drive. We used the Montagnard Tribesmen because they were fierce, loyal and clever. And they were outcasts. A minority. We came to a village that had been attacked by the Viet Cong. They resisted them. Then the Vietnamese government sent in troops to punish the villagers for collaborating. No-one will admit it, and you'll never see it in a report, but what happened in that village..." Miller paused to swallow and take a long breath. "I found Tiên on the floor of one of the huts. Her sister was in her arms. Dead. The wounds in her chest were so deep. Machetes..." he said. "Tiên was bleeding too. I did what I could, before the village was attacked by the VC. We took casualties and called in for a Medevac. I put Tiên on that helicopter, but when we got to Saigon, they wouldn't look at her. It had been a busy day, there were too many wounded, and she would have to wait. That's when I met Frode. I've no idea why he was there, or what he was doing, but he had a Jeep, and he took us across the city to a French asylum. They treated her there."

Miller squeezed my fingers. He tried to smile, tried to look at me, but the corners of his mouth flattened, and he looked away. I let go of his hand and wiped at the tear welling in the corner of his eye.

"You'll ruin your make-up," I said.

Miller swallowed, and then tugged at one last strap on my webbing. He took a canteen of water from his belt and secured it in the empty pouch on mine.

"You stay right beside me," he said. "On the helicopter and on the ground."

"Yes," I said.

"You've got three magazines on your webbing. There's thirty rounds in each. Don't shoot unless you have to. Don't leave my side. Don't..."

"What?"

Miller shook his head. "Never mind. We need to go."

The Strikers assembled into groups as Miller led us to the makeshift airstrip. I pressed my hand onto my hat and ran behind him to the last in the line of helicopters. The door gunner reached out to grab my wrist, yanking me inside the cabin and nodding at one of the bucket seats. Miller sat down beside me, turned his carbine barrel-down and gestured for me to do the same. The pilot increased the pitch and tilt of the rotors and we left the ground.

The wind dried the paint on my face and slipped under the collar of my shirt. My Somchai disguise, with my close-cropped hair and bare neck lifted my spirits for the first part of the flight. But my heart sank when the gunship pulled away from us, and I saw the first streak of smoke from the rockets beneath its wings, followed by the dull crump and flash of the explosion on impact. Miller tapped my arm, and then tapped the cover of his watch with two fingers.

"Two minutes," he said, his lips pressed close to my ear.

They were the longest and the shortest two minutes of my life.

The helicopter pitched onto one side, as the pilot flew a crazy S on his approach in anticipation of ground fire. The helicopter levelled and flared at the edge of the clearing. The skids had barely touched the ground when Miller leaped out of his seat, grabbed the straps of my webbing, and hurled me out of the cabin. He jumped into the long grass a second later, grabbed the back of my webbing and pulled me towards the thick vegetation and tall trees between the clearing and the village. Miller stopped in the well of deep tree roots and pushed me to the ground, kneeling beside me and scanning the jungle as the Strikers fell into position on either side. The shudder and thud of the helicopter's rotors receded as the pilot took off and joined the other helicopters in a high orbit above the village.

"Stay with me," Miller said, as he walked in a crouch towards the village. The Thai Strikers fanned out behind him and I followed.

The sound of light weapons fire crackled and chattered through the broad leaves and stringy trunks of the trees. Miller held up his fist for us to stop three times, as we approached the village. We waited beneath the trees in a thin steam of condensation as the sun warmed the musky earth. Miller waved one of the Strikers to his side and pointed at a trail leading between the huts. I saw the muzzle flash of rifles to my left, and then Miller was up, and the Striker behind me tapped me on the shoulder, nodding for me to move.

We jogged along the narrow trail to the first hut, pausing and crouching on either side of the trail, until Miller signalled for us to move again. More muzzle flashes, and the crack and splinter of bullets ripping through the huts slowed us down, as Miller waited for the other teams to move across our path. He turned away from the trail leading to the centre of the village, choosing to follow a thinner trail leading around and to the north. He stopped beside a large rotten stump, and the Strikers took up covering positions.

"There," Miller said, as he waved me forwards. "See the hut in the trees?"

"Yes," I said, following the direction Miller was

pointing. "Will Eko be there?"

"He should be. That's the plan. But he must have cleared the village. There are no people."

"That's good."

"Yes, but it means there's nothing to slow our guys down. We have to move now, before they find him, or before he leaves." Miller pressed his hand on my carbine and checked the safety selector. "Semi auto," he said. "Aim. Breath. Squeeze."

"Okay."

"Ready?"

I thought I was. I nodded, and moved to follow Miller, but I stalled at the sight of a second team charging down the path towards. The men in front were taller than the Thai – Americans, with Perkins leading from the front.

"Friendly," Miller said, raising his carbine above his head.

The approaching team slid into firing positions, as the jungle ahead of us erupted with a burst of gunfire, shredding the leaves, and tossing Miller onto the trail. Blood splashed onto the earth as he rolled onto his side. I leaped up to run to him, only to be pulled back behind the tree stump by one of the Thai Strikers.

"Wait," he hissed, before pushing me to one side and returning fire.

The Americans on the trail leading down to us, opened fire with long bursts, walking their bullets along the trail and into the tree line. Miller rolled to one side, ducking his head behind a metal bucket and a wooden feeding trough, as he tugged a bandage from his webbing and tied it around his head. He wiped the blood from his eyes, and then flashed a quick thumbs-up to the Strikers huddled around the tree stump.

The shooting from inside the jungle stopped, and the Americans paused to reload. They shouted at Miller through the smoke, and Perkins risked a peek around the side of the hut from where he was firing.

"Where are they?" he shouted, his voice piqued with adrenaline.

"In the tree line," Miller said. "Moving north. Maybe two shooters."

"We'll take them," Perkins said. He slipped out of cover and ran down the trail, ignoring the two Americans calling for him to wait.

A streak of bullets ripped into the earth in front of him. Perkins stumbled off the trail and fell onto his side. Miller rolled onto his knee and fired into the tree line. Between short, measured bursts, he got to his feet, moving steadily forwards until he was flanked by the Strikers and the jungle attack was suppressed. Miller supervised the positioning of his men behind the available cover, and then waved for me to come to him.

Perkins stood up at the same time as I did. He stepped onto the trail as I clambered out from the hollow by the tree stump. The loop of my hat caught on a fleck of bark, tugging the hat off my head as I stepped onto the trail. Perkins stopped, open-mouthed as he stared at me.

"You," he said.

He raised his weapon a second later.

I left the hat hanging on the stump, tightened my grip on the carbine, and ran down the trail towards the landing zone. I could hear Perkins pounding along the trail behind me, the metallic clack of his rifle as he changed magazines, and Miller's voice, pressing at my back.

"Run, Inniki. *Run.*"

Chapter 31

I was never going to make it to the clearing. I veered to my right, felt the sweat bead on my neck and slip down my collar, as I ran along a broad path into the heart of the village. The pounding of boots behind me, echoed through the earth and bounced into my soles. I didn't have to look behind me to know that Perkins was close. I leaped over a goat straddling the path. I heard it bleat as Perkins crashed into it, followed by a curse and the clack of metal as he fiddled with the M16 assault rifle he carried in his hands.

The path broadened as we ran towards three large huts. I ducked around the first and inside the second, holding my breath as Perkins followed. Smoke drifted out of the stone hearth in the centre of the hut. I stared at it, watching it curl up and away through the hole in the roof, as I pressed my hand to my chest and fought for a regular breath. I almost choked on the humid gulps of air within the hut, pressing my hand to my mouth as Perkins slowed between the huts.

"I know you're here," he said, kicking at a small pile of empty pots. They crackled into shards as he crushed them. "You think you're so smart, don't you? Cutting your hair, wearing fatigues. But you've run out of luck. This is where it ends – beyond the camp walls, far from that little VC bitch, and your Captain friend."

Perkins slowed his step and stalked closer to the hut I was hiding in. The walls were thin and curved. I pressed the side of my face to the wall, felt Perkins' footsteps vibrate along the smooth surface. I held my breath when he stopped, and I caught the adrenaline-charged stink of his sweat as it seeped around the open door. I could see the tip of his boot.

"I'll let Fritz deal with Captain Miller once we're back at camp. But you won't have to worry about that. I'll deal with you here."

I pressed a sweaty thumb on the safety selector switch and chose full *auto*. Perkins reacted to the metallic snick of the switch, and I saw his shadow flinch in the sunlight.

"So close," he said.

I pushed off the smooth earth side of the hut, and turned to spray a full magazine through the wall. The bullets thudded through the wall, tearing it into fist-sized chunks of earth, and ripping into Perkins' side. The impact threw him across the path, and I charged out of the hut, raising the carbine in my hands and tugging it into my shoulder.

I remembered to aim, to breath, and to squeeze. But the mantra was useless, without a fresh magazine of bullets. Perkins kicked at my shins with blood-streaked boots, knocking me onto the path as he drew the Colt pistol from the holster at his belt.

Perkins aimed and squeezed, but the breathy rasps of air bubbling out of his lungs threw the bullets wide as he pulled the trigger.

"Inniki," Miller shouted, as he ran along the trail.

I didn't hear him – I may even have ignored him, but as Perkins waved the pistol towards me, I rolled onto my knees, tugged it out of his hand, and fumbled it into mine. I gripped the pistol in two hands, pressed the barrel into his chest, felt the heave of his lungs, and squeezed the trigger. I was too close to aim, and I didn't trust myself to breathe. If I breathed, I might think, and I didn't want to think. I just wanted it to end. I wanted *him* to end, and he did. Perkins' life ended in the red earth of northern Thailand, between the abandoned huts of a drug-baron's village.

The echo of the shot was all I heard for the next five minutes. Miller slid the pistol from my hands, pulled me to my feet, and pressed the carbine into my arms. He changed the magazine, tucked the pistol into his belt, and then dragged Perkins' body inside the hut.

"Come on," he said, as he stepped onto the path. "We have to go."

Miller pulled a grenade from his webbing, removed the pin and tossed it inside the hut. He pushed me along the path, further into the village. The grenade exploded with a muffled pop and a shower of sparks, followed by the crackle of the grass roof as it caught fire.

"White phosphorous," Miller said, as he grabbed my arm. He picked a path leading to the north of the village and started to run. "It'll burn everything."

"Where are we going?" I said.

The path softened and our boots squelched in thick mud, as Miller led us over a thin fence and through a pig yard.

"To complete your mission," he said.

"I don't want to," I said. "I'm tired. I just want to rest."

Miller stopped in his tracks and pulled me onto my knees. He tapped my arm and pressed me into the undergrowth. My knees slipped in the mud that stretched from the yard along the path, and I dropped the carbine.

"Shit," Miller whispered. He raised his carbine and fired two short bursts into the trees where the path curved ahead of us. The crackle of incoming bullets forced him into the mud alongside me. "There's at least three of them," he said. "I'll cover you. Now, crawl through there."

"What?"

"Through the bushes, Inniki. Just crawl." Miller flinched as another round of bullets slapped into the mud. He cursed when one of them sliced into his thigh. I reached out for him, but he pushed me away. "Through there," he said. "There'll be a path, or you'll make one. The hut is maybe sixty or a hundred yards that way. Go. He's waiting for you."

Miller cursed as another streak of bullets shredded the leaves above our heads. He rolled onto his side, firing up and along the path.

"Go," he said.

I left Miller beneath the leaves and my carbine in the mud. I heard him curse and cry out twice more before I crawled out of the trees and onto a narrow animal track leading north. Miller's weapon had a lighter bark than the ones the bandits used. I heard it as I ran along the track, held my breath when it stopped, and then breathed again when I realised he must be changing magazines. The bandits pressed their attack, and I heard them shout from their covered shooting position inside the jungle as I ran past. A single shout and the crack of a bullet above my head encouraged me to run faster. I ducked beneath low hanging branches, brushed curtains of stringy leaves to the sides with my arms, and then stopped at the sight of a small hut ahead of me.

I caught my breath, pressed my hands on my thighs, and bent forwards. The morning sun steamed through the jungle canopy, and the hut drifted in and out of a thin white cloud. Someone stepped out of the hut, placed light feet on the ground, and padded towards me. The mist cleared and I saw the man's bare feet, his dark blue cotton trousers, tied at the waist with a loop of rope. His chest was bare, nut-brown but with raised ridges of angry scar tissue. I looked up into the face of Eko Simigaq and cried.

"Inniki?" he said, as I collapsed onto my knees. "I was told to expect someone, but I didn't dream it would be you. Inniki, is it you?"

Eko ducked to tug my arm over his shoulder. He pulled me to my feet and led me the last few steps along the track to the hut.

"Sit here," he said. "I'll find some water."

I slid my back down the wall and pressed my hands onto the rough fibres of the bamboo mat covering the floor of the hut. Eko pressed a wooden bowl of water to my lips and I drank.

"Frode should know better," he said. "He should never have sent you."

"He wanted me to tell you something."

I pressed my fingers against the lip of the bowl and pushed it away.

"What?"

The frown on Eko's forehead was almost hidden beneath the thick hair pressed tight around his head with a sealskin cord. I reached up to pinch the cord between my fingers. Eko crouched in front of me and took my hand.

"Tell me what, Inniki?"

It was almost like shooting a gun – *aim, breathe* and *squeeze.*

"He's your father," I said. "He sent me here to find you, to make sure you knew the right side from the bad. He sent me to bring you back."

Eko rocked back onto his heels and then lounged on the mat beside me. He plucked at my fingers as a smile played across his lips.

"You knew?" I said. "All this time."

"What I know…" Eko said. He lifted his head to look me in the eye. "What *I* know, is that Frode Worsaae is not my father."

"What?"

"We let him think that. Sure, he slept with my mother. We know this. But she was already pregnant with me. The hunter Frode thinks was pretending to be my father? He *was* my father. But my mother knew that Frode would look after us – money, and things, every time he came to Thule. She took that secret to the grave. We used to call him *Nissimaaq* – Father Christmas. Because he always came with gifts."

"You used him."

"Only a little." Eko shrugged. "No more than he has used us – both of us." Eko sat up and brushed his fingers on my neck. "I almost didn't recognise you," he said. "What have you done with your hair?"

"To get to your world, I had to cut it off." I flicked my head towards the door, as the sound of gunfire drew closer.

"Come," Eko said, as he stood up. "We should go now."

"I can't go. I have to deliver the message."

"You have."

I slapped at Eko's hand as he thumbed at the paint on my face. "Not that message. You have to tell me what's going on, give me information about the drugs, how they are being taken out of the country. I have to give that information to Frode. I have to tell him that you are still undercover, that you can still be trusted. We have to convince Fitzpatrick."

"Fitzpatrick?"

"*Aap*," I said. "He's the one that ordered the attack on the village. They are his men looking for the drugs."

"There are no drugs here," Eko said.

"But they traced the heroin they seized in America back to this village. Eko, this is why there are soldiers here. It's why Miller contacted you and arranged the meeting. Fitzpatrick thinks you are working for the traffickers. Frode says you are working for him. It's all about you, Eko. Don't you see?"

Eko pulled back the mat and pulled a canvas satchel out of a hollow in the earth. He tucked the strap over his head and shoulder, and said, "I see many things, Inniki. Sometimes these things are plain to see. Other times I must call on the spirits."

I looked at Eko's arm and stretched my fingers towards the crook of his elbow. The skin was red with rash and needle pricks. Eko pulled away from me. He stood up and swung the satchel around so that it hung in the small of his back.

"I saw you many times," he said, as I stood up. "You had long hair, the kind Kunuk could sit on." Eko smiled. "I saw him too. And all our Greenlandic brothers and sisters. That's why I'm here, Inniki. To help them. Just like *Inuarakasik*, I had to go to the end of the world, so that I could save our own."

"I don't understand," I said.

"Then you must come, and I will show you." Eko turned his head at the sound of more gunfire. "We should go."

He took my hand and led me out of the hut. I paused at the trail and looked back towards the village. Eko reached for my elbow, urging me to hurry with a nod of his head. But I had seen something, or *someone*. It might have been Miller. I wanted it to be him. He had taken me this far. I couldn't leave him. I *wouldn't*.

"Inniki," Eko said.

"*Naamik*," I said, shaking my head. "I have a mission. *You* are my mission. I have to get you back to Frode. That's what I promised to do.

I turned my head at the snap of a twig, less than ten yards away. Miller stumbled out of the jungle and onto the track. There was a bloody bandage around his thigh, and another wrapped tight around his head. He waved as he limped along the track towards us.

"See," I said to Eko. "Miller is here to help us. He's on our side. He'll get us back to the camp." I reached for Eko's arm, but he brushed me away.

"*Naamik*," he said, as he slid the satchel from his back to his belly. Miller stopped just a few feet from us, as Eko reached into the satchel and pulled out a pistol. "I'm not going back, Inniki."

Chapter 32

Eko's eyes shrank to two hard black beads, as he raised the pistol and pointed it at Miller's chest. I could feel the familiar Greenlandic wind on my cheek, but instead of the salty tang I was used to, an oppressive rush of fetid air pressed against my face – hot and rank like chunks of meat caught in a bear's maw, black with rot. Eko's arm shook with the weight of the pistol, and the thin veins in his arm popped with the effort, snaking beneath his skin in raised ridges. Eko said he had found another way to the otherworld, an easier means of talking with his spirits and familiars. It might be easy, but it came with a cost – physical and emotional.

Frode had groomed me to fall in love with Eko, and to be loved in return. I had let him, from the moment he suggested what I wear to the prison, and for every meeting thereafter. Eko was my way back to Greenland, my home, and my people. He had shown me my country. He had guided me through the pain of accepting Kunuk's death, my mother's failure, and he had opened my heart to the land, the sea, and the ice. In return, I had loved him, followed him across the world, and let myself be trained, let myself suffer, just to be necessary, to secure the bond between us. And now, in Thailand's damp, fetid, claustrophobic jungle, a million miles from the icebergs and huge open spaces of Greenland, I was going to break that bond. I had to. For Eko, for Miller, for Tiên and Frode, and for me.

I had to do this for me.

I had been beaten, shot at, and manipulated for this man. I had even killed for him, or because of him. I struggled to understand what I had done to Perkins, understanding only that it had been necessary to survive. And if I was going to *survive* Eko, I had to break our bond.

I stepped between the two men, and walked up to Eko, stopping when the barrel of his pistol pressed through the sweat-stained fabric of my shirt and into my sternum.

"Inniki?" The pistol wavered in Eko's grip. "You must move," he said.

"*Naamik*," I said, stepping to the side, as he tried to move around me.

That same brush of air smelled sweeter now, as it cooled the sweat beading between my lip and my nose. I felt the camouflage paint blister around my mouth, and for the first time since Perkins' death, my heart slowed to something approaching a normal beat. Suddenly, things felt right. What I was doing felt right – it had purpose. *I* had purpose. I was no longer just a tool or a reward. The jungle had taught me that. With Miller and Tiên's guidance, with their selflessness, I had discovered myself. Frode couldn't control me, and the moment Eko pulled the pistol on Miller, he too had lost his hold on me. Although, on reflection, I realised it had started on the bathroom floor of the hotel in Dartmouth. The shaman's magic had lost its allure.

"Step aside, Inniki," Miller said, his words measured and clear. "It's all right. Let me handle this."

"He has to come back with us," I said, staring into Eko's eyes. "You must come back."

"Don't do this, Inniki," Eko said. "I love you."

"*Naamik*, you only think you do." I reached for the pistol, wrapping my hand around the barrel as I pushed it down towards the jungle floor. The bear just beneath the surface of Eko's skin retreated for a moment, and his eyes softened. I saw the man I had loved then, the man I had chased halfway across the world, the one I would have run away with. But the other man, the other *Eko*, was not the man I loved. I didn't know if he ever could be, not truly, not without some transformation. He would have to find another route back to this world and leave the otherworld behind. He would have to make a decision. When his eyes hardened, and the bear returned, I realised that he already had.

Eko yanked the pistol out of my grip, shoved the barrel into my thigh, and fired.

It took a second to realise what had happened, to truly understand what he had done. I crumpled to the floor, screaming, clawing at Eko as he raised the pistol and fired three times down the path at Miller. I heard the wet slap of impact, as the first of Eko's bullets ripped into Miller's chest. The second and third bullets flew wide, thwacking into the trees, splintering the bark. Gun smoke flittered out of the end of the pistol as Eko looked down at me, staring with the black beaded look of the polar bear. He stuffed the pistol into the satchel, turned and ran.

"Eko," I shouted, reaching for him, only to grasp handfuls of jungle air.

The slap of Eko's sandals along the trail was lost beneath the crack and zing of bullets blasting down the trail, as a team of Thai Strikers burst out of the jungle and gave chase. One of the Strikers stopped beside Miller, and another kneeled in the earth next to me.

"Your leg?" he said, ripping a bandage from his webbing. "More?"

"More?"

"More wounds. Where he hit you?"

"No," I said. "Just my leg."

The sound of gunfire continued, slower, more measured, as the jungle thickened, and the trail thinned. The Striker bound my thigh, nodding and smiling as he told me it was a good wound.

"Through and through," he said. "No artery. You lucky."

"Miller?" I asked.

"Not so good." The Striker lifted his head at the sound of the helicopters landing. "Maybe he will be okay, but we have to leave now." He stood up and offered me his hand. "We leave now."

I stared down the trail, turning my head at the occasional crack of a bullet, a shout, and then the tramp of more boots along the trail, the heavy tread of the larger American soldiers, and another squad of Strikers.

"They will find him," the Striker said, as he pulled me to my feet.

"No," I said. "No-one will. Not anymore."

The bond had been cut. Eko was free. We both were.

The medics carried Miller out of the helicopter just seconds after it landed at the base. I watched from above, leaning out of the door of the helicopter behind Miller's. Frode was waiting for me as we landed. He ducked as he walked to the skids, reaching out to help me step down. I turned my head to watch the medics disappear inside the doctor's hut with Miller.

"I need to see him," I said.

"No," Frode said. "No time for that."

"He saved my life."

"I'm sure he did. Now let me do the same."

Frode slid one arm around my waist and tucked his shoulder beneath my armpit. He walked me across the packed earth between the huts towards a Jeep idling beside the raised barrier at the gate.

"You remember Thaksin?" he said, as we approached the Jeep.

"Yes."

"Good." Frode stopped on the passenger side of the vehicle and helped me into the seat. "Let's go, Thaksin," he said, as he climbed into the back of the Jeep. I glanced over my shoulder as Thaksin drove through the open barrier and bounced onto the dirt road leading away from the camp.

"All the way to Chiang Rai?" Thaksin said.

"Yes," Frode said. "All the way. Don't stop." Frode switched to Danish and continued. "Fitzpatrick was ordered back to Washington the second it was confirmed that the village contained no drugs, or people. He thinks Eko was warned."

"Miller did it," I said. "So that we could meet."

"Yes. I'm afraid that was one of my biggest mistakes. Fitzpatrick isn't the only one to be recalled. We'll be flying all the way to Copenhagen," he said. "We have to face the wrath of P.E.T.'s board of inquiry for professional conduct."

"You must have known Eko would empty the village."

"Of people, Inniki. You saw the gunship. I couldn't

have that on my conscience, and neither could Miller. That young man has seen far too much death already. We discussed this when I contacted him about looking after you. He did what I asked, and I believe there will be consequences."

"But you can help him, like you helped him before?"

"I can try, but I'm running a little low on currency, and have probably used up all the favours anyone ever owed me."

"But you'll try?"

"Yes, of course."

Frode was silent for a moment, holding onto the side of the Jeep, as Thaksin bumped the vehicle through a series of deep potholes.

"What about me?" I asked. "I killed Perkins."

Frode flattened his lips into a sad smile. He reached forwards and squeezed my shoulder. "Leave it in the jungle," he said.

The road levelled out and Thaksin accelerated. He pointed at the footwell between us and I almost smiled when I recognised my holdall.

"I brought it to you," he said.

I gritted my teeth and leaned forwards to grab the holdall. I knew there was a small towel inside, and I used it to remove some of the camouflage paint from my face. I looked in the side mirror, barely recognising the older me that stared out of the mirror. My hair was shorter than it had been when Frode found me outside the movie theatre in Copenhagen. I struggled to remember what movie I had seen.

"It was with Brigitte Bardot," Frode said. "When I met you on the street, you had just been to the movies." He shrugged when I caught his eye in the mirror. "It's a long time ago."

"Yes," I said. I dropped the towel into my lap and turned in my seat to look at Frode. "What really happened? What was Eko doing, really?"

"Protecting his people," Frode said. "Albeit in a misguided way."

"I don't understand."

"You're aware of the backlash against Denmark?"

"In Greenland?"

"Yes." Frode leaned forwards, ducking his head below the flow of air streaming over the windscreen. "It's been getting worse, with a lot of clashes, demonstrations, a lot of anger. There's even a Greenlandic band singing about a revolution."

"I've heard of them," I said, thinking back to the song Eko talked about in the prison.

"I haven't confirmed it, but I have my suspicions, that Eko is financing a revolution of his own. I sent him undercover to expose a drug trafficking route, and instead of exposing it, he exploited it. I hate to admit it, but I think Fitzpatrick is right; Eko was never on our side. I just hoped – I even prayed – that you might be able to discover the truth."

"I did," I said. "He turned on me in the jungle. It was Eko who shot me."

Frode pressed his hand to his face and rubbed his eyes, nodding as he reached out to take my hand.

"I was afraid he would," he said. "I used you, Inniki."

"I know."

"I put you in danger. I put my own needs – personal and professional – first."

"*Aap*," I said. It was my turn to squeeze Frode's hand. "There's something else." I waited for Frode to look up, and then said, "He's not your son. They used you. The whole village knew. You were their Father Christmas, bringing gifts, giving money. You say you used me, but Eko has been using you, from before he was born."

I let go of Frode's hand, as he sank bank onto the bench seat in the back of the Jeep. The rush of air curled over the windscreen, as Thaksin picked up speed along the wider road to Chiang Rai. The lines on his face softened, but if it was from relief or despair, I couldn't tell. He didn't say another word until we reached the airport.

I washed my face in the washroom basin, before boarding the flight, climbing up the steps and sitting down in the back seat of the aircraft. Frode sat next to me, explaining the different legs of the journey. He said nothing more, and I left him to his thoughts. As the pilot taxied to the runway, I lifted my hand, as if to grab Frode's so that he might calm my nerves before flying. But after all I had been through in the jungle, a few take-offs and landings, even a little turbulence, were nothing compared to what I had done in the jungle. I had new horrors to keep me awake at night. New terrors to live with.

The sudden thrust of the engines pushed me back into my seat. I dropped my hands into my lap and closed my eyes.

Epilogue

The Danish National Hospital in Copenhagen is on *Blegdamsvej*, the same road as the prison. Greenlanders are flown to the *rigshospital*, as it is known in Denmark, when they can't be treated in Greenland. I was there because it was the easiest place to keep an eye on me, and convenient, if I they decided to move me further along the road to the prison.

In the two weeks since leaving Thailand, I had seen little of Frode. He came by when he could, explaining each time to the head nurse, that my stay at the hospital was temporary, and yes, he did understand that my wound did not require such an extended stay, that the beds were needed for other patients, not just VIPs.

I laughed when he told me I was a VIP. A Very Important *Prisoner*, perhaps. The nurses dressed my wound, and the doctors prescribed physiotherapy. I took long walks in the hospital garden but resisted the temptation to leave the grounds. Frode had said it would not help matters.

"There's an inquiry," Frode said. "They want to talk to you, but I said you were recovering. I may have exaggerated the nature of your wounds, but it's for the best. You must play along, Inniki. It's for your own good."

"For how long?"

"Just a little while longer. I'm working on something."

"And what about you?" I asked.

"Yes, I'm working on that too."

I wanted to ask about Miller and Tiên. And I needed to hear if they had found Perkins' body – not because I wanted to. But Frode had a way of ending our conversations with a look, suggesting he had more to say, but didn't want to tell me, not before he had to.

I decided to wait.

Three days went by without a word from Frode since his last visit. I chose to walk closer and closer to the edge of the garden, testing my leg, knowing that I could run if I had to, knowing too that the nurses wouldn't react. They just wanted my bed.

I took a longer walk the day *he* came. One of the nurses from the ward found me in the garden and told me to hurry because I had a visitor. She didn't say *Frode*, which surprised me, because they knew his name, all of them did.

I avoided the lifts, choosing to take the stairs, as I wondered who would visit me. I paused at the door leading into the corridor, wondering for a second if it was Eko, and what I would do if it was. I opened the door, stepped into the corridor, and walked the last few yards to the ward. The curtain was drawn around my bed, but I saw a pair of boots poking out from beneath it. Miller smiled when I pulled back the curtain.

"They said you were out in the garden," he said, as I looked at him.

Miller's face was paler than I remembered, and the thick blond hair on his head was parted with a long scar, and red spots of skin running along the sides, where the stitches had been. But the smile was the same, lifting the corners of his mouth. There was a light in his eyes, dancing brighter than it had in the jungle. He reached for my hand, and I took it, sitting next to him on the bed, saying nothing.

"Tiên is fine," he said, after a moment's pause. "Freddy helped her out of Thailand. I think she's in Laos. He wouldn't say. He said he didn't know. But she sent a letter." Miller patted his pocket. He plucked at my fingers, glancing at my face, before commenting on my hair. "It's a little longer than last time I saw it," he said.

"I'm growing it, for Kunuk."

"Kunuk?" Miller's smile faded. "Who's he?"

"My brother," I said, as I pulled Miller's hand onto my thigh. I cradled it in both hands. "He's dead. But he liked my long hair. I'm growing it for him. Because I want to," I said, frowning at the sudden thought of taking charge of my own look, for me, not for some purpose, but because I wanted to.

"I'm sorry," Miller said. "About your brother. Not about your hair. I liked it long."

We sat in silence for another minute, before I found the courage to ask, "Why are you here, Miller?"

"You can call me *James*," he said, and laughed.

"I prefer Miller," I said. "At least for now."

"Freddy sent for me." Miller let go of my hand and reached into his shirt pocket. He pulled out a thin cardboard wallet containing two airline tickets. He fished a passport from his other pocket and placed both in my hand. "We," he said, "have been given a job, if you're interested."

"What kind of job?"

"Look at the tickets," he said.

I opened the cardboard wallet and traced my fingers beneath my name, and then the destination. "Greenland?" I whispered.

"Yes," Miller said.

I felt the frown crease my forehead and turned my head to look at Miller. "Why?"

"They're sending us after Eko," he said. "And if you want to catch a Greenlander, you have to go to Greenland."

"They're sending us? Who's *they*?" I refused to think about going home to Greenland, before I knew at least *who* was sending me. "It's Frode," I said. "It has to be."

"Not just Frode. This is a joint operation. There are other interested parties."

My stomach cooled as my muscles contracted. "Fitzpatrick..."

"Amongst others, yes. Despite everything, Inniki, there are some people who think you and I are best suited for the job, if you think you can do it."

"I can do it," I said.

"Maybe you need some time to think."

I shook my head. "No more time to think. I'm ready."

"Okay then," Miller said. "But it might help to think of him as *The Greenlander*. Yes, it's Eko, and we're going after him, but it's important to be clear about the mission."

"The mission is the man," I said. "It hasn't changed."

"You're right, but..." Miller paused. "There were some emotional attachments, and I need to know if you still have them," he said. "Attachments."

"He shot me, Miller."

"Yes."

"So," I said. "No more attachments."

"Then you're ready to leave?"

"*Aap*."

"And I still don't know what that means."

"It means *yes*," I said. "I'm ready."

The End

Author's Note

_____

Eko, Inniki and Miller will return in The Greenlander.

About the Author

Christoffer Petersen is the author's pen name. He lives in Denmark. Chris started writing stories about Greenland while teaching in Qaanaaq, the largest village in the very north of Greenland – the population peaked at 600 during the two years he lived there. Chris spent a total of seven years in Greenland, teaching in remote communities and at the Police Academy in the capital of Nuuk.

Chris continues to be inspired by the vast icy wilderness of the Arctic and his books have a common setting in the region, with a Scandinavian influence. He has also watched enough Bourne movies to no longer be surprised by the plot, but not enough to get bored.

You can find Chris in Denmark or online here:

www.christoffer-petersen.com

By the same Author

THE GREENLAND CRIME SERIES
featuring Constable David Maratse
SEVEN GRAVES, ONE WINTER Book 1
BLOOD FLOE Book 2
WE SHALL BE MONSTERS Book 3

Novellas from the same series
KATABATIC
CONTAINER
TUPILAQ
THE LAST FLIGHT
THE HEART THAT WAS A WILD GARDEN
QIVITTOQ
THE THUNDER SPIRITS
ILULIAQ
SCRIMSHAW
ASIAQ

THE GREENLAND TRILOGY
featuring Konstabel Fenna Brongaard
THE ICE STAR Book 1
IN THE SHADOW OF THE MOUNTAIN Book 2
THE SHAMAN'S HOUSE Book 3

CHRISTOFFER PETERSEN

THE POLARPOL ACTION THRILLERS
featuring Sergeant Petra "Piitalaat" Jensen and more
NORTHERN LIGHT Book 1

THE DETECTIVE FREJA HANSEN SERIES
set in Denmark and Scotland
FELL RUNNER Introductory novella
BLACKOUT INGÉNUE

THE WILD CRIME SERIES
set in Denmark and Alaska
PAINT THE DEVIL Book 1
LOST IN THE WOODS Book 2

MADE IN DENMARK
short stories *featuring* Milla Moth set in Denmark
DANISH DESIGN Story 1

THE WHEELMAN SHORTS
short stories *featuring* Noah Lee set in Australia
PULP DRIVER Story 1

THE DARK ADVENT SERIES
featuring Police Commissioner Petra "Piitalaat" Jensen
set in Greenland
THE CALENDAR MAN Book 1
THE TWELFTH NIGHT Book 2

GREENLAND NOIR POETRY
featuring characters from Seven Graves, One Winter
GREENLAND NOIR Volume 1

47062177R00168

Made in the USA
Lexington, KY
04 August 2019